Duels & Deception

Cindy Anstey

READS

SWOON READS · NEW YORK

A Swoon Reads Book

An imprint of Feiwel and Friends and Macmillan Publishing Group, LLC

DUELS & DECEPTION. Copyright © 2017 by Cynthia Ann Anstey.
Excerpt from *Love, Lies and Spies* © 2016 by Cynthia Ann Anstey.
All rights reserved. For information, address Swoon Reads,
175 Fifth Avenue, New York, N.Y. 10010.

Our books may be purchased in bulk for promotional, educational, or business use.
Please contact your local bookseller or the Macmillan Corporate and Premium
Sales Department at (800) 221-7945 ext. 5442 or by e-mail
at MacmillanSpecialMarkets@macmillan.com.

Library of Congress Cataloging-in-Publication Data
Names: Anstey, Cindy, author.
Title: Duels & deception / Cindy Anstey.
Description: First edition. | New York : Swoon Reads, 2017. | Summary: In 1800s London,
    a young heiress and her lawyer are caught up in a kidnapping plot to steal her fortune,
    but as their investigation delves deeper and their affections for each other grow, Lydia
    starts to wonder what she truly wants.
Identifiers: LCCN 2016029131 (print) | LCCN 2016043439 (ebook) |
    ISBN 9781250119094 (pbk.) | ISBN 9781250119087 (Ebook)
Subjects: | CYAC: Heiresses—Fiction. | Kidnapping—Fiction. | Love—Fiction. |
    London (England)—History—19th century—Fiction. | Great Britain—History—
    1789–1820—Fiction.
Classification: LCC PZ7.1.A59 Du 2017 (print) | LCC PZ7.1.A59 (ebook) |
    DDC [Fic]—dc23
LC record available at https://lccn.loc.gov/2016029131

Book design by Anna Booth

First Edition—2017

swoonreads.com

For my family,
especially Mike, Deb, Christine, and Dan

Chapter 1

In which a sensible young lady must choose between the peril of a careening carriage and mud . . . deep mud

$\mathcal{H}$ad Miss Lydia Whitfield of Roseberry Hall been of a skittish nature, the sound of a rapidly approaching carriage would have caused considerable anxiety. As it was, the clatter behind her did nothing to stay her steps. Besides, she recognized the bells on Esme's harness and Turnip's nicker of protest—poor creature hated to canter. The vehicle could be none other than the family landau.

However, as the nickering changed from protest to panic, Lydia was certain the carriage was now descending the steep hill too quickly. The road from Spelding was rocky and rutted, especially in the spring, and it made for a rough ride. Most drivers took it at a walk.

But not this driver.

With a glance over her shoulder, Lydia ascertained that said person was none other than Uncle Arthur. While the distance between them prevented a close examination of his facial features, there was no doubting the tension in the rigid way he held himself.

Uncle was in a mood.

With a sigh, Lydia frowned at the pretty rill beside her as it babbled its way down to the bottom of the hill. She was less than enthused with the idea of stepping off the road and into the deep mud. Instead, she quickened her pace. The rill veered away from the road around the curve, a more promising spot to allow a carriage to pass. She was confident she could make it to the turn before the landau barreled down on her.

As she hastened to safety, Lydia was surprised by a small sound as it broke through the noisy approach of her uncle. But then, the sound wasn't really that small.

It was a shout.

Lifting her head, Lydia examined the road ahead of her. The scene was nature at its finest, for not a house, chimney, or steeple was in sight. Even the sizable gates to Roseberry Hall were hidden around the corner. Past the entrance, the road rose again, coming back into sight from where she stood, and it was there that Lydia spied a carriage and an occupant.

It was a smaller vehicle than the one rumbling behind her . . . a gig, perhaps; it was hard to tell exactly from this distance. And the driver appeared to be a gentleman of indiscernible age—again, because her squint could not render the figure any clearer. Still, it was definitely not a woman.

There seemed to be a problem of some sort, for the man was

standing in his gig—not a wise thing to do even on the smoothest of roads. And he was waving. Rather frantically.

Lydia waved back to acknowledge the hail and increased her pace even more. As she did, she noted that the stranger dropped back onto his seat and flicked the reins, setting his horse at a quick trot. Trying to understand what necessitated this untoward greeting, Lydia considered the possibility that he might be lost or injured in some way. She would know soon enough, for their paths would meet just around the corner.

However, Lydia could tell by the increasing noise behind her that she did *not* have enough time to reach the dry ledge before the landau would be upon her. She was forced into the ditch—and the mud. Though she saved her skirts from the worst of it by lifting them higher than was seemly, her boots were covered in sticky brown goo clear up to her ankles. She was not best pleased.

As Lydia watched her uncle rush past, she was surprised he did not slow for the corner, taking it at a dangerous clip. Surprise turned into concern when she realized his anger was affecting his driving—erratic and ill-considered. Did he see the other carriage up ahead? The narrowness of the road would require one driver to give way, but at that speed, would either be able to react quickly enough?

The answer was not long in coming. The sound of a collision reached Lydia just before she rounded the corner. Horrified for men and horses, Lydia lifted her worsted Pomona green skirt even higher and ran.

The sight of the two carriages sitting on opposite sides of the road was at first a great relief. Both men were atop their seats, and the horses were neither down nor screaming in fright. However, with closer scrutiny, it became clear that the gig—while veering right—had broken its wheel on a collection of rocks and was listing rather dramatically, threatening to dump the driver onto the road. The stranger jumped of his own accord, likely preferring to land on his feet rather than allow gravity to deposit him in an undignified sprawl.

Uncle's carriage—or rather the Roseberry Hall landau—had fared better when it veered off the road, although its cargo had not. A large box, which must have been on the seat beside him, had slid to the ground, throwing the cover and contents into the rill. It was to this that Uncle Arthur was pointing when Lydia hastened toward him.

"There, Lydia, I hope you are happy. I was bringing you a surprise, a pretty little peace offering, a gift for your birthday. And you ruined it. Yet again your obstinacy and disregard for anyone but yourself has brought about a disaster."

Other than slowing her pace, Lydia did not know how to react to such a speech. It was laden with so much injustice that she could only stare in wonderment and question Uncle's grasp of reality. The accident had not been her doing; it had been his excessive speed. Had the road been clear of pedestrians or other carriages, his speed would still have made negotiating the turn without mishap near impossible.

Then there was his reference to obstinacy and disregard for others. Never had she been so accused. Her sister, Ivy—who was as stubborn as the day was long—carried that trait proudly on her ten-year-old shoulders. And as to disregard for others—well, perhaps he should look in the mirror, for *he* himself wore that characteristic, and it fit like a glove.

As to the peace offering/surprise/birthday gift, well, that, too, made no sense. It could not be all three things at once. . . . And to make matters worse, the *gift* was nothing more than an allusion to what he perceived as her immaturity. For as Lydia's gaze followed the pointing finger, she saw that a large, exquisitely dressed porcelain doll stared up at her with its one unbroken eye. This was not a present for a young lady about to turn eighteen but for a girl of ten or eleven. In short, it was a mockery.

Anger and insult fought for supremacy and control of her tongue, leaving Lydia momentarily at a loss for words. Fortunately, Uncle was too wrapped up in his own emotional swirl to take advantage of Lydia's unusual speechless state.

"There. It's all yours. I hope you enjoy it," Uncle Arthur shouted in hypocrisy. And then with a great huff, and in complete indifference to the young man he had just run off the road, her uncle dropped back onto the seat and flicked the reins. Esme and Turnip reacted immediately, trotting through the Roseberry Hall gates and quickly disappearing down the long drive.

"I am terribly sorry your, um, present has been ruined."

Lydia started. She had momentarily forgotten about the stranger and looked up with surprise. Finding him standing a little too close, Lydia back-stepped off the side of the road and would have rolled her ankle had he not reached out to steady her.

It was all so naturally done that when she met his eyes, she was comforted rather than embarrassed by his touch. "I'm sorry," he said again, only this time Lydia was certain he was referring to scaring her rather than sympathizing about the disastrous doll.

The well-dressed gentleman looked to be twenty at most, with dark, wavy hair brushed forward in a windswept look. The style served to accent his square jaw and Grecian nose. A classic example of tall, dark, and handsome, and yet it was his eyes that were his most arresting feature. It wasn't the color—for they were an ordinary shade of brown—or the shape. No, it was the emotion emanating from them. Deep set under heavy brows, his kindness shone through, blanketing her, filling her with the calm she had struggled for not minutes earlier.

"Charming fellow. Relative of yours?" The stranger jerked his head toward the gates. "Seems a might dicked in the nob."

"Yes, I'm afraid I have to claim him. An uncle—my mother's brother."

"Drives like a demon, but he did bring you a present." Pivoting, they both stared back down at the figure on the soggy ground. "Very nice of him. Do you collect dolls? Large, frilly ones?"

The poor thing was covered in mud, the delicate lace dress was ripped, and the right side of its face was smashed. There would be no recovery from this accident.

"I did—once."

"I'm afraid she's quite done for."

His words sounded so tragic that Lydia looked up to reassure him . . . and noticed his laughing eyes. "I think the doll was not bought out of charity but spite—meant to put me in my place, so to speak. Reestablish the pecking order," she said with no little asperity.

"Not terribly subtle."

"No, but then tact and delicacy have never found a home in Uncle." Lydia didn't usually speak so freely.

Strangers were few and far between in this little corner of Somerset, but Lydia found the unfamiliar territory quite pleasant. In fact, Lydia might go so far as to say exhilarating. She quite enjoyed the intensity of the stranger's gaze whenever their eyes met, and her sudden shortness of breath was not in the least alarming. Perhaps she should cultivate more encounters with strangers if this were to be the result.

They stood some moments watching the dirty water seep farther up the doll's white lace, and then Lydia sighed and turned toward the man's gig. It was a functional sort of carriage rather than showy. With burgundy leather seats and a folded black hood, it was well adapted to reasonable distances in a variety of weather conditions. However, one of its two wheels was splintered and wedged up the side of the incline; the man would not be traveling any farther today—at least, not in this vehicle.

"I am not an expert, but I do believe your carriage is in need of repair." Lydia scrunched up her nose and shook her head for emphasis. "Were you going much farther? The village of Spelding is within walking distance, but it will take you the better part of half an hour to get there. I can offer you a pause at Roseberry, should you wish us to attempt the repair. It is the least we could do considering Uncle—Well, our coachman, Mr. Hodge, is quite handy with this sort of happenstance."

"This sort of happenstance? Pushing strangers off the road? Does it occur that often?"

"No. You would be the first *traveler* abjectly affected by my uncle's ill humor."

"My luck, I suppose."

Lydia shrugged with a hint of a smile on her lips—an apology of sorts without using words. He seemed to be the sort of young man who understood these types of indications. Then she recalled the waving and his hurried approach. "Was there some sort of urgency to your journey?" His expression indicated confusion, so she quickly explained. "When I first saw you across the vale, you were standing in your gig, waving—in what I thought was a worrisome manner."

"Ah, yes. That."

"That? Was there a problem?"

"Oh, most definitely. I was trying to warn you about the carriage, the one behind you. I could see it racing down the road. . . . And your back was turned."

"Oh, you mean the large, heavy carriage that clattered and clanked and rumbled so noisily that it might have woken the dead?"

"Yes, that would be the one."

"I was somewhat aware of its approach."

"Yes, so I gathered."

"I do appreciate the gallantry, though."

The stranger bowed. "It was my pleasure."

Lydia shifted her stance and tried to ignore the flush that was working its way up her cheeks. She did not lean toward the stammers and blushes of most young ladies her age and was surprised by her racing heart. Likely caused by too much sun . . . or an awareness that time was passing. Yes, that was it. She could dawdle no longer by the side of the road; if she didn't return soon, there would be abject consternation—well, curiosity at the very least.

With renewed focus, Lydia turned the conversation back to the problem of the carriage wheel. "Would you like Mr. Hodge to take a look at your gig?"

She waited, giving him time to decide. She rather hoped that he would take up her offer; he was quite personable and didn't upset her sensibilities whatsoever. There would be shock and disapproval at Roseberry should she return with a stranger in tow, but an occasional deviation from the norm was good for one's character . . . as long as one's actions never hinted of inconstancy. Lydia was certain she could never be so accused.

Hunkering down, the man checked the underside of his gig. "It might not be an easy fix; the axle might need to be replaced as well."

"All the more reason not to try for Spelding." Lydia leaned across the gig's seat. She grabbed the reins and then secured them to a nearby bush. "I'll have Jeremy fetch the horse, and we can leave the carriage in Mr. Hodge's capable hands—a very competent man in regard to coaches and carriages. He won't steer you wrong."

Standing back up, the man dusted his hands together in a slow, deliberate move. When he looked up, meeting her gaze, he nodded. "Well, it would be most convenient as Roseberry Hall was my destination."

Lydia frowned, straightened her back, and unconsciously lifted her chin. "Really, sir? You are expected at Roseberry Hall?"

"Might you be Miss Lydia Whitfield?"

"I might be." Lydia was uncomfortable with such a personal question issued from the lips of a stranger, no matter how handsome and gallant. It just wasn't done.

"Excellent, most excellent." The gentleman nodded, seemingly unaware of her sudden uneasiness. "I had hoped for a proper introduction. This is a little awkward, but one must make the best of a bad . . . or rather an inelegant . . . situation, don't you think?" As he spoke, the stranger reached inside his caped coat.

"I have here a letter of introduction. I was expecting to give it to your uncle, Mr. Kemble." Glancing at the gate again, where Uncle Arthur had disappeared, the young gentleman hesitated a moment and then continued. "But I think in these circumstances, I had best give it to you directly."

"Indeed?" Lydia was flummoxed. This was highly irregular; all delicacy dictated that she . . . that she . . . bother! The situation was such that she had no precedent on which to lean. She was quite at a loss.

"From Mr. Alfred Lynch."

Lydia's hand went out instantly, but she slowed it just enough to take the letter with great dignity and solemn interest. "Mr. Lynch of Bath? My solicitor?"

"One and the same."

The letter was not long and took mere seconds to peruse. "You are Mr. Newton? Mr. Robert Newton? Mr. Lynch's clerk?"

Mr. Newton leaned forward, looking down at the paper as if he were going to read it upside down. "Clerk? Is that what he calls me?"

Edging back, Lydia instinctively pulled the letter to her bodice. "Are you not his clerk?"

"Well, I am. But he offered me an apprenticeship just last week. Though I will admit he did not state exactly when it was to begin. Still, he might have referred to me as an apprentice-in-waiting."

"A somewhat unwieldy title."

"True enough. Though it's more likely that he forgot."

"Seems unlikely. The man's mind is as sharp as a tack."

"Been a while since you've seen him?"

"At my father's funeral, three years ago. Not that long."

"Yes, well . . . a lot can happen in three years."

Lydia thought about how much *her* life had changed and reluctantly agreed—though silently. "Mr. Lynch's letter does not explain why you are here to visit us."

"No, it does not."

Lydia waited for him to continue, but he didn't seem disposed to enlighten her. "So why have you come all the way from Bath to Roseberry Hall, Mr. Newton?"

"Bath isn't all that far. It only took me a couple of hours." He glanced over at his gig and shrugged. "Would have been faster on horseback, but Mr. Lynch did insist. Thought it looked better. More official."

Lydia's heart skipped a beat, and she swallowed with a little difficulty. "Do you *need* to look official?"

"In some eyes, yes, I would say so."

"You aren't being very clear, Mr. Newton. Rather cryptic."

"Mr. Lynch said you were clever."

And so it was that Lydia stood on the side of Spelding Road just outside her own gates, observing that the day had grown chilly and that the splash of the rill was rather boisterous, in a less than charming manner. Had she been of the right disposition, she might have snapped at Mr. Newton for his uninformative conversation. She was now overburdened with thoughts of tardiness and broken wheels while her solicitor's emissary thought nothing of being mysterious.

Perhaps Mr. Newton didn't realize that an official visit from a solicitor had preceded the retrenchment of several households in the area. Or he might not know that Mr. Pibsbury, the estate land agent, had just retired and that a ninny had been hired in his stead. Still further, he might not know that arriving without an invitation or warning was highly irregular and boded ill.

And as those thoughts passed through her mind, Lydia hit upon another possibility—a reasonable and nonapocalyptic reason for his visit. It was just a seed at first, but it grew until it blossomed in the form of a smile and brought out the sun again. "My letter about Mr. Drury—the new land agent. Mr. Lynch sent you in response to my letter."

"In part, yes."

The sense of relief was such that Mr. Newton's hesitation barely registered.

"Oh, excellent. Most excellent. Come, Mr. Newton, let us wend our way to Roseberry."

With a quick step back to the gig, Mr. Newton grabbed his satchel, pulling it free. Joining her by the estate entrance, he half-raised his arm toward her and then, likely realizing they were too newly acquainted to offer such an intimacy, he dropped it back to his side.

However, Lydia found that she was not disinclined to take his arm; in fact, the prospect was rather exciting, in a daring sort of way. Feeling somewhat roguish, she stepped to his side and placed her hand in the crook of his arm. He smiled down at her in a manner that caused a strange flutter in her belly, and then he led them through the gates.

Chapter 2

In which Miss Whitfield must fob off a dandy before dealing with the merits of pineapples

Robert Newton, third son of the Earl of Wissett, was visiting Roseberry Hall at the request of Mr. Lynch, as he had stated. It had been hinted that well-executed duties such as these would lead directly to the start of his apprenticeship. Still, Robert had not been keen on rushing into the country—an absence from Bath didn't seem necessary. Nor, when Mr. Lynch had described the child at the center of the . . . complications had he been drawn to the character that was supposed to be Miss Whitfield.

Clever, yes, that had been part of the description—but not used in a flattering sense. "Too clever for her own good" was how it had been put. Mr. Lynch had then gone on, at some length, to complain of Miss Whitfield's interference—a tendency whose fault was laid at the feet of her deceased father, who had *overeducated* his elder daughter.

And yet here Robert was walking down a pleasant, elm-lined drive with an elegant young woman whom Mr. Lynch would not have recognized. It was clear that Lynch had thought Miss Lydia Whitfield to still be the fourteen-year-old child he knew three years earlier. But he couldn't have been more mistaken. Gone were the braids, the pinafores, the awkward scuffling gait, the red face, and the watery eyes—tears most likely—that were part of Lynch's description.

The Lydia Whitfield that Robert had just met was a completely different young lady—in countenance and temperament. Tall, for a woman, and willowy, she walked with the loping grace of a deer—without the skittishness. Rich black curls spilled out from under her green bonnet with enough haphazard profusion to indicate a thick head of hair, and her features were soft and fine. Although some might say her nose was overlong and her chin a trifle sharp, Robert found both features appealing. Swaying, their gait in harmony, he quite enjoyed her proximity. Quite.

As to her character, Robert was pleased with her readiness to laugh, her compassion toward a stranger, and her barely disguised impatience with his boring observance of the passing storm clouds. As to the other facets of her personality, well, Robert was surprised to discover that he was looking forward to getting to know them.

"Well, here we are, at last, Mr. Newton."

Robert looked up, for despite Miss Whitfield's words, they had only just come in sight of the house. It was the typical hodge-podge of a sixteenth-century manor, with irregular additions, mullioned windows, and timber beams. The moss-covered tile roof was dotted with chimney pots and embellished with a chapel tower. Everything about Roseberry shouted antiquity saturated with grandeur. This was, of course, no great surprise as Miss Whitfield was the heiress of a large fortune made in the sugar industry over the past two generations of Whitfields.

"Very nice," he said, nodding with approval and noting her smile of pride.

However, Miss Whitfield's smile suddenly disappeared, and she came to an abrupt halt, frowning as she stared at her boots.

The reason for her frown became quite clear—well, muddy.

Miss Whitfield set about stamping her feet—knocking off a significant amount of caked, dry mud. "Oh dear, this will not do." She dropped into a squat to wipe away the last of it, and as she did, she glanced down the tree-lined drive. Her frown deepened.

"Miss Whitfield? Is anything amiss?"

"No . . . not really. It's odd more than anything else. Shadows that seem out of place. It has happened several times this past week." She continued to focus on one particular bush.

"Really?" He squinted toward the object of her concentration, noticing only that it had been trimmed recently.

"Indeed. I know the grounds down to the last blade of grass. . . . And yet the shape of that silhouette is somewhat odd—as if a person is lingering and watching from behind the greenery."

"That will not do," Robert said as he stepped forward, marching on the shrubbery in question. However, upon gaining said bush, he found nothing untoward. "All is well," he called as he circled around and then returned to her side. "Not to worry, Miss Whitfield. Merely a trick of light."

Laughing, somewhat weakly, she stood and then shook her head. "My imagination is running amok. I shall endeavor to keep it in check."

Robert found Miss Whitfield's flight of fancy as charming as it was surprising. They lapsed into silence until reaching the arched front entrance.

There, the wide door opened, seemingly of its own accord. Miss Whitfield glanced over her shoulder toward the elm trees, shrugged, and stepped across the threshold. Thanking her butler, by the name of Shodster, she then arranged for the rescue of Robert's horse and gig before stepping farther into the great hall. Partway across the marble floor, she stopped abruptly. And so, of course, did Robert.

"Mr. Chilton, what are you doing here?"

Miss Whitfield's tone was so frosty that Robert expected the object of her disgust to freeze on the spot. Instead, the man, who had been seated on a narrow chair beneath the balcony of the upper hall, leaped to his feet and minced toward them. He was a fleshy fellow in his midthirties, dressed with the eye-popping flair of a fop. His waistcoat was an exotic, beaded bright orange with a clashing cerulean blue jacket. Worse still, the man's overly starched neckcloth pushed his chin up and his jaw out, forcing him to drop his shoulder to see forward.

"Miss Whitfield, what a wonderful coincidence. I was just on my way to Spelding when my—"

"Mr. Chilton," Miss Whitfield interrupted, "I believe I asked you not to darken my doorstep again."

"No, no, my dear. You asked me not to visit . . . which I am not doing. I was on my way to *Spelding* when my horse threw a shoe."

"How is it, then, that I find you cluttering up my hallway?"

Robert glanced uncomfortably around the cavernous hall, taking in its impressive fireplace and abundance of dark paneling, preferring to be elsewhere for what was turning into a heated discussion. He spied an alcove off to the right with a collection of small landscapes and decided art appreciation might be a worthwhile enterprise for a lawyer's apprentice. Still, with only fifteen feet separating him from the confrontation, Robert could hear the conversation without any effort.

"Why, the shoe came off just outside your gates, my dear Miss Whitfield. If it had been anywhere else—"

"Is your horse being taken care of?"

Robert thought the painting of a flower garden was nicely rendered—the light shining through the trees added an ethereal atmosphere.

"Oh, yes, my dear. The hospitality of Roseberry Hall is renown. Your dearest mama arranged for—"

"Have you been offered any refreshment while you wait?"

It was a shame that the varnish of the seascape had darkened. It required a squint and a closer look to make out the crashing waves and jagged rocks.

"Oh dear me, no, my dear. That is most kind of you to—"

"Shodster, could you have Hugh show Mr. Chilton to the kitchen. I'm sure Cook can find him a glass of beer—"

"Kitchen? Beer?" Mr. Chilton squeaked, clearly astonished by the offer of such an unrefined libation and made worse by being relegated to the back of the house.

"And a bite of cheese and bread. There you are, Mr. Chilton, the staff will have you back on the road in no time. But on the next occasion that your horse loses a shoe in front of my gate, please find your way to the servants' door, because you will not be granted entrance here."

Hugh arrived before Shodster could do anything as demeaning as seek the liveried footman, and soon the hall echoed with the steps of the two men as they vacated the grand entrance. Shodster quietly disappeared, too. Miss Whitfield joined Robert in the alcove, where he was, for want of a better word, hiding.

"A most interesting collection," he said, staring at a depiction of four cows in a field by a stream, with a boy fishing and a lady on a black stallion riding through the background; a busy place, this pastoral landscape.

"Yes, indeed, in a very pedantic way."

Robert turned to see that Miss Whitfield's color was higher than it had been. It was most becoming, but as it was caused by either anger or embarrassment, he was sorry to see it.

"I should not have subjected you to such a scene. I do apologize."

"Think nothing of it. A solicitor, if possessing no other qualities, should have selective hearing. Excellent practice."

"Still, I should have seen you settled first before dealing with . . ."

As Miss Whitfield labored to find a polite description of the scene he had just witnessed, Robert replied as if it were already stated. "Yes, but if you had done so, I would not have had the pleasure of casting my eyes upon a waistcoat of which I am sure never to forget."

In a superlative attempt to hide her levity, Miss Whitfield gestured Robert out of the alcove with a serious expression, only the twitching corners of her mouth offering up her true reaction to his words. "Yes, indeed. Such a superior example of . . . beadwork . . . I have yet to see."

Back in the center of the hall, Miss Whitfield looked to the first floor and then toward a door off the main entrance. "Were you hoping to see the family in an informal setting, such as the drawing room . . . ?" She paused, obvious in her attempt to have Robert explain more fully.

He wished that he could put her out of her misery, but again Mr. Lynch interfered. Robert had been instructed that impartiality was most important in dealing with this situation. He could not explain until all involved parties were gathered together.

"Actually, I would prefer a more secluded location, if you don't mind. And just the presence of Mr. Kemble and Eric Drury."

With a nod, Miss Whitfield turned and reached for the bellpull hanging next to the ornate mantel. However, before she could give the bell a tug, a voice floated down from the upper balcony.

"Is that you, Lydia?"

Robert could not see the questioning person, but the tonal range assured him that it was, in fact, a she.

"Yes, Mama."

"Oh, I am so glad. I quite expected you back a full ten minutes ago. It doesn't serve my nerves well when you do something irregular. You are usually as timely as clockworks."

"There was no need to worry—" Miss Whitfield lifted her hand in Robert's direction. It seemed to be an indication that he should step forward and provide the excuse needed to calm her mother's poor nerves, but her hand stopped moving as soon as her mother interrupted.

Unsure of his role, Robert hesitated as well.

"Oh, I was not worried, no, I was anxious . . . anxious that you would miss Mr. Chilton. No, perhaps I mean excited. Yes, that's it. Did you see him?"

"I did, Mama. I wish you wouldn't encourage Chilton."

"Oh, Lydia, how can you be so unromantic? He is smitten, can think of no one else but you." This was stated in a slightly different voice quality, telling Robert that it was a quote rather than an original thought.

"As I have told you before, Mama, Chilton's pockets are to let. His interest in me is financial, not romantic. Besides, you know that I am already betrothed."

Robert frowned. Lynch had not mentioned an engagement.

"Don't talk like that, Lydia. It is not official. You are not obligated—"

With a flick of her hand, Miss Whitfield indicated that she wished Robert's presence to be known, and he stepped into the open part of the hallway.

"Could we talk about it at another time, Mama?" The request sounded suspiciously like an order. "I have business to discuss with Mr. Newton."

"Mr. Who? Oh my, why did you not say that you were not alone, Lydia? Hello, Mr. Elton. I don't believe we have been introduced."

The situation was a little awkward as Miss Whitfield seemed disinclined to take Robert up the stairs for a proper introduction and Mrs. Whitfield seemed disinclined to come down. However, both ladies overlooked this and merely adjusted the level of their voices. Miss Whitfield enunciated Robert's last name clearly while performing the honors, and Robert bowed neatly to the woman leaning over the rail.

There was no doubting the relationship; Mrs. Whitfield was very much like her daughter but without the bright smile, slim figure, thick hair, and intelligent eyes. On second thought, perhaps the family resemblance was encapsulated only in the shape of her chin and the length of her nose.

Once it had been established that Robert was not at Roseberry Hall to visit the family but as a representative of Mr. Lynch, Mrs. Whitfield lost interest and shrugged, returning—one had to assume since it was not visible from where he was standing—to the drawing room.

In quick succession, Miss Whitfield's bell summoned the butler, the housekeeper, and the returning footman, Hugh. Shodster was sent in search of Uncle Arthur and Eric Drury with a request to meet in the study. Hugh, after being laden with their outdoor clothing, was sent to ensure that Robert's horse and gig had arrived safely—the doll was not mentioned. And, despite Robert's protest, Mrs. Buttle was asked to prepare a room for their guest.

"If I need to stay longer, Miss Whitfield, I will take a room at the inn in Spelding. That was my intention from the outset." While Robert had prepared for the possibility that his quest would require an overnight stay, he did *prefer* to return to Bath at day's end.

"Please, Mr. Newton, there is no need. Mr. Lynch has stayed at the house—since you are here as his representative, it only stands to reason that if our meeting goes longer than expected, you will not have to travel in the dark—not to Spelding or Bath. A precaution, nothing more. We have the room."

Robert was given little opportunity to protest, although he retained his satchel as a token of resistance. Miss Whitfield led him down a smaller windowed hallway that ran along the front of the house. A few twists and turns later, they entered what was called the study: a book-lined room that looked suspiciously like a library except for the desk and the chairs grouped at both ends. The study was of such proportions that it possessed not one but two huge fireplaces. There was a sense of grandeur to it all, but it was the books that impressed Robert the most, for he was a great reader. With a smile, he noted that there was no whiff of mustiness. The room had the atmosphere of a well-used and well-loved haven, despite its size.

They did not have to wait long for the others to arrive; Robert had only just set down his satchel and made himself comfortable behind the desk, as Miss Whitfield had indicated, when the irritated and irritating Arthur Kemble stormed into the room. Robert jumped to his feet, offering a polite nod, but it was of no consequence as the man didn't so much as glance in his direction.

"What is all this? I will not be summoned like a dog, Lydia." Although clearly he could. "You should have come to me. I am your elder and your guardian, and I *will* be treated with respect." Kemble shook his head with such vigor that Robert, standing quietly to the side, suddenly came into view. "Who are you?"

Robert was a little taken aback, as their encounter on the road could not have been more than half an hour earlier. The man was either woefully thick or purposefully antagonistic.

Miss Whitfield provided the official introduction. The formality didn't go as smoothly as one would suppose. Kemble would not be persuaded to accept a gentleman who could only *claim* an association with Mr. Lynch. The protest was quickly cast aside on the strength of Lynch's letter and one of Robert's printed calling cards. They were presented and studied carefully, and then Kemble turned his attention to Robert, now ignoring Miss Whitfield.

"Glad you're here, Newton. Been arguing with Missy here for days. But will *she* listen? No. Will *she* let it be? No. Needs to be put straight—told *her* place."

"Uncle. Please." The "she" and "her" protested quite loudly.

"That's why you are here, right? To tell her to stick to ribbons and frills and all those gewgaws that females adore. Leave the estate to me."

Even Robert felt nonplussed by Kemble's attitude. There was a proprietary air to his words and stance that were out of kilter with the true state of affairs. This man was not Oliver Whitfield's heir. No, indeed not. He was Mrs. Joan Whitfield's brother.

Oliver Whitfield's will had provided Kemble with a healthy allowance should he agree to uproot his family and move to Roseberry as Lydia's guardian. The Kembles were to live at Roseberry Hall until Miss Whitfield reached the age of majority, when she could take up the running of the estate. Had Oliver Whitfield any closer male relatives, Arthur Kemble would still be living in his small, financially strained manor two counties away.

"As you have surmised, sir, I am here to clear up the misunderstanding that has put the estate at odds."

"Tell her she's wrong and then be on your way. Mr. Lynch

has not interfered before, and I don't expect him to interfere now. I have the right to manage the estate as I see fit."

"In conjunction with Mr. Lynch, sir. It is a *joint* trusteeship. And I have been authorized to say that there will be no more funds forthcoming—"

"What!"

"Until the misunderstandings have been addressed. That is why I am here. I will be making my recommendations to Mr. Lynch upon my return to Bath."

"Who do you think you are? Coming in here, telling us what we should or shouldn't do."

"As you saw in the letter, sir." Robert enunciated each syllable as if he were dealing with someone of inferior wit. "I am here under Mr. *Lynch*'s authority. I am here to understand and then to pass on that understanding to *Miss Whitfield*'s solicitor as stipulated by Oliver Whitfield's will." He glanced at the subject of their discussion, admiring her restraint, and then returned his eyes to Kemble.

"Yes, yes. Fine. Let's get on with it. I have better things to do."

"We will wait, Uncle, for Mr. Drury." Miss Whitfield glanced casually at Robert as she made a task out of choosing a chair close to the nearest fireplace. "He should be here presently."

No sooner were the words spoken than a lanky man, somewhere in his fifth decade, entered the study with a hurried step. Though his face was narrow, wide, bushy side whiskers balanced the attributes of his face, and while he sported a broad smile, the congeniality did not reach his eyes.

"Hey ho, Shodster thought you were in need of me, Miss

Whitfield. And here I see you are occupied with company, so I will take myself off and see you at some other time. Much to do: busy, busy, busy." Turning, Drury almost made it out of the room before Robert called him back by uttering his name.

"Do I know you?"

Robert noted the lack of the word *sir* and the upward tilt of Drury's nose, but he soon had all three seated and silent and waiting.

Robert cleared his throat, hooked his thumbs into his waistcoat pockets, and tried to sound lawyerly. "In the past fortnight, Mr. Lynch has received three heated letters regarding Roseberry Hall and the running of the estate."

"Three?" Miss Whitfield was clearly surprised.

"Yes, three. These letters included words such as *inept, ignorant,* and *disaster.* Mr. Lynch had no choice but to divine the true nature of these complaints."

"Drury, you didn't." Kemble fixed a glare on the land agent.

"You told me to."

"I did no such thing. Told you I'd take care of it. Yes. No. Never asked you."

"Indeed, you did . . . yes, yes, yes. Well, perhaps not in so many words. But, well: Missy won't let me do this; Missy natters about that; if Lynch knew the half of it, he'd put a stop to Missy an' all her opinions. Couldn't be clearer."

Robert intervened. "Gentlemen, if I could have your attention. Thank you. Now, first we shall address this year's crop choice. There is a wide disparity: apples, tea, or pineapples."

"Pineapples?" Drury's surprise outshouted Miss Whitfield's.

"Yes." Kemble nodded with supreme authority and then turned toward Drury. "You made mention of a new strain that would grow in these cooler climes. Just developed, you said. Could fill the Roseberry coffers tenfold. Well, I think it a most estimable idea, but *Missy* here thinks she knows better." He studiously didn't look in Miss Whitfield's direction.

"Yes," Drury said with heaps of derision. "Exactly. But I said tea."

"Gentlemen, be it tea or pineapples, both are experimental and require time to establish." Miss Whitfield turned back toward Robert. "Digging up the apple orchards and planting them with tea . . . or pineapples . . . makes no sense."

"This is not for you to say, Lydia. You have not been running this estate; I have—"

"I beg to differ, Uncle, but that is not true. Until three months ago, Mr. Pibsbury has been overseeing—"

Kemble stood, knocking his chair over in his haste. "Nonsense. Do not listen to this green girl, Mr. Newton. Tell Mr. Lynch that I have decided to plant pineapples—"

"Tea!" Drury's tone was heated.

"Yes, right. Tea. It is agreed then. Off you go." And off Kemble went instead, rushing out the door.

"Well, that won't do . . ." Robert started to say, but there was no audience save Miss Whitfield to talk to as Drury had followed on Kemble's heels. "Hmm."

"Yes, indeed." Miss Whitfield sighed. "You see the problem."

Robert nodded—family politics were always complicated. "I'll have to talk to the gentlemen separately, I suppose."

"That is a wise idea. I'll tell Mrs. Buttle to set another plate. . . . Well, I mean to say—would you care to join us for dinner, Mr. Newton?"

"Why, thank you, Miss Whitfield. I would be honored." There was no helping it. Robert knew it would be dinner and an over-nighter. Ferreting out the reason behind Kemble's irascible and belittling attitude—toward his fellow trustee and his niece—would take more than an afternoon.

It could be that Kemble truly did not see that Miss Whitfield was interested in more than gewgaws. While Robert had been in Miss Whitfield's company long enough to know that she possessed a large helping of common sense, it was possible that her uncle had not noticed the transformation of child to young woman.

Glancing at the figure bending over to right her uncle's chair, Robert made a pleasant observation. Miss Lydia Whitfield had definitely grown up.

Chapter 3

*In which an important discussion takes place in the garden
and Lord Aldershot refuses to be pushed around*

Finding no excuse to remain in his company, Lydia reluctantly left Mr. Newton seated comfortably at her father's desk scribbling out a few notes; his description, not hers. Deep in thought and distraction, she wandered into the morning room at the far side of the manor, where she could be alone. With a sigh, she worried at her bottom lip.

There seemed to be some urgency to Uncle's manner and choices that Lydia did not understand. Was it all too much for him—the burden of the estate—too much weight for him to bear? To buckle after such a short duration, well, it smacked of weakness. It was a most abhorrent condition to her father, and one that he must not have foreseen or Uncle Arthur would never have been named as a trustee. The whole situation was beyond perplexing.

If only Mr. Pibsbury were still there. He would call Uncle a ninny, quietly under his breath, and toss Mr. Drury out on his ear. Tea would get short shrift, and pineapples wouldn't even merit a comment—a smirk, perhaps, but no more than that.

Yes, a wonderful, competent man, Mr. Pibsbury. He was a font of information, kindness, and chuckles—a bonhomie sort. His pensioning-off had come as a complete surprise to all. Thirty-five years of knowledge swept away in one fell swoop.

This whole state of affairs was nothing short of a disaster.

Frowning, Lydia plopped—very unladylike—onto the firm morning room settee.

Disaster. Her father would not appreciate the word's use—too much emotion, smacked of an indecent amount of sensibility. Histrionics at its worst. Perhaps *farce* would be a better word. Yes, digging up a productive orchard to plant tea . . . in Somerset, no less . . . could be nothing but a farce.

Still, there was little Lydia could do—farce or disaster—at this point other than appeal to Mr. Lynch, which she had already done. Rubbing at her forehead—completely mussing her carefully placed curls—Lydia considered one more option . . . one more person to whom she could turn. Yes, despite a qualm or two, she considered involving her neighbor, Lord Aldershot, in this tug-of-war of authority.

Indeed, Manfred Barley, Lord Aldershot, had authority in spades simply for being who he was—Lord Aldershot: friend of her father (or, rather, the son of her father's friend), member of the peerage, and the gentleman to whom Lydia was unofficially engaged.

Yes, that might do the trick.

Barley would be like-minded—he always agreed with her. No reason to think he would have his own opinion in regard to crops; it would be uncharacteristic, for he was a compliant and easily led individual. And while he knew nothing of running an estate the size of Roseberry, which was three times larger than Wilder Hill Manor, he had a vested interest.

All and sundry knew that their engagement was not official—no contract had been signed, none of the larger issues settled. Yet, had their betrothal not been generally bandied about, Barley would have had to retrench, so deep were his debts. Forced into Bath or, worse, Bristol—to live a quiet life off a rented Wilder Hill Manor. It was a horrifying thought to any who knew him. Barley was a country gentleman: horses, hounds, and high living were his lifeblood . . . and his financial drain.

It stood to reason that Barley would not wish his future jeopardized.

Jumping up, Lydia exchanged her seat on the settee for the chair at her escritoire. She stared at the rosewood grain for some minutes as she composed the missive in her head and then dashed off the carefully worded note. Then, after giving the sealed letter to Shodster, she adjourned to the first-floor drawing room to await Barley's arrival.

The drawing room was a pleasant apartment: of a good size, lately redecorated in floral pink and green with a bank of windows overlooking the formal gardens. As expected, the room contained six ladies, and did so daily—Lydia, being the seventh female of the household, was somewhat inconstant.

Lydia had a deep affection for all members of the Whitfield family circle. Cora Shipley, the governess of Cousin Tessa and Lydia's sister, Ivy, was included under that umbrella, for they were, in fact, close friends. However, the family was not without flaws. Cousin Elaine, almost three full years Lydia's senior, could be annoying at times—prone to exaggeration or melodrama. Mama was . . . Mama. And Aunt Freya, Uncle Arthur's beleaguered wife, well, the poor woman fancied herself a gifted but unfulfilled artist and constantly regaled them with anecdotes of flower arranging or matching ribbons or choosing wallpaper.

Walking sedately into the room, Lydia allowed the bubbling conversation and laughter to distract her from her worries . . . her uncertainties. Ivy joined her on the couch with an embroidery sampler, asking how best to correct a stitching error. Once Lydia had fixed her sister's needlework, Cousin Tessa traded places with Ivy for no particular purpose. Tessa lolled against Lydia, as only a worshipping nine-year-old could. The scene was so untouched by the tea-and-pineapple hostilities that Lydia's abating tension was soon no longer a pretense but truly realized.

Even Mama's pointed remarks did not nettle.

"How is dear Shelley, Lydia? Have you heard from her lately?" Mama turned to look at Aunt Freya, who was seated next to her on the couch by the fire. "Shelley is a fast friend of Lydia's from Miss Melvina's Finishing School for Young Ladies—"

"And of Cora's, Mama." Lydia glanced toward the window seat, where her friend sat sideways with a book on her lap; she was lost in her own world, staring out at the trees. The picture of a demure governess, Cora wore an unembellished dove-gray gown, a serene expression with a hint of melancholy in her pretty blue eyes, and a sensible upsweep of her dark blond hair. It was quite disturbing, for Cora was of a flamboyant nature in dress and character, normally tending toward laughter and spirited discourse.

When Lydia had offered her the position of governess six or so months earlier, Cora had been extremely grateful. Cora had been at wit's end as her brother's wife had made it plain that Cora's presence was tiresome and that she was no longer welcome at the Shipley manor.

Lydia had offered her friend a home at Roseberry Hall with no obligations, but Cora called it charity and would not agree. It was then decided that a girl well versed in elocution, deportment, and dancing could provide the two youngest girls of the Whitfield-Kemble menagerie with a worthwhile education. And so, Cora Shipley acquiesced.

Now, not for the first time, Lydia observed that her friend had become withdrawn this past month. Quiet afternoons were spent staring out the window with an ever-growing expression of sadness. Even the mention of her name had not distracted Cora from the complicated process of staring at nothing.

With a sigh, Lydia returned her attention to her mother's conversation.

"Yes, Shelley is newly married," Mama continued. "Shelley Dunbar-Ross, as she is known now."

There was a hint of satisfaction in her mother's voice that Lydia didn't quite understand . . . after all, Mama had nothing to do with it.

"It was a *love* match." Mama stressed the word *love* as she turned her eyes to her elder daughter. "Is she back from her bridal tour?"

"Yes, indeed. I received a letter from her not two days ago. I had written to her while she was away to verify the timing of her return; I did so hope she would be back by the beginning of May."

In a little less than two months, Lydia was going to celebrate her eighteenth birthday at a private ball in Bath, with two hundred of her closest friends: well, her mama's closest friends. Over two dozen would be Lydia's nearest and dearest, including Shelley and her new husband, Edward Dunbar-Ross.

Shelley, who had—as her mother had just mentioned—fallen instantly in love with her eligible bachelor, had surprised the whole of their society by marching up the aisle after knowing Mr. Dunbar-Ross for a mere four months. It was surprising that her parents did not object as Shelley was not yet nineteen and might not know her own mind. But Shelley was adamant and would not let anyone dissuade her.

The circumstances of Shelley's marital bliss circled once again through Lydia's mind. Yes, Shelley was eighteen, and she was married two months ago. . . . And other than a few uncharitable remarks about counting the months, the marriage was generally celebrated as a great coup. Everyone enjoyed a love match. . . .

Yes, Shelley was only six months older than Lydia. She had been—

"Is she going to be able to come?"

"Hmm?" Lydia looked up from the midway point of the floor and her thoughts, confused momentarily by the question.

"Shelley. Is she going to be able to join us at your ball? You know, travel into Bath . . . in two months' time."

"Of course. There is nothing to prevent her from attending." Lydia ignored the implication of her mama's words—one, the girls were present, and two, she would not dignify such a suggestion. As far as Lydia knew, Shelley was not in the family way; and if she were, then there should be congratulations, not snickering behind raised fans.

Just as she was about to fix her mother with a decided glare, the door to the drawing room opened, and Shodster announced the arrival of Lord Aldershot. All seven females jumped to their feet to bob their greetings. Only Lydia was not surprised by his visit.

Manfred Barley was not a tall man—standing only two or three inches above Lydia. Neither was he handsome, although he was considered presentable. He dressed well but not too stylishly, and, other than a pointed nose, his face was unremarkable for a man of three and twenty. His character was somewhat bland, and his manner was pliable.

Lydia was not particularly fond of the baron, but then neither did she find him offensive, and in this she was content. Marrying Barley would allow her to remain close to Roseberry Hall—something that factored high in her mind. The title was a nice additive but not as important to her as it had been to her father.

Not of a romantic nature, Lydia was well satisfied with her matrimonial future. She saw no need for sleepless nights and anxieties over a hopeful attraction. She had only to look at Elaine, who at the advanced age of twenty threw herself at any and every bachelor in the neighborhood. Her cousin could talk of little else; it was not something Lydia ever wished to emulate.

Barley was twitching with visible impatience as he spoke pleasantries to her mother and aunt—about their health and the weather. While they reciprocated in kind, Lydia wondered if she had been too forceful in the language of her note. She remembered using the words *problem*, *lawyer*, and *help*. Was he worried? Was that why he had arrived so promptly? If that were the case, Lydia was prepared to be impressed and to take her assessment of him up a notch.

After everyone had decided that it was not likely to rain, Lydia took advantage of that pronouncement and suggested a stroll through the garden. There was no possibility for privacy in a room full of women, no matter how large it was or how much they pretended disinterest. Barley readily agreed, and soon they were arm in arm, wending their way through the boxwoods.

Conversation was frivolous until they were sure their discussion would not be overheard. They had not seen each other for a few months and had to catch up on the latest litter of pups, Barley's new stallion, and an author of whom Lydia was quite enthused. Eventually, the reason for his visit was approached—with far less gallantry than Lydia had hoped for.

"It was not a great inconvenience, Lydia. I was heading into Spelding anyway when your note arrived." Then he sighed as if he were encumbered by a significant burden. "So tell me what great woe has befallen you, and why I should be involved? I am a busy man. Places to go, people to see."

"Really, Barley. I did not expect you to drop everything and rush over. . . . Though I will say this whole situation is, or at least should be, of as much concern to you as it is to me." And with that, she proceeded to tell him all about the impending tea fiasco.

"And what do you expect of me? I'd just as soon have the pineapples."

"You missed the point entirely; pineapples will not grow here any more than tea will. If Drury and Uncle are not stopped, Roseberry Hall will not make any money this year—at all." Frowning at the vehemence of her statement, Lydia shifted her gaze lest Barley see the depth of her anxiety . . . and irritation. She rested her eyes on the wall of the conservatory and was startled from her pique by a strange shadow. It reminded her of the one on the front lawn a few hours ago.

"Well, be that as it may, anything *I* say will be considered interference, and since everyone knows that my agricultural knowledge is limited at best, they will know that I am merely spouting your words. I will not be your marionette, Lydia; I am my own man, you know."

Lydia shook the odd silhouette from her mind and lifted a brow. "Yes, of course you are. And I would not ask your involvement were it not of great importance to our financial future." She felt the sudden tension in his arm and knew that her words had finally sunk in.

"Be that as it may, I have no official capacity here. We are not betrothed as yet."

"I thought we could rectify that."

"What?"

"I am going to be eighteen in two months. I thought we could announce our engagement at the ball and marry this summer."

Looking askance, Barley stepped away from her side—an awkward move as they were still walking arm in arm. "Really, Lydia, I am the one who is supposed to make the offer—it's traditional—and I hadn't planned on doing so for several more years. Eighteen is still rather young to be taking on such heavy responsibilities—the estate, the duties of a wife, et cetera. Don't you want a Season?"

"I don't see the need. I am going to enjoy my birthday ball—"

"The need? Need has nothing to do with it. Well, yes, there are some who need to find a husband during their Season but not always."

"I believe it is more the rule than the exception."

"Please, Lydia, I am trying to educate you about the ways of the world." He stepped back to her side, and they continued down the path. "A Season is all about balls and concerts. Seeing and meeting new acquaintances. It's full of frivolity and flirting."

"You want me to flirt with you?"

"No, of course not. It wouldn't be seemly. Everyone knows that we mean to be married."

"Then you want me to flirt with other men?"

"No, of course not."

"Barley, I am confused."

"Well, that is because you are not listening. As I was saying, you need to kick up your heels. Live a little before you take on your domestic role." And then, under his breath, as if Lydia was not meant to hear, he added, "Sow some wild oats."

"Oh, I understand perfectly now. *You* want to kick up your heels and live a little."

"That is not what I said."

"Yes, but it is what you meant."

The heavy silence lasted several steps. It was broken when Barley cleared his throat—in discomfort. "I think we should hold off a little longer. Until you are twenty, at least."

"I don't believe we have that luxury, Barley. Though we might not need to be married right away, our engagement *should* give you enough authority to question Mr. Drury's management. A right to an opinion—"

"Your opinion."

"Yes, of course, unless you have gained some sort of knowledge in crop rotation of which I am unaware."

"I don't even know what that means." Again, he sighed heavily. "I will have to think about it."

Lydia stopped in her tracks. "Do you not wish to marry me?"

"Really, Lydia, not wishing to be pushed around is not the same as not wishing to be married. I have control of my own life, thank you very much—even if my purse strings are tied around your waist. . . . Oh, I do beg your pardon; I did not mean to mention any part of your body . . . err, umm, person. I should have said bodice . . . or wrist . . . or something else of that nature."

Lydia ignored the reddening of his complexion, amused by his sense of delicacy. "Why don't I have the papers drawn up, just in case?"

"In case of what?"

"You decide that an announcement will serve us best, after all."

"Perhaps. Yes, we could start the process. Iron out the wrinkles, as Mrs. Candor would say."

Lydia had not heard Barley's housekeeper use any such expression before, but then she hadn't spent a lot of time with Mrs. Candor. That, too, would change when Lydia moved into Wilder Hill Manor. A cold, drafty, massive place without a single marble statue . . . and dusty books—such a disheartening thought.

"Yes. We can iron them out." Lydia planned to arrange a life interest for her mother and sister at Roseberry. They needed to be secure in knowing that they could stay at Roseberry for as long as they wished—something her father had failed to consider.

"Indeed. You will be twenty soon enough. It will come quickly." He lifted his head, staring at the empty sky, and nodded in agreement to some internal thought. "Two years should be sufficient."

"Sufficient?"

Dropping his gaze back to Lydia, he smiled. It was full of charm and humor; the very reasons Lydia knew that their life-long union would be comfortable. "Yes, places to go, people to see."

Returning his smile with one of her own, Lydia shrugged. "Fine," she acquiesced. "A two-year engagement is not overly long."

"Engagement?"

"Isn't that the purpose of the contract?"

"Yes, yes, of course it is."

"And then, once the paperwork is out of the way, you can offer your hand. At the ball, perhaps?" She lifted her cheeks even farther and tried to look wistful.

Barley's frown returned. "Please, Lydia, you are trying to control everything again. You will have to wait until I deem the time appropriate."

"No announcement at the ball?"

"We shall see."

"But I really do need you to help me in this disagreement with Uncle Arthur, Barley."

"I think you should be concentrating your efforts on this lawyer chap, your Mr. Lynch. He's the one with the true power—control over the money is key. And this here fellow he's sent around . . . Newbury?"

"Newton."

"Yes, quite. He's the one—sounds sensible enough. Work on him, Lydia. There's your answer."

Lydia dropped her smile. "So it would seem." Then she brightened. "I say, Barley, why don't we take advantage of Mr. Newton's presence? Yes. We can start working on the marriage contract right away. . . . Hmm, let's see. Why don't you come over tomorrow afternoon around two o'clock? I'll forgo my usual constitutional; this is far more important, and I do like to be impulsive." She ignored Barley's snort of derision. "Yes, that would work. . . . Oh, are you free tomorrow at two?"

"Might as well take the bull by the horns. Tomorrow it is."

Lydia watched Lord Aldershot wend his way out of the garden, taking the west gate to the stables. She wasn't too sure that she liked the analogy. A bull? Was she the bull or its horns? Neither sounded flattering.

Glancing at the conservatory wall, she was glad to note that the strange shadow had disappeared—and again dismissed it as a consequence of a distracted mind.

The tableau that greeted Lydia when she returned to the drawing room had changed little since her departure a quarter of an hour earlier. However, there was an addition. Robert Newton was now on the settee that she had vacated, and Cousin Elaine sat beside him—holding up Ivy's needlework.

"Just a little cut, right here, if you don't mind, Mr. Newton. It is vastly important to get the length exact."

The accommodating gentleman proceeded to open a penny knife from his pocket—despite the presence of a pair of scissors on the table beside Elaine.

Giggling, her cousin leaned closer in an overt display of flirtation. Lydia found it most irritating. Elaine had been setting her cap at every handsome bachelor she encountered since she was fifteen, but this bachelor was Lydia's. Yes, hers . . . her . . . Mr. Newton was here on business. This vulgar display was inappropriate.

Lydia's mother was the first to speak.

"Ah, there you are, Lydia. Mr. Newton was looking to speak with you—you are very popular today, I must say. I told him you would be but a moment, and, look, here you are."

Mama did have a tendency to ramble or blather, but even this speech was a little too vacuous for her. Was she nervous? Or was that a sparkle of excitement? And her eyes, why was she moving them about so oddly—from Cousin Elaine to Mr. Newton and back again? Surely she wasn't intimating an attraction between them?

"I'm sure you don't need to pull Mr. Newton away from *our* company so soon."

Lydia was at a loss for words. Though she had known Mr. Newton for only a few hours, she was almost certain that his taste did not, would not . . . should not . . . run toward a girl who thought the length of thread a grievous matter. Lydia's first inclination was to protest this travesty. Fortunately, Mr. Newton knew his way around a drawing room.

"As much as I would like to stay, Mrs. Whitfield, I *am* here on business, and until it is concluded, I must soldier on." The words were spoken with just the right amount of world-weariness to elicit an accepting sigh from the ladies. "I look forward to seeing you at dinner," he concluded.

"Oh, yes, of course. Soldier on, Mr. Newton, soldier on." Cousin Elaine spoke in a breathy voice laden with intensity. "We *will* see you this evening."

Mr. Newton nodded, glanced at Lydia with humor in his eyes, and then rose, slipping his penny knife back into his coat pocket. They said nothing to each other until they had descended to the ground floor, and even then, Lydia made no reference to the obvious matchmaking that had been going on in the drawing room.

"Are your meetings with Uncle and Mr. Drury already over, Mr. Newton? So soon?"

"Would that it were so, Miss Whitfield. I'm afraid that both gentlemen have made themselves unavailable."

Lydia gritted her teeth for a moment and then smiled—somewhat wanly—at the man walking beside her. "Perhaps we should use the morning room to continue our discussion," she said, gesturing away from the study. "It's brighter, and I feel a sudden need of a lighter atmosphere. Might even open a window for fresh air. Roseberry is getting quite stuffy and overbearing." They both knew she was not talking about the manor.

Chapter 4

*In which Mr. Newton is afflicted
with an odd state of the dismals*

The morning room was a much brighter chamber than the study, Robert observed. It seemed equally beloved, with its large bay windows, yellow walls, and charming watercolors of gardens and farm children. There was an informal atmosphere in the room that was unexpected. Not that such a place existed in Roseberry, but that Miss Whitfield had chosen this room to continue their conversation.

It was a business conversation, or so he thought.

"Mr. Newton, there is a matter other than the governing of the estate that I would like to discuss with you."

Her words did not sound ominous, but there was a sudden stiffness to the way she was walking that garnered Robert's attention. He waited for her to explain, but she, instead, waved him to one of the chairs by the unlit chimneypiece and seated herself on the settee opposite. And still he waited.

"Is there something wrong, Miss Whitfield?"

She was now staring out the window, skyward, as if there were something of particular interest in the empty air.

"Miss Whitfield?"

"Oh. I do apologize. I was thinking about sowing oats."

Robert didn't remember the mention of a grain crop. "Instead of apples?"

"Pardon?" Miss Whitfield brought her gaze back down to earth and into the morning room of Roseberry Hall. "No, no." She laughed a very pretty trill. "Poor Barley. He said something about sowing wild oats—Is something wrong?"

Shocking revelations would be part and parcel of a solicitor's daily routine, and Robert thought himself prepared, but to hear that Lord Aldershot had used such an expression in Miss Whitfield's hearing was appalling. Though it was apparent that she did not know that men sowed *wild* oats in the company of light-skirts.

Without comment, Robert nodded for her to continue— reestablishing his attitude of nonchalance with only a smidgen of difficulty.

"As I was saying, Barley has not had the funds to sow any oats—wild or otherwise—nor to kick up his heels and live a little. It's no wonder he feels . . . Well, that is easily rectified. We shall add an allowance to compensate—throughout our betrothal. Yes, that will give him the chance to go to London and be frivolous before he has to settle down and play the devoted family man. Yes, that will do quite nicely."

Robert remained silent. He thought it might be a worthwhile policy when a client was being enigmatic. He would understand soon enough . . . or he wouldn't. There were only those two possibilities.

"Yes, that is just what I'll do."

Her smile was full of life and mischief, and for a moment, Robert could think of nothing other than how appealing Miss Whitfield looked when her eyes sparkled. Overcome by a sudden desire to join her on the settee, he shook the distracting thoughts from his head and tried to focus on the topic at hand. What were they talking about? "An allowance?" he said, finally remembering.

With a sigh of what seemed to be satisfaction, Miss Whitfield nodded. "Yes. Can we add that to the contract?"

"Contract?"

"Yes. Oh, I do beg your pardon. I am starting at the end rather than the beginning. I would like a contract to be drawn up—a marriage contract—between Lord Aldershot and me. I have asked Barley to return tomorrow at two to discuss it—I hope that time is convenient for you."

Robert barely had time to say "of course" before Miss Whitfield continued.

"I thought we could go over the particulars of a usual

contract, then add in what I hope will be agreeable to Barley. I am concerned about the welfare of my mother and sister when the estates are joined, and I would like to retain control of as much of Roseberry as possible."

This time when Robert offered the standard "of course," Miss Whitfield hesitated and tossed him a thoughtful look. He should have hidden his amusement a little better. He had noticed her wish to regulate everything—and everyone—around her, and while he found it both unusual and impressive, it was an opinion best kept to himself.

"I imagine Barley will have a few stipulations of his own. We can discuss them tomorrow. . . . Oh, yes, and an allowance should be included."

"Are you sure you wish to offer Lord Aldershot money before the marriage?"

"It smacks of paying him to marry me, doesn't it? I'm not, I assure you. Well, I suppose some will see it that way—probably best to keep that tidbit confidential. I'm sure Mr. Lynch and Barley will agree—to the confidentiality, that is. Now, where were we?"

And so the afternoon continued as Robert noted Miss Whitfield's addendums. While there was much he had to learn about contracts of this sort, he could explain that her father's estate would essentially become Lord Aldershot's property, to be passed down to their children. She was unaware that the law did little to support her claim once they were conjoined.

"Barley has never shown any interest in the farm."

"I hope that it is ever thus, Miss Whitfield."

"Yes, so do I."

$\mathcal{B}$y the time Robert went down to dinner, he was sure he had served Miss Whitfield well in regard to the marriage contract. He knew that Lord Aldershot would wish to add unforeseen clauses—negotiation was fairly standard in these kinds of dealings—but Robert also knew that Mr. Lynch would find his notes thorough.

However, rather than sporting any sense of satisfaction, Robert was afflicted with an odd state of the dismals. The condition had begun in the morning room while they were discussing the union of the two estates. Somehow it didn't seem right; he felt the need to protest, but on what grounds he couldn't say. Perhaps this undefined melancholy had nothing to do with Miss Whitfield's nuptials but stemmed from the incompletion of his original task—that of clarifying the problems with the estate management.

Yes, that had to be it. He would corner both Drury and Mr. Kemble in the morning and then return to Bath with the situation, if not solved, at least better understood. Yes, he would lose this sense of sadness as soon as he returned to Bath.

And yet, even that thought brought no sense of release. Distancing himself from Roseberry Hall was no longer a priority. He quite liked the lively conversation to be found within its walls. Robert had a sneaking suspicion it had more to do with the way he felt when his eyes met those of Miss Whitfield than with bricks and mortar.

The footman, Hugh, opened the drawing room door with a flourish, ushering him in. The ladies were waiting, dressed in their finery and ready to be taken down to dinner. Lydia—as he was beginning to call Miss Whitfield in his mind—had warned him that dinner was usually a formal affair but that he was not to feel uncomfortable about not having a dress coat. There was nothing he could do about it; he had not planned to join the family for dinner and could not pull an evening coat out of his satchel when one had not been put in.

Still, while the party of women—for there was no sign of Mr. Kemble—was in full evening gowns, Lydia wore an elegant but simple dress of pale green-gray that was cut to form. It was clear that Lydia had done him a kindness in her restrained mode of dress, to make him feel comfortable. But in doing so, she stood out as an antithesis to her relatives' ostentation and Miss Shipley's lacy gown.

"I'm afraid we have a problem this evening," Mrs. Whitfield greeted him with a nod of acknowledgment. "Gentlemen are in short supply. It will be even worse when Ivy and Tessa are out of the schoolroom."

"It's a problem that we have every evening, Aunt Joan," Miss Elaine tittered. There was no other apt descriptor; it was definitely a titter.

Robert said nothing.

"Indeed, it is true." Mrs. Whitfield glanced at Mrs. Kemble for confirmation. Once given, the conversation continued. "We had hoped to have the arms of two gentlemen to lead us into dinner, but . . . Well, I suppose Arthur can be forgiven for picking today, of all days, to visit the Major. Major Ryder has been his dearest friend for . . . I'd say two decades now; although, they seldom get together. His wife passed away some years ago, and the Major lives a bachelor lifestyle that some consider—"

"Mama."

"Yes, Lydia dear. Oh, am I doing it again? Yes, well. I am told by *some*, Mr. Newton, that I have a tendency to veer off topic. I don't see it at all, as my late husband had no problem following my conversation. In fact, he often said—"

"Mama."

"Oh, yes, for heaven's sake. Where was I?"

"I believe you were lamenting the lack of male company." Robert smiled in what he hoped was a benign manner.

"Oh, yes. That's right. Well, it would be traditional that you would take me into dinner, as the only gentleman present and I, the mistress of the house."

Robert did his best not to look toward Lydia at that pronouncement.

"But that would not be fair to the other ladies—and rather selfish of me. And I will not have it said that I am a selfish person, for I am quite interested in charity. The president of the Children's Educational Society has often complimented me on my good heart. Just last week, we—"

"Mama."

"So over time, we have developed a system—a way to share, as it were."

"We have?" Lydia's surprise hinted at a little prevarication.

"Yes, we have. And it's Elaine's turn tonight."

Miss Elaine was no longer tittering but grinning. She tipped her head to the side and batted her eyes in a manner, one can only assume, she considered coquettish.

Neither was appealing, but Robert knew his duty; he bowed to the young lady in question, observed that the yellow of her gown suited her complexion admirably, and offered her his arm.

On their way down the stairs, Robert inquired after her enjoyment of the day and the progress of her needlework, and he offered the possibility of rain on the morrow. Miss Elaine laughed at most, if not all, of his comments—even those about the weather. She wove her fingers together atop his arm, thereby turning her body and drawing Robert closer. It would seem that Lydia's cousin was a determined flirt.

After leading Miss Elaine to her chair, Robert placed himself farther down the table, next to Miss Shipley. However, Mrs. Whitfield was not satisfied with the arrangement; she required the whole of the company to move. Only when Robert was once again at Miss Elaine's side did the seating plan obtain Mrs. Whitfield's approval. Fortunately, this secured him the position across from Lydia.

Though, try as he might, he could not ease the furrows from her brow. He spent the first two courses wordless, trying to understand the cause of her discontent. It wasn't until they were enjoying the third course that the conversation gained his full attention.

"So you *will* have property one day?" Mrs. Kemble continued her questioning, which was beginning to feel more like an interrogation than a conversation. "You won't have to work all those terrible hours to the end of your days."

Running the discussion back through his mind, Robert could not find any reference to terrible hours. It was true enough, though, and he could only assume that Mrs. Kemble knew someone in the legal profession.

"Slotten House is a pretty but small manor in Worrington, Salisbury way."

"Excellent. Yes, excellent, very good. That is only fifteen or so miles from here." She glanced significantly at her daughter and nodded.

"Actually, I believe it is closer to twenty-three miles, give or take." He waved a pointed finger toward the window as if it were visible in the distance.

"And why is it that your *brother* is living at Slotten House, not you?"

"Well, until last year, Slotten House was his to inherit, and I have the town house in Bath for the same reason—with a career eventually in law. It is what is expected of a third son, as well you know."

"I'm not sure I understand." This was the first time that Miss Elaine had looked at him with genuine interest and, therefore, forgot to giggle. "What changed?"

This was a subject Robert did not like to discuss. The pain was still too raw. Even after seven months, the shock was not yet behind him. His life had changed in a flash—a flash of gunpowder. An imagined insult and hotheaded idiocy had taken Lloyd's life.

"My eldest brother was killed last August." He spoke the words with tight lips, hoping that that would end it. He would not discuss the whys and wherefores—not only was dueling illegal, it was as great a folly as any that had been invented.

"What do you think of the venison, Cora? Has Cook not outdone herself?" Lydia smiled and nodded, as if encouraging her friend to speak.

"Indeed. Very good." Miss Shipley lifted her cheeks briefly and then returned her gaze to the table.

Lydia stared at the top of Miss Shipley's head, her brow folded. She sighed softly and then turned back to the company. "Do you enjoy living in Bath, Mr. Newton?"

Appreciating her efforts to lead the conversation to safer ground, Robert smiled. "Yes, I do. Although my work often keeps me too busy to enjoy its diversions."

"That is a shame. No frivolity for you, then?"

"On occasion." He nodded incrementally as an acknowledgment of her kindness and, on close observation, watched her return the motion.

"So Slotten will be yours on your father's death." Mrs. Kemble, however, was *not* sensitive to the emotions of others and brought the topic right back where Robert didn't want it to be. "Your other brother will take the title and seat of Wissett. What is the name of your ancestral manor . . . Tonington Hall?"

"Please, Aunt Freya, you are talking about the death of Mr. Newton's father. It is a subject best avoided." Lydia gave her head a vigorous shake and glared at the foot of the table. Then, after visibly taking a deep breath, she turned back toward Robert. "Would you be able to take time to attend a ball? We are going to celebrate my birthday with a moderate gathering of two hundred or so in the Lower Rooms in May."

She grinned with such enthusiasm that a polite acceptance was out of Robert's mouth before he even considered it. Fortunately, when he did, he came to the same conclusion. Yes, it would be something he would be pleased to attend. Very pleased, indeed.

Lydia talked for several minutes about the plans for the big day until, at last, the other ladies were infected. The discussion then bounced from person to person, with opinions getting louder and laughter that was truly contagious. Robert could add little to the discussion. He knew nothing of the latest fashions, what punches were best served at a ball, or how many nights' accommodation would be required before the big day. And yet he enjoyed their excitement—the way Lydia's eyes lit up when she talked about seeing friends and her smile of patience as she listened to her cousin describe her dancing slippers in excruciating detail.

Just when it seemed that the meal would conclude in this general sense of goodwill, a voice penetrated the doors and, suddenly, the dining room was silent. When the voice shouted again, Mrs. Kemble flushed and glanced at her sister-in-law.

"You'll have to excuse me. I believe I am needed."

Robert stood as the lady gathered her skirts and slipped into the hallway. For the brief period that the door was open, Mr. Kemble's irritation echoed through the cavernous entrance and bounded into the dining room. The reverberation and the slur of his tongue distorted the meaning of his words, but there was no doubt of his inebriated state.

"Dear me, I believe Arthur and the Major might have indulged a little too much." Mrs. Whitfield looked uncomfortable and offered Robert a waxen smile. "It happens so rarely that we must overlook it."

Lydia snorted—in a most unconventional manner—while Miss Elaine began a loud summary of a letter that had been received from an acquaintance. Her oration drowned out the voices from the other room, as it was meant to, but it also left the rest of the table uninvolved, staring at the plates in front of them. By the time dessert was finished, so was the letter's summary and the hallway conversation, but rather than adjourn to the other room, Mrs. Whitfield suggested calling it a night.

After having made his bows, Robert climbed the stairs mulling over the day and all that had transpired. He didn't mean to overhear the conversation between Lydia and Mrs. Whitfield, but the entrance, with its grand stairway, had the acoustics of a theater.

"Mama. You have to do something about Uncle's over-indulgence."

"No, Lydia, I don't. It will all come right in the end."

"Ignoring a problem does not make it go away. It can, and likely will, make the situation worse."

"That sounds like something your father would say."

"Thank you."

"It wasn't meant as a compliment."

"I know. But I will take it as such."

Robert, who had unintentionally paused at the head of the stairs, smiled and went about the business of finding his room.

*A*s agreed, Robert waited in the study for Eric Drury at precisely—Lydia's qualifier, not his—nine in the morning. He was not surprised when the clock on the mantel chimed the hour and the man did not appear. Rising to his feet, Robert opened the door and found the hallway was not empty as he expected, though the person without was not Drury.

Suddenly his mouth was dry, and his heart thrummed in a quick-time march.

"Drury isn't here, is he?" Lydia looked fresh as a daisy for such an early hour; ladies didn't usually make an appearance until midmorning.

"No, Miss Whitfield, I'm afraid not." Robert took a calming breath, disguising it as a sigh.

"I will find him and bring him here, even if he is at the far reaches of the estate. I will not have you forced to stay another night when you have more important things to do."

Robert could think of nothing significant when placed beside the needs of the lovely Miss Lydia Whitfield, and he was about to offer to stay another night . . . or two . . . when she continued.

"I am so convinced that this has to be settled today that I will forgo my usual period of correspondence between half past nine and ten minutes after the hour of ten—"

"Precisely?"

"Yes. What? Pardon?"

"Excuse me. I did not mean to interrupt."

"Oh, well, where was I?"

"Forgoing your letters."

"Yes, that's right. And Mama might need to review the menu at eleven, if Uncle wants to play the same game. Not her favorite task, but if I am otherwise occupied, she will have no choice. It is a topsy-turvy day, Mr. Newton. Everything is in a muddle, at sixes and sevens. . . . Well, we shall overcome. One day of confusion will not set the world aflame."

"Count yourself privileged, Miss Whitfield, that it might only be one day."

"Why do you say that?"

"My days are anything but routine. . . . But then, I would be bored if every day was like the last."

"There is security in routine—calm, peace."

"But no adventure, no surprises."

"Surprises can be overrated."

"Or they can be fun. That's part of the adventure."

"A strange philosophy for an apprentice solicitor."

"We are not all cut from the same cloth, Miss Whitfield."

"So I see." The words might have been biting had the comment been made with the right inflection, but they weren't. They were uttered with a smile and a gleam of mischief. Robert had a feeling that, one day, Lydia Whitfield would find routine, not surprises, overrated.

A half hour later, Drury walked into the study with Lydia hard on his heels. "My apologies, young man. Lost track of time. Miss Whitfield happened to be looking for the coachman just as I was readying my horse to ride out. Would have been gone in a trice, you know."

"Yes, indeed, chance was on our side, sir. Please, sit down." Robert nodded toward Lydia in recognition of her success and saw that she had something to say. "Yes, Miss Whitfield."

"I thought you would be pleased to know that your carriage has been repaired and will be made ready for your return whenever you ask for it. I told Mr. Hodge that it would likely be late afternoon. Was I correct?"

"Yes, that should give me enough time to get back to Bath before dark. Excellent, thank you." Robert did his best to sound enthused—it wouldn't do for Lydia to think that he wished to stay longer, that he wanted to hang around her skirts like Mr. Chilton. Taken aback by the direction of his thoughts, Robert looked down at the desk and shuffled his papers around until he had control of his expression . . . and emotions. When he looked back up, Lydia was gone, the study door was closed, and Drury was staring at the ceiling.

"So shall we start at the beginning? Why pineapples?"

"Tea. Really, Mr. Newton, I have never advocated anything but tea. That I know and understand."

"Good to hear. I shall make a note of it. So where did you get your expertise, sir? Have you been to India . . . China?"

"No, no." The land agent laughed weakly. "I drink it, you know. Buckets of the stuff."

"I see." Yes, Robert could see that it was going to be a long morning.

$\mathscr{B}$y the time Robert sat down with Miss Whitfield and Lord Aldershot at two in the afternoon, precisely, he had a very good idea of what his recommendations to Mr. Lynch would be in regard to the tea-pineapple debacle. He had found Drury every bit as ignorant of estate management as Lydia had stated. The man needed to be replaced and quickly. The problem, of course, was the timing. Most land agents, the good ones, would already be in place; it was spring after all. Growing season was right around the corner.

Problem One: Replace Drury.

Solution to Problem One: Have his brother, Charles, and/or the Slotten House agent, Mr. Brandon, make inquires; Slotten was far enough away from Roseberry that Arthur Kemble would not have any influence over those applying.

Which led him directly into the next quandary.

Problem Two: Uncle Arthur.

During the second, more explosive interview of the morning, Robert was praised and harangued in equal measure. Shouted at and then slapped on the back in jocularity. The man was unpredictable at best, a drunken lunatic at worst. But through it all, Kemble made it more than abundantly clear that his only interest in Roseberry was to feather his own nest. Whether it was with tea or pineapples, he didn't care. Kemble just wanted to make some money—fast.

It was hard to imagine how wrongheaded Oliver Whitfield had been—that he had trusted this beetle-brained elbow-crooker enough to watch over his precious, captivating daughter . . . er, precious estate . . . after his demise. Something must have changed, and not for the better. As a result, Kemble resented Lydia in more ways than could be counted. Her rosy future, her wealth, her opinions, etc. Everything from the colors she wore to the way she walked were part of Uncle Arthur's tirade against the monster called Lydia.

Perhaps it came down to simple greed: Kemble had become used to the niceties of Roseberry and hated the idea of being forced to return to his small house, with limited funds, and two unmarried daughters. That he had squandered his own inheritance on horses and gambling was not considered significant. And now, to be backing a questionable decision based on the promises of an ignorant man put paid to the whole deal.

If only Robert could replace Kemble as well, but male relatives were few and far between in the Whitfield line.

Solution to Problem Two: Suggest that a commission or bonus system be set up based on the success of the estate. Kemble could "earn" the money—a concept that might be abhorrent to the upper crust but well understood by those in need.

So the quest was complete—Robert knew the source of the complaining letters, and he could provide the particulars and possible solutions. Robert could return to Bath with a clear conscious. Well, almost clear. He had yet to resolve the task for which they were now ensconced in the study. A landed lady with money marrying an impoverished title—though the players changed, it was an old game. Even the bride-to-be's young age was not an issue with parental consent.

No, the only difficulty with which Robert was dealing was a personal one.

As he looked across the room at the charming, laughing eyes of Miss Whitfield, for the first time in his life, Robert wished that he were a firstborn son expecting to inherit a title.

Chapter 5

*In which Miss Whitfield prevents abject
despair by extending an invitation*

"*I*'m quite happy to allow you the choice of land agent, but that is where it shall end, Lydia. You will not *direct* the agent or me. I will not look a lemming in my own house, nor will I let it be said that my wife deals in business. Really, a lady should know nothing of plants save where the roses look best in a vase of flowers."

"Yes, I understand—"

"No, you don't. The expectations of society will change the instant we are wed, and you will have to change with them. I'm sorry to say this, but your father, as much as I admired his acumen, did you no favors in your education. A lady should—"

"Barley, you do realize that I'm not ever going to be a mouse sitting in the background, nodding in agreement whenever you bother to glance in my direction?" Lydia stared intently and directly at Lord Aldershot. If Barley did not understand who she was, then she foresaw a heavy slog while they found their footing in the quagmire of married life. She would do it, and eventually she would bring Barley around to her point of view, but the prospect of starting their life together with such misguided expectations . . . well, it made her tired. She suddenly felt old, as if she were nearing five and twenty instead of eighteen.

Lord Aldershot sighed deeply as if he, too, felt older than his years, and then he grinned. "Of course, you silly goose. I know you." His eyes left Lydia's and settled on Mr. Newton, who had leaned forward. "When she was ten, I found her trying to climb a tree—in skirts, no less. Did she ask for help down? No, she insisted that I help her get *higher* to replace the nest that had fallen to the ground."

"Four little chicks were desperate for their mother," Lydia explained. "There was no need for them to die simply because the Whitfields couldn't produce a son to climb the tree in propriety."

Barley laughed, as she knew he would, but Mr. Newton's brow furrowed for a fleeting second.

"Do you regret being born a girl, Miss Whitfield?"

Lydia almost snorted in agreement, but she saw that it was a serious question. No one had ever asked her that before, not even her father when he made her the son he never had.

And as she deliberated, Lydia found that she couldn't look away. She was locked in Mr. Newton's gaze. It was a most unusual prison; she was quite happy to be there. Her heart started to beat faster, and her breathing became shallow. A sense of exhilaration flooded her mind and . . . well, something that could only be described as excitement raced from her toes to her head and back again. She felt as if she could fly, and yet all she wanted to do was stay right where she was, forever.

"I should say not." Barley was still chuckling, unaware of Lydia's stupor—for which she was heartily glad.

Giving herself a shake, Lydia hoped that Mr. Newton was as obtuse as her to-be husband. She shrugged with a pretext of nonchalance and saw no change to Mr. Newton's expression. Luckily, her solicitor-in-waiting seemed unaware. . . . Not that he was *her* solicitor-in-waiting; it was just a figure of speech. Just as anyone would say *their* butler, or *her* sister. . . . Not as if it were a possessive sort of relationship. Not that there was any relationship—

"Lydia?"

Lydia started; fortunately her eyes had wandered over to the window while her thoughts had been tripping over themselves, and so she had not been caught staring. "Yes? Oh, my apologies. I was woolgathering."

"Now, that should settle it."

"Pardon? Settle what?"

There was a pause, a frown, and then a very confused expression stole over Barley's face. Lydia tipped her head, trying to fathom out the misunderstanding. Silence reigned for some moments until there was a loud clearing of a throat from the other side of the desk. They both turned toward Mr. Newton.

"The added clauses have been duly noted. I will discuss them with Mr. Lynch, but I would not expect there to be any changes.

So, as Mr. Lynch does not like to venture out of Bath anymore, I'm afraid you will need to come into the city to sign the papers. Might I suggest you allow two weeks for preparations? Would Thursday, March twenty-seventh, suit everyone? Say at one? Precisely?"

The modulation of his last word seemed to hint at some sort of humor. Was it a joke? It must have been a private one, for Barley's perplexed expression had not changed one iota. Best to ignore such things. "Yes, that will work for me. I have to make some final arrangements regarding my birthday ball—" She opened her mouth to explain about the musicians that had to be hired and the flowers that had to be chosen; but when she saw that neither of the men looked in the least curious, she left the explanation on the tip of her tongue.

"Me as well. That should be fine." Barley shifted in his chair as if he were about to rise. "Unless. That isn't Holy Week, is it?"

Lydia blinked, amazed at Barley's question—not that he didn't know Easter's date, but that he should care. "No, that is the following week."

"Oh, good." He nodded. "I have promised the rector to take part in the Maundy Thursday service."

"Have you? That is a surprise." Lydia thought Barley might be having her on but chose to react as if he was in earnest.

"Really? How so?"

"I didn't know you to be a religious man."

"I will admit that it is a recent inclination, but I find the Reverend Caudle inspiring and his thoughts uplifting."

Reverend Caudle and his family were a fairly new addition to Spelding, having only taken up the living four or so months ago. Lydia found his sermons overly long, particularly as he had a tendency to mumble, and his conversation dull. "Really. I must have missed something. I will have to listen more intently next Sunday."

"Yes. That you must." There was no disapproval in his words, as they were spoken with an air of distraction and followed with a smile. "Will you invite him to your ball?"

"Oh, yes, of course. He and Mrs. Caudle. I'll also include his son and daughter—I believe she is out." Lydia had not had much opportunity to speak to Mavis Caudle as she was usually tucked in behind her mother.

"I believe so. Yes, I think the Reverend said Miss Caudle came out last summer."

"Excellent. Then the entire family will be added to the invitation."

"Are they going out soon?"

"The invitations? Yes, I was hoping for them to go out next week, but Mama has decided to help. So I believe it will be closer to a fortnight now."

"Do I have your permission to mention it? Mrs. Caudle has heard the talk, of course, and despaired over the possibility of not being included."

"Oh dear, we can't have that. I will say something next Sunday. That should put her mind at ease."

"No, no, I'll do it. I'm on my way to the rectory now."

"Are you?" Lydia sat back in her chair to look at Barley from a different angle. It didn't make any actual difference, but, still, she concluded he was not jesting; he really was quite in earnest.

"Yes, the Reverend expressed an interest in my almanac of Somerset fishing rivers. I'm dropping it by. He is particularly fond of trout."

"Is he?" Lydia glanced at Mr. Newton's bland expression and then back to the animated one of her betrothed . . . soon-to-be betrothed. "Then, by all means, mention away."

"Excellent. I will do just that."

Lydia smiled wanly and wondered if a visit to one of those rivers was in her future. She certainly hoped not.

"*Y*ou should have devised something, Lydia. Was it too much to ask?" There was hostility and resentment in her aunt's tone; she sounded so much like Mama.

"No, Aunt Freya, not too much to ask. However, you did not mention your desire for Mr. Newton's continued presence until this very moment. He has already been gone an hour. I can hardly race down the road after him."

Aunt Freya grimaced. "Elaine will be so disappointed. Can you call him back? Invent some sort of need for legal advice—a boundary dispute or a troublesome tenant. Something of that nature."

"I can't without its being an obvious ruse. Perhaps when I go into town to see Mr. Lynch, I—"

"You are going to Bath? Oh, yes, that will do quite nicely. Yes,

yes, Elaine and I will accompany you. You can talk to Mr. Lynch while Elaine . . . oh, yes, this will do quite nicely."

Lydia's aunt continued to congratulate herself on her quick thinking for some minutes before turning away from the railing where they had been standing in the great hall; she was still muttering. Forgotten, or ignored, was that neither Aunt Freya nor her cousin had been invited, and, more important, that her aunt did not know when the outing was planned. Still, Lydia could hardly travel to Bath on her own—at least Aunt Freya would not complain of the discomfort all the way, as her mother was most likely to do.

With a sigh, Lydia made her way to the morning room to work on the invitations to the birthday ball. She could hear squeals of delight issuing from the drawing room. Aunt Freya was no doubt enlightening everyone about her brilliant strategy to catch Mr. Newton for Elaine.

For some reason, the thought made her peevish, and Lydia had a hard time focusing on the task at hand. She stared at the invitation list for some moments before she realized that she had written Mr. Newton's name down . . . three times. Scratching off the superfluous inclusions, Lydia set about the task of writing out a few notes, but her mind wandered yet again. She wasn't certain of where it wandered to, just that she had not finished a single invitation by the time the bell echoed through the hallways to remind everyone that dinner was imminent.

Jumping up, Lydia shook her head. "Papa would not be impressed." She scolded the empty air. "This will not do."

Hurrying to her room, she quickly changed into an evening gown of pale mauve that flattered her figure quite nicely. She tried not to think of the effect as being wasted or wonder if Mr. Newton would have noticed the pretty pearls that her maid was using to dress her hair. These were all distracting thoughts that had no place in her head; with an even firmer resolve, Lydia cast them aside.

Not surprisingly, the drawing room was empty when Lydia peeked in; she was a full five minutes late. She hastened down the stairs to the dining room and slipped in unnoticed. At first, it seemed odd that such a travesty could occur without great consternation, but Lydia soon learned that another topic of conversation, of much more import, was being tabled.

"A new dress, of course." Aunt Freya was facing Cousin Elaine as she spoke.

"Can I have one, too?" Tessa gave the impression of bouncing up and down in her seat.

The two youngest often joined the family for dinner when there were no guests. Mama thought it made the evening livelier and offered the little ones a chance to observe proper etiquette. Unfortunately, manners were a little lacking this evening.

"Tessa, don't bounce. Ladies don't bounce."

"Oh, but Cousin, I can hardly sit still. I am thrilled to pieces."

Lydia smiled at this exuberance. "Are you, indeed? And to what are you referring?"

"We are all to Bath. It shall be such a lark; I have never been there before."

"My goodness. That is exciting." Lydia reached for her glass. "And when is this wondrous excursion to take place?"

The silence that met her words pulled Lydia's eyes away from her glass. She frowned, looking from face to face, finally meeting her mother's gaze. "Mama? Is something amiss?"

"Well, no. It's just that we cannot tell you the when of our trip when *you* are to tell *us*."

"I'm confused."

"You are headed into Bath to see Mr. Newton . . . I mean, Mr. Lynch. Did you not invite us to accompany you?"

Lydia felt a surge of frustration and swallowed her ire with a shudder before replying. "No, actually, I didn't. I have business to conduct and hadn't planned on any frivolity. Aunt Freya thought of joining me . . . with Cousin Elaine."

The silence was now filled with tension.

"You mean, we can't go?" Tessa's chin began to wobble.

It was one thing to foil the schemes of a matchmaking mama, it was another to disappoint an adorable nine-year-old. "A week from next Thursday," Lydia relented. "And we'll have to take both the coach and the landau if we are to be comfortable with all seven of us. Don't want anyone forced to sit on the roof or, worse yet, with the coachman."

She laughed weakly and then sighed. She wondered if she might not be better served by asking Shelley Dunbar-Ross to help with the final arrangements of the ball. Her friend did live close to the ancient Roman town and might have some insights to make the process easier.

"Can't have the landau."

Again, Lydia was required to swallow her irritation. She turned her gaze toward her uncle, sitting at the head of the table—in her father's place. "I beg your pardon?" She showed her teeth in a way that only a drunken sot would call a smile.

"I'm going to visit the Major the next two Thursdays." Uncle Arthur's hands shook as he lifted, and spilled, his wine. Drops of red stained the crisp white cloth.

"Could you not go some other day?" Lydia was hard pressed not to mention that the landau was, in fact, hers and that he was only using it by her good graces.

"Certainly not. Told him I'd be there, and that's what I'll do."

"Perhaps you could ride, leaving the carriage to us ladies."

There was a gasp from Aunt Freya before she spoke. "No, Lydia. That will not do. Riding can be dangerous at night."

Lydia was aware, even if Uncle Arthur was not, that Aunt Freya knew he would be in his cups upon his return.

"Fine. So be it. I shall hire an additional coach for the day."

"Excellent solution, Lydia dear. I knew you would put family first."

Lydia tucked into her whitefish with much more vigor than needed and wondered how she was going to rid herself of this effusive horde of females before arriving at the lawyer's office.

Before journeying into Bath, Lydia made time to visit Mr. Pibsbury. She wanted not only to see how the old gentleman was faring but also to glean any tidbit of farming knowledge that might sway Mr. Lynch to her way of thinking. She was quite sure common sense would rule the day, but there was no reason not to "hedge her bets"—as her papa used to say.

Mr. Pibsbury had been given one of the larger tenant houses on the east side of the estate, an easy walk from the manor. As Monday was a day of spectacular sunshine—rare in this part of Somerset in the spring—Lydia left just after luncheon on her own two feet. She was pleased to note that all shadows were appropriate in size and shape to their source and that her sense of being observed had dissipated.

She found Mr. Pibsbury working in his garden, which was still more mud than soil. They spent a good half hour chatting, reminiscing, and generally having a convivial time. The subject of tea and pineapples was quickly laughed away—so quickly, in fact, that Lydia came away with no new information but a stronger resolve to see Mr. Drury tossed out on his ear.

She was on her way back to Roseberry Hall when she heard a carriage approaching. Squinting into the sun, Lydia realized it was more of a cart than a carriage and then soon after recognized the shape of Reverend Caudle—he wore a distinctive hat, with a shallow crown—and a passenger. The cart slowed and pulled aside.

"Miss Whitfield, well met, well met. I hope you are well on this fine day. Out and about, are you, out and about? Oh, you remember my daughter, Mavis."

Lydia smiled and inclined her head. She was about to begin the usual banal conversation with inquiries into the health of the family and discussion of the weather and then move on, but she was not given the chance.

"Hope you don't mind us using your road, Miss Whitfield. Wilder Hill has the most atrocious drive—covered in mud. All those dips and hills. Thought we might approach from your side of things."

Again, Lydia was about to speak—generously giving the pair leave to do just what they were doing—but the good Reverend continued.

"Off to see Lord Aldershot. We have so much to discuss, fish and fowl, yes, fish and fowl."

"Thank you for including us in your birthday celebration, Miss Whitfield." Mavis Caudle interrupted her father with a hand placed lightly on his arm. Her voice was soothing and calmed her father's twittering.

It also brought Lydia's attention to her, which previously had amounted to a glance. Lydia was surprised to note that Miss Caudle was a pretty girl, not in that insipid vacuous way that seemed to attract the gentlemen, but with character in her countenance and intelligence in her eyes. It was a pleasant discovery, for Lydia had been hobbling through Spelding without any sort of clever conversation for years until Cora arrived. And now, it would seem, another active mind was about to enter their midst.

"You are most welcome. The proper invitations should be in the post within the next fortnight . . . or so. But I am glad that Lord Aldershot heralded its arrival."

"Yes, I believe he understood dearest Mama's excitement. We have not been to a ball since Christmas."

"Christmas. Well, that is not so long, then."

"No, our dancing shoes have barely gone cold." Miss Caudle smiled. They both knew that "dearest Mama" was trying to establish her social position and importance within the community. Being friendly with Lord Aldershot, and now the Whitfields, would take her up several rungs of the ladder.

"Well, I hope it to be a pleasant affair. Not too much of a crush."

Miss Caudle nodded, opened her mouth to speak, and then closed it again.

"Yes?" Lydia encouraged.

Wisely choosing not to play ignorant, Miss Caudle smiled—broadly, as if caught in a mischievous act. "I know this is most inappropriate . . . but . . ."

"Yes."

"I was hoping to . . . well, the library at the rectory is quite small. . . . And I have gone through the complete collection already."

"More than once," Reverend Caudle interjected.

"Indeed." Miss Caudle turned her smile briefly toward her father. "And I have heard that the library at Roseberry Hall, your study, is exemplary and vast."

"That might be overstating it a little, but yes, it is a very good library. And yes, you are more than welcome to visit us with the intent to borrow a book or two."

"Oh, thank you, Miss Whitfield. You are most generous."

"Not at all. Might I recommend week's end. Perhaps Saturday the twenty-second?"

"That would be lovely."

Reverend Caudle foreshadowed his next words by lifting the reins. "Excellent, excellent. Now that that's settled, we must away. Well met, Miss Whitfield. I'll bring Mavis, here, over on Saturday."

"Or I can walk up on my own." It was Miss Caudle's turn to interject.

Lydia smiled and quickly agreed to the latter. Without saying so, she planned to include tea and a chat with Miss Caudle's visit to the Roseberry library. The idea of getting to know her better and perhaps even forming a friendship was very pleasant. Perhaps Cora could join them—a distraction from her melancholy.

Indeed, a productive afternoon.

"*Tessa*, where is your sister?" Lydia stood in the great hall with her bonnet fastened and her gloves on. It was now approaching eleven, and Lydia's temper was building into a grand passion.

It had been agreed the previous evening that the party would set off for Bath at ten in the morning. It was the earliest that the ladies could be persuaded to leave. Even at that, luncheon would have to be a hasty affair if the appointed hour at the law firm was to be met. With each passing minute, the likelihood of a late arrival became more and more evident even without a stop for sustenance.

It was irresponsible, intolerable, inconsiderate, and just plain rude.

"I don't know where she is." Tessa had joined Lydia in the hall without the requisite family at her side a full quarter hour ago. "I'll go see."

"No . . . no, Tessa, just . . ." Lydia's protest went unheeded as her cousin lifted her skirts and skipped back up the stairs.

A few moments later, Tessa's disembodied voice echoed through the hall. "Ellie, why are you changing your gown?"

Lydia sucked in a noisy gasp and looked daggers at the offending staircase that had not produced the ladies. She turned to Cora, who was seated on the narrow chair beneath the hall balcony, waiting with patience—far more patience than Lydia could muster.

"Hugh," she said in a calm voice that deceived no one. "Might you ask Betty to check on the preparedness of my mother and sister?"

Hugh, who had been standing silently by the door waiting to see them away, nodded and headed toward the back of the house. While it seemed like an hour to Lydia, Hugh returned fairly quickly with his unwelcome news.

"Another half hour!" Lydia didn't even *try* to tamp down the volume of her protest. "That is not acceptable. It will not do. Let's go ahead, Cora. Frustration is making me fret—a condition, as you know, that I—"

"Abhor. Yes, I do know." She stood and joined Lydia in the center of the hall. "There is no need for you to wait. It is your appointment and your schedule that should be met. Not to worry, I will explain."

Slowly turning, Lydia stared out the window at the two waiting coaches and considered her options. The hired coach was the smaller of the two; a party of four could be accommodated but certainly not more. The Roseberry Hall coach, however, could seat six in a pinch, though it would not be a comfortable journey. Even five would be uncomfortable. . . . But, well, there had to be consequences for such inconsiderate behavior.

"You shall not be forced to wait, Cora. There is no need."

"I will be expected to care for the little ones, Lydia. I can hardly shirk my duty."

"Stuff and nonsense. We are ready; they are not. I won't have you squished into a carriage because of their tardiness. They won't thank you for the sacrifice, either. No, we will go together. Besides, I need a chaperone."

Cora laughed, only slightly, but it was the first time in days that Lydia had seen her smile. "I can hardly be your chaperone; we are of an age."

"True." Lydia returned her smile. "That might lift an eyebrow or two. Still, we are companions, and that will have to serve. Come now, the longer we argue, the more the delay. . . . And I will triumph in the end, you know. I always do."

"You usually do. It is not the same thing."

Lydia's smile broadened into a grin. She could feel good humor trickling back into her psyche when she realized that a timely arrival was still possible.

Turning toward her footman, Lydia straightened her perfectly placed bonnet. "Hugh, could you tell the ladies, when they arrive, that we have gone on ahead. Time and decorum now dictate that we go straight to Mr. Lynch's, but we will wait for them there before going any farther." That should keep complaints of impropriety at bay.

Chapter 6

*In which there is a rude awakening and an
informative carriage ride*

Many hours earlier, before dawn had even thought about peeking over the horizon, a distant pounding had awakened Robert from a deep, and deeply needed, sleep. It sounded like a fist hammering on the front door of his town house, but Robert ignored it. Longdon would send the interloper away. He rolled over and returned to the ethereal world of dreams.

Within moments, or so it seemed, the pounding became more insistent. This time, it sounded like a fist beating against Robert's *bedroom* door. He knew that to be unlikely, bordering on impossible, and he once again closed his eyes. However, the squeak of the door hinge startled Robert into a fully awake state.

"Sir?" a voice drifted toward Robert from the far side of the room.

"Yes, Longdon. Is there a problem?"

"I'm afraid it's Mr. Cassidy, sir."

"Cassidy? Lawks! Has he done himself an injury?"

"In a manner of speaking, sir. He's so far in his cups he couldn't remember how to get home. . . . An' he sent the chair away what brought him. I put him in the study for the time being. Do you want me to make up the spare room?"

Robert resigned himself to the inevitable. "Yes, indeed. Thank you, Longdon."

Dropping his feet to the floor, Robert grabbed his robe and shoved his feet into his slippers. He hastened down the stairs with a little apprehension. Usually his friend sought his company at a more reasonable time of day—certainly not in the wee hours of morning. And while Cassidy was always cutting up a lark and making a mull of something, he was not prone to such overindulgence that he couldn't recall his own address.

Perhaps he had had another set-to with his father. Yes, that could precipitate excessive drinking and not a bad memory, but no desire to find his way home.

Opening the door to the study, Robert was pleased to see that Cassidy was still upright, sitting in one of the wingback chairs by the unlit fireplace. Unfortunately, he held his head in his hands and swayed in a manner that had Robert glance around the room for a receptacle of some sort, just in case. The ice bucket was the closest possibility.

"You don't look your best, my friend," Robert said quietly.

Of that there was no doubt. Robert had known Vincent Cassidy all his life, growing up on neighboring estates, and Robert had never seen his friend quite as . . . well, he looked green—bile green. His brown hair was clumped rather than carefully arranged around his long face; his deep-set eyes were more like canyons; and his nose looked sore, as if it had suffered a collision with something solid—such as a wall or floor.

Lifting his head, Cassidy smiled weakly. "Foxed, I'm afraid."

"So foxed you don't remember the way home? A pretty story— one that worked on Longdon. But I am less gullible. What is it really? Did you have a set-to with Lord Tremont again?"

"What? Oh, no. Father isn't even in Bath right now. No, this is worse . . . so much worse."

"Really. Best you spit it out, but wait, let me sit. I only just woke up, you know, and my faculties are not yet fully engaged." And so saying, Robert chose the chair opposite to watch for signs that might necessitate the use of the ice bucket. Perhaps his faculties were working better than he had stated.

Robert waited, and waited, but Cassidy seemed more inclined to stare at the carpet than discuss what it was that had brought him to Robert's door. "I'm all ears." The prod didn't produce much more than a start, and Robert suspected that Cassidy was drifting off to sleep. "Well, I can only assume that you have reconsidered the dire nature of your problem. Let us find our beds, and you can tell me tomorrow . . . um . . . later today."

"No." Cassidy's head shot up, and he flushed as the volume of his objection produced an echo. He continued in a more subdued manner. "I can't believe what I have done."

"So, tell." Robert shrugged; it was feigned nonchalance. Apprehension was climbing back into his lap.

"I have accepted a challenge."

The bald statement brought with it a swirl of dismay, horror, and memories. Robert had not been present when his brother stood in front of a bullet, but he had been there for the duel's aftermath—the blood and glassy eyes, his mother's sobs, and his father's laments. Robert's recollections were still so raw they brought pain with them—true physical pain. The relentless cramp in his gut was superseded only by the ache in the general region of his heart.

Robert's silence must have penetrated Cassidy's fogged brain, for he sat up straighter and cringed at some unexpressed thought. "Didn't mean to, Robert. I don't even know what I did to cause the insult. Really, truly. I was just sitting at the Black Duck with some of my fellows. . . . Hmm, can't remember who was with me. Well, I was just sitting there minding my own business. We were laughing and joking, and then everyone looks up . . . over my shoulder. Someone says, 'I will not allow such liberties. You must answer for your words.'" Cassidy shook his head and sighed . . . and lapsed into silence.

Robert, too, shook his head, though not likely for the same reason. He waited, but Cassidy was once again lost in his thoughts. "And you calmly said, 'I apologize, no insult was intended.'"

"Hardly. Wouldn't be here, then, would I?"

"No."

"Don't rightly know what I said. Only know that Peterson . . . oh, yes, Peterson was there. Anyway, after the blighter leaves, Peterson looks at me an' says, 'That was ill-advised. The man's known to be a crack shot.'"

Robert groaned—inwardly. "So you have two choices: Apologize publicly or ignore the challenge."

"Three."

"Three?"

"Three choices. I can show up at Daisy Hill at dawn next Wednesday."

The famous, or infamous, Daisy Hill on the outskirts of Bath had obtained its cheery moniker by way of a cheerless reference. Those who dueled there were known to push up daisies not long after.

"Next week? That is strange; a duel should be fought within forty-eight hours."

"Perhaps he has a busy schedule. He might have other duels on the go."

Robert snorted at Cassidy's gallows humor and then frowned at the thought. "You cannot possibly wish to put your family through the consequences of such foolishness."

"Honor requires it, Robert. Imagine the shame if word got around. I'd be labeled a coward or worse. A stain across the family name."

"Better than being dead."

"I'm not sure my father would agree—"

"Don't say it. Don't even think it. Your father would be devastated. You are his heir."

"He has a spare."

Anger, too acute to share, forced Robert to clamp his jaws together. He breathed through his nose for some minutes, looking for calm. He found it at last, but not until he had come to two conclusions: He had to find out the cause of Cassidy's insult, and he had to find a way for Cassidy to make amends . . . that did not involve pistols at dawn.

"I know you are not that cavalier with your life, Cassidy. If you were, you would not have come here at this ungodly hour. You would have shrugged at the challenge, gone home to your own bed, and thought nothing more of it until next week. No, I am the one person you knew who would not allow it; this duel will not take place."

"I . . . I don't understand, Robert. How did it happen? I meant no disrespect to anyone. How can I insult someone without intent to the degree that requires a challenge? I . . . I . . . I'm not a good shot, Robert. I'm almost as bad as you."

Robert laughed despite himself. "I'm sure you could hit the broad side of a barn if it was required."

Cassidy snorted, no longer looking quite as green around the gills. "You'll help me?"

"Of course. We'll talk about it later, when the port has worn off."

"It was brandy."

"Matters not to your brain. It will hurt like the devil when you wake up."

Robert stood, ushering Cassidy ahead of him. Even as they climbed the stairs, Robert amended his schedule to include a visit to the Black Duck, though it would have to wait until late afternoon or even the evening. Lydia Whitfield was due at the firm of Lynch and Associates at one o'clock, precisely. He did not want to leave her in Mr. Lynch's befuddled hands. Yes, that was the only reason he needed to be present for the meeting. It had nothing to do with missing someone he had only just met.

*N*ow that the journey was under way, Lydia could relax. There was nothing more she could do. Their tardiness, or lack thereof, was in the hands of the coachman. And she had impressed upon the fellow her need to arrive at the law office at one o'clock, precisely.

As expected, the verdant scenes of tranquil fields, charming village churches, and vine-covered cottages brought Lydia a sense of calm. Though it did take a full quarter hour for those wonders to penetrate her high state of tension. Another quarter hour and she was feeling quite mild.

It was somewhere in this vicinity that Lydia noticed a great deal of silence emanating from across the great expanse of two feet, and her heightened mood returned. "Cora, is all well?"

Cora, who had been staring out the window in a posture similar to that of Lydia's, started. She turned toward her friend and frowned, then smiled in a somewhat lackluster display. "Of course. Why do you ask?"

"Well, you have been so quiet of late. I noticed it some weeks back and was loath to point it out lest doing so would exacerbate the . . . but perhaps . . . well, a moving carriage couldn't be more private to discuss any number of problems. If there is a problem requiring privacy . . . that is."

Cora's weak smile disappeared entirely, and she eyed Lydia in such a way that Lydia began to regret her approach. But the die was cast—the deed was done, in for a penny, in for a pound. Might as well take the bull by the horns. Lydia was fully aware that in her anxiety she had overused her metaphors.

"Finding your way in a new household can be difficult; I know that. Family norms are different—odd to those unused to the various personalities. Still, I was certain that you would feel at home, thought your well-being secured, when you were newly arrived at Roseberry. But . . . well, you have not been your usual self for some weeks. Very subdued, even your manner of dress has changed, rather restrained. I would have said it to be against your nature to be so prudent. But, well, there you are dressed head to toe in gray without the least embellishment. No hint of color.

"I could not be more sorry that our experiment has not succeeded. That you do not feel comfortable and happy. I thought it a grand plan—but in trying to help, I see that I have made a mull of the situation. You should not feel obligated to remain at Roseberry if it is not to your liking. I'm sure we could prevail upon one of our school chums to—perhaps Shelley might . . ."

Lydia was babbling, but she was not quite certain how to stop the flow of words; they seemed to keep falling from her mouth of their own accord. "Or find you a position more suited to your needs in Bath or even London. Perhaps it is the monotony of country living that is giving you this fit of the dismals."

Thankfully, Cora lifted her hand, stemming the flow and rescuing Lydia from her runaway tongue.

"Dearest Lydia, I am not unhappy at Roseberry. It is my sanctuary. Ivy and Tessa are delights, as is the *restfulness* of country living. No, all is well in that regard. Please do not trouble yourself."

"And yet you have changed."

"Have I? Yes, I suppose it is true." Cora turned back toward the window, but with no apparent interest in the passing scenes.

"Cora?"

"Hmm?"

"Is there anything I can do to help?"

"Can you make my heart see sense?"

Perplexed, Lydia frowned. She opened her mouth to ask her friend's meaning, but before she had the chance, Cora continued.

"I am not the first to be disappointed in love and likely not the last."

It was such an unexpected statement that Lydia agreed without thought. But in the lapse of Cora's conversation, Lydia cast her mind into the past. She remembered a gentleman much taken with Cora's exuberance during their school days—the brother of one of the other girls, if she was recalling correctly. It had not seemed to be significant at the time, and yet, now on examination, Lydia remembered a comment or two in Cora's letters. A surprise visit upon her return home.

"Mr. Granger? From Fullerton?"

Cora's pursed lips said more than her silence.

"Did you have an understanding?"

Cora sighed and turned back to meet Lydia's eyes. "Very nearly. In fact, that is why I delayed leaving Fardover until the autumn. I did so hope . . . I quite expected a visit and a . . ."

"An offer?"

"Yes. Mr. Granger was quite attentive for several months; we got to know each other well, and I became very fond of him."

"And if he had made an offer, would he have found favor in your answer?"

"Oh, absolutely." Cora's eyes were suddenly bright, and she laughed. "How could I not agree? Not only was Mr. Granger blessed with good looks and the means to support us, a jollier gentleman I have never encountered. Our conversations were as much levity as anything else." She sighed in a wistful manner. "His estate was some distance, and his excuses for coming all the way to Fardover were . . . well, excuses. At our last meeting, he expressed a desire to speak to my brother." Cora shook her head and glanced down at her tightly clasped hands. "It would be hard to mistake that meaning. And yet it seems I did, for that was the last I saw of him."

"Perhaps he was delayed and does not know you are no longer at your brother's house."

"I thought the same at first, and as much as Suzanne and I did not get along, I was fairly certain that she would give Mr. Granger my direction when he finally did call. I was disappointed to leave Fardover without hearing from him, but I did not become overly concerned until a month ago. By then, I thought I should not count on my sister-in-law's benevolence and undertook my own means of contacting him. As I could not write Mr. Granger directly, I wrote to his sister, Gloria, instead."

"I'm trying to put a face to the name. A quiet girl with her nose always in a book—reddish curly hair."

"No, indeed. Chocolate-brown hair—like her brother—and her nose was always in the air."

"Oh. Surely not. You cannot mean Gilded Gloria, the one who put a spider in Miss Jury's pillow."

"Yes, one and the same. More dissimilar siblings you will never find."

"I should hope so."

Lifting her eyes, Cora sighed again. "I sent her a chatty letter and asked after her family . . . mentioned her brother, casually, of course. I received my reply a few weeks ago."

"And?"

"Mr. Granger is engaged to Tatum Brownlow, Gloria's closest and dearest friend in the whole world." Cora's tone dripped with caustic honey. "It was settled at Christmas," she added.

"Oh, Cora, I am so sorry."

"If it had hurt less, I would have been able to share this with you sooner. But I was quite taken with the idea of being

Mrs. Granger. And now, I must toss away my foolish dreams and expectations. Yes, foolish, foolish dreams."

Silence returned to the carriage, but this time it was companionable. Cora looked relieved, as if by imparting the reason for her melancholy she had eased it somewhat, and Lydia now understood that the true source of her friend's distress had nothing to do with her residency at Roseberry.

The quiet accompanied them for another mile or so before Lydia voiced a possibility.

"Cora, as I recall, Gloria Granger was known for her prevarication. It is possible that she was cutting shams when she wrote of Mr. Granger's engagement."

"To what end? There is no need for her to lie."

There might be if Gloria guessed the purpose of Cora's letter and was less than pleased with her brother's association with a lady of no means. But this might be a little too honest an opinion.

"Did she need a reason to splash ink on Venetia Winworth's favorite gown? Or accuse the gardener of lechery?"

"We were schoolgirls then, Lydia. I'm sure Miss Granger is no longer the careless girl she once was."

"It's nice to think that adulthood has tapped us all on the head equally, Cora. But while some of us have undoubtedly matured, not all the girls will be so affected. Some characters need a little more time to ripen. And we are only talking about last year. Not a decade or two."

"All right, if we suppose Gloria was not telling the truth, why has Mr. Granger not sought me out?"

"He can hardly do so if he does not know where you are."

"But Suzanne would have—"

"Would she? Suzanne has not been blessed with a genial nature."

"Then my brother—"

"He is often from home several hours at a time. Visiting the tenants and the like."

"Yes, avoiding Suzanne."

"Exactly."

"So there is a possibility that it is not true . . . that Mr. Granger is not engaged and . . . well, doing everything that he can to find me."

Not overly attached to romance, Lydia found this statement a little too emotional for the situation, but she refrained from saying so. After all, the man only had to visit the minister to ask for Cora's direction . . . or the grocer. Any number of village people near Fardover could have supplied the information—but Lydia would not allow common sense to wipe away the bright grin on Cora's face.

"I think we will have to be direct in an indirect way." Lydia threw her hand down to maintain her balance as the coach negotiated a rather sharp curve.

"I'm not sure I understand."

"Let us write Miss Melvina and ask her if the rumor is true. Her school is near enough to the parish of Fullerton that gossip about the Grangers will have traveled to her. . . . And you know how she loves to share tittle-tattle."

"Oh, Lydia, that is an excellent idea."

Lydia nodded, barely aware that she was approving her own words. Her mind was occupied with other thoughts. It had skipped away from the fictitious engagement—as she was certain it would prove to be—and landed on the next hurdle. How could they contact Mr. Granger without upsetting propriety, and then, how could Cora ease back into his society, where the courtship could begin anew?

As they approached the outskirts of Bath, Lydia was reminded of Mr. Newton. She couldn't help but put the two together. Might she not prevail upon Mr. Newton to facilitate a meeting? It might require a little subterfuge, but Lydia was fairly certain he would be pleased to offer assistance. It was a reasonable expectation. . . . And Mr. Newton was a reasonable sort of gentleman—reasonable and interesting, with engaging eyes, a winning smile, and a character that drew one closer. . . . Yes, indeed, she was quite certain he would help.

Lydia turned her grin to the window.

Chapter 7

In which a person is tossed and a person is trussed

$\mathcal{Y}$awning, Robert glanced at the mantel clock on the other side of the office. Miss Lydia Whitfield would be there in ten minutes, precisely. And here he sat, half asleep at the desk outside Mr. Lynch's closed door.

Another yawn suggested to Robert that he stand up, walk about, or get some fresh air before he was obliged to think clearly. Of all nights for Cassidy to knock on his door, last night couldn't have been more poorly timed. While there was no doubt that Cassidy was in a pickle, it was not a new occurrence; Cassidy was always getting into one scrape or another and relying on Robert to get him out. This one, however, might require significant intervention, even if that involved tying Cassidy to a chair next week.

A duel.

Robert sighed and shook his head. How was it that Vincent

Cassidy, who only a few months ago agreed on the general stupidity of the rite, had been manipulated into participating in one?

To Robert, all sides of a duel were the wrong side—no matter what the reason. His tolerance for the illegal but still prevalent manner of defending honor was never high, but his brother's needless death had erased any acceptance he might have had for something that could only be described as a perilous huff.

If feathers were to be unruffled before the momentous day of stupidity, Robert would have to gather as much information as possible before approaching the offended person . . . a person who must have known that Cassidy had dipped far too deep and was well in his cups. How could a gentleman be insulted by the words of a young man making a cake of himself? Robert needed to understand the motives of the man involved; his investigation would begin with a conversation, a *long* conversation with a sober Vincent Cassidy. Tonight.

Standing, Robert stretched and glanced at the clock; five minutes before Lydia's arrival. It was time for a breath of air to clear his head and get him out from behind his desk. With a glance at Mr. Lynch's door, Robert headed down the stairs. He would wait on the sidewalk, ready to hand her down.

The fresh breeze brought some revival, and pacing smartly in front of the tawny stone building for a moment or two brought the remainder. At one, precisely, Robert was in position, standing straight and proud. Glancing around, he saw that the busyness of the street was limited to a milk wagon, two drays, and a tilbury. A mother and child meandered across the road, and two men loitered, leaning on the corner streetlamp. It was quiet in a semibustling way. Perhaps stating it was quiet in a non-Lydia sort of way would be more apt to Robert's way of thinking, for the street was decidedly Lydia-less.

With a frown, Robert pulled out his pocket watch. Hmm . . . five after one. Looking around yet again, Robert saw that the two men were no longer leaning, sauntering instead in his direction, and the mother and child had been replaced by a gentleman in a bowler, marching with purpose on the opposite side of the road. And still no carriage or travel coach appeared—nothing that would indicate the arrival of the usually punctual Miss Lydia Whitfield.

With a sigh of resignation, Robert was about to determine that Lydia was late when he spied a small coach rolling down the road from the right direction. It was still too far away to ascertain that the driver was Mr. Hodge, and yet Robert was fairly sure that the young lady was indeed about to arrive.

He was rather surprised by the quickening of his heartbeat and the sudden need to throw out his chest. Ignoring both, Robert replaced his foolish grin with a benign smile and nodded to the coachman as he pulled up in front of the law office. The driver was not, in fact, Mr. Hodge, nor was the face at the carriage window that of Lydia's. However, there was no mistaking Miss Shipley, so Robert immediately opened the door and offered her his hand as she stepped down to the curb.

While greeting the young lady, who was all blond curls and polite smiles, Robert presented his hand again and was very pleased to see Lydia lean into the light. However, just as she gripped his fingers, the carriage door on the other side slammed open, and Lydia glanced over her shoulder. The coach dipped on its springs as if someone had entered. Lydia gasped and was jerked backward.

Hauled halfway into the coach by Lydia's hold, Robert sprawled across the threshold, feet pedaling for the step. Catching the edge, he launched himself inside, only to land on his knees on the carriage floor. Intending to spring up, Robert was instantly halted in his ascent by the press of cold, hard steel against his neck just below his jaw. It was an untenable position, kneeling with a knife at his jugular, while Miss Shipley's piercing scream filled the air.

The carriage dipped again, and a guttural voice barked out from the driver's bench. The coach pulled away from the curb, picking up momentum as it sped away. The door banged shut behind Robert, and Miss Shipley's distress faded into ominous silence.

Blinking hard to adjust to the semidark carriage, Robert tried to turn his head.

"Ah, ah, no ya don't. Make yer self comfortable right there."

The rigidity of his muscles was meant to mask Robert's fury, his planned attack. But the knife was pressed deeper.

"I'd sooner slit your throat, my boy. Don't give me the excuse."

A gasp from Lydia stilled his fury. Suddenly he was cold with fear—fear for the safety and sanity of Lydia Whitfield. He had to protect her at all costs. Swallowing with difficulty, he breathed deeply through his nose, struggling for calm and balance.

Would she faint and become entirely vulnerable? How could he reassure her? Would she cry in terror—

"Here, take my bag and be done with it." Lydia's tone was almost as sharp as the knife against Robert's throat.

"Don't want yer bag, silly cow."

Suddenly the carriage jerked, rattling into and out of a deep rut; Robert tensed against the inevitable slice and was surprised by how little it hurt.

"Have a care!" Lydia shouted with obvious distress. "You have cut him."

"Oh," the villain snickered. "Look at you. Red after all—ay. Not a blue blood—ay. Not to worry, just a nick, me boy. Don't get yer drawers in a bunch."

And yet the pressure was eased—the damage to his throat minimized.

"Are you all right, Mr. Newton?" There was a slight tremor to her query, but Robert could neither voice an answer nor move his head.

"Ah, don't you worry none, me girl. Just a drop of blood . . . thimbleful at most."

"How can you be so cavalier? You are putting his life at risk," she snarled. "And for what? What do you want?"

"Ah, Missy. Not gonna answer any a yer questions. I were warned about you."

"Warned? You know who I am? Have you been watching me?"

"This be me not answerin' again. Told ya I wouldna. Now, lean yer pretty self forward and pull them drapes. That's a way. Oh, Oh. Careful. There. Now, sit back and enjoy the ride. Don't get no ideas."

As the light inside the coach dimmed even more, Robert tried to assess the situation with a clear head. It was hard to do, as his awkward position was becoming more painful with every jolt and turn and his thoughts were occupied with the necessary task of avoiding the knife at his throat by maintaining his balance.

"Perhaps now you might let Mr. Newton up off the floor. He is dripping blood on your boots, and you cannot continue to hunch over him in such a manner if we are going any distance. Are we going any distance?"

Robert would have laughed if there hadn't been the danger of slitting his own throat by doing so.

"Thinking of my comfort, are you, my girl? So kind. No, no. The boy will stay right where he is fer now. Won't be long."

Silence reigned in the coach for some moments as Robert, and likely Lydia, considered the ominous meaning of "won't be long." However, the villain's idea of *not long* was not the same as Robert's. The time seemed very long, indeed; he was still on his knees, after all—still in pain, and still trying to avoid the knife.

"I will do as you say if you remove your weapon from Mr. Newton's throat—"

"Leave off, my girl. Knife stays right where it is till I say so." There was exasperation in the villain's tone.

"Holding a knife on Mr. Newton is counterproductive. If you cut . . . kill him, I will most definitely *not* cooperate."

The laugh was nasty and harsh. "Yah, but till then, you'll be a little lamb, now won't you, my girl. Quiet little lamb that makes no fuss, no bother. So good I don't need to tie you up. No need to put the gag to ya. So quiet and calm I won't get twitchy—don't want a man with a knife to get twitchy, do ya?"

"No, indeed. Twitchy would be disadvantageous."

More likely fatal, but Robert was not about to quibble.

"Knew you'd see it my way."

As the eon of ten or so minutes passed, the noise of the city diminished, and Robert was certain they were being taken out of Bath. The irregular rattling across cobblestones gave way to the haphazard ruts of packed earth. He couldn't decide which was worse: the shaking or the dipping.

Finally, the villain directed Lydia to lift the curtain, allowing him and Robert a quick glance outside. The amount of greenery flashing by confirmed Robert's fears; they were, indeed, passing through the countryside, well away from prying eyes that might alert the Watch.

As he squinted at the window, Robert's pain-fogged brain was slow to understand the release of pressure on his neck and the unexpected rush of air behind him. Suddenly he was pitched backward through the door, out into emptiness. Robert landed hard in a tumbling, violent roll, and his momentum left him breathing in dirt, winded and confused . . . but only for a moment.

A scream brought him to his senses, and he was up and running before he could put two thoughts together. But his legs no longer worked, and he landed on his poor, abused knees, shouting out in useless frustration as the coach raced away.

"Lydia!"

*L*ydia glared. There was not much else she could do at this point and time as she was trussed like a Christmas goose. . . . Well, as she thought a Christmas goose might be trussed. She was not a cook, after all. Her bonnet lay in tatters on the coach floor, and her gloves were rags held on more by the rope around her wrists than the delicate stitching around her fingers.

And, the most insulting of insults, she was gagged.

As her only weapon, glaring really was quite ineffectual. The villain seemed unmoved by her outrage, frustration, and appraisal of his character. Breathing in as deeply as she could around the tightly bound rag in her mouth, Lydia decided that a scowl might penetrate the man's calm better than the glare—but he seemed not to notice the change.

He was a thin brute with hardly any hair and a ragged ear; his complexion was swarthy in a weather-beaten way. Though he did not have the demeanor of a farmer, perhaps a fisherman? No, what was she thinking; he was a kidnapper. That was enough of an occupation for any man; it would keep him very busy.

Abducting innocent girls, asking for money—she thought

this his most likely motive—collecting his ill-gotten gain, and then running from the law. Yes, that was why he was out in the sun. Running, running away. Coward!

Lydia tried to shout the word, but it came out more like a grunt than an accusation and only brought a smile to the villain's mouth—revealing a maw of rotten teeth.

"Almost there, Missy."

Lydia shook her head in disgust and turned her gaze to the window. It was not much of a view as Robert's awkward exit had precipitated the trussing—despite her valiant struggle—and a reclosure of the curtain.

Lydia swallowed in discomfort. Poor Mr. Newton. What a terrible landing he must have had. She knew him to have survived; she heard him call out to her as they raced away. Flushing slightly, Lydia heard the echo of her name in her mind. So distraught, Robert Newton had used her first name. Highly irregular—she wasn't sure whether she should mention this slip when she saw him next . . . whenever that might be. Perhaps it would be best to ignore the overly familiar address—after all, in distressful situations, it was easily done.

Despite the heartfelt conviction that she should *not* consider Robert's possible condition, Lydia found her mind continually returning to that very subject. It became apparent that approaching it directly and then moving on would serve her better.

So, at worst, Robert had broken something—a leg, an arm, his head . . . yes, no, she wouldn't get carried away. And at best, he was fit as a fiddle and chasing down the coach . . . or a magistrate. It was likely somewhere in the middle, and rather than allow her imagination any more rope, she should deal with her own pickle.

No sooner had that thought entered her head than Lydia felt the coach slow and negotiate a sharp turn—to the right. They continued to travel farther, but at a much-reduced gait and not for long, a minute. Perhaps two. Another sharp turn, this time to the left, and then the carriage pulled to a stop.

Lydia's heart began to beat at a rate more akin to a brisk walk of some miles than a half-hour sit. Suddenly she felt that there was more security in the foreign coach than the out-of-doors and deplored the idea of stepping into the unknown.

For the first time in Lydia's life, she didn't know what awaited her. It was a very strange circumstance—one that she would not recommend to any but the most frivolous of persons.

The door was jerked open from the outside, and yet another thug made his presence known; he thrust his head inside, taking a long look at Lydia before turning to his mate.

"Yer late," the new villain barked his words—shooting spittle onto the vest of her traveling companion. "Startin' to think ya weren't comin'. Thought we were in the suds."

"Hey now, Morley, calm yerself down, relax and help me get this here baggage inta the barn."

Barn? Did the villain say barn?

"What'cha tie up 'er feet for, Les? I'm not carryin' 'er."

"Lazy sot. Help me get her down, an' I'll do the rest." And so saying, Les shoved Lydia's feet out the door toward Morley and yanked her off the seat.

Within the confines of a coach, the distance to the floor is not excessive; however, as the move was sudden and unexpected, Lydia did not have time to prepare. Though how she could have been ready, she could not conceive. As it was, she connected with the floor in a bruising jolt. That pain had barely subsided when Les grabbed her shoulders and shoved her out the door, banging her elbows and then her shoulders against the sharp edges of the jamb. The process was obviously not a practiced maneuver.

Gritting her teeth, Lydia neither helped nor hindered; she observed and tried to plan an escape. Her resolve to wait it out—to see which way the wind blew—crumbled when lewd remarks about her skirts riding up proved to be too much for her delicate sensibilities. Writhing like a serpent, Lydia kicked out at Morley, catching him on the chin. The move proved to be very ill-considered. The nasty piece of work lost his grip, and her feet slammed to the ground. Les, juggling the whole of her weight, slipped and banged her head against the step.

In that instant, Lydia lost her hold on consciousness.

Chapter 8

In which words such as <u>rats</u>, <u>cell</u>, and <u>rapid descent</u> are strangely pertinent

*L*ydia was brought back to awareness by an odd sensation. A collection of pins ran up her leg, stopping somewhere about her hip. There was a slight weight associated with these pins, and her skirts shifted. It was almost as if a mouse were sitting on her. . . . But that was absolutely absurd.

Opening her eyes, expecting to see a cheerful blue-and-white coverlet, Lydia was momentarily confused to discover that she was lying on her side with her face mushed into straw . . . in a very dimly lit space that reeked of an unpleasant earthy odor. It made no sense until she suddenly recalled her abduction and the possibility of a mouse on her hip was no longer absurd.

With a gasp, Lydia sat up in a dizzy stupor and came perilously close to issuing a most undignified scream. Had her training at Miss Melvina's Finishing School for Young Ladies been anything but exemplary, she might have done so, for the creature was not a mouse; it was a rat.

Lydia had nothing against rodents, but they were not her favorite animal, and she much preferred them in the stables or running through a cornfield—away from her. Certainly not sitting on her person. Fortunately, the process of sitting up served to dislodge the creature from its perch, and it scrambled across the room and disappeared through a hole at the base of the wall.

Grateful that there were no witnesses to her temporary loss of poise, Lydia looked around her enclosure and frowned. Perhaps her gratitude was misplaced; being alone was not a boon in this situation. A person could be worked upon, but this emptiness was not advantageous—certainly not to her.

The little room . . . stall, no, she would call it a cell, for it felt like a prison—not that she had ever had occasion to visit a prison, but it was what she imagined a jail cell to look like. This cell was long and narrow, the floor was covered with a less-than-generous helping of straw, and there was no window. Weak blades of light shone through the cracks and splits of the old wooden walls, where most of the chinking was gone. There was a door—Lydia pushed on it, shook the handle, and changed her description. There was a *locked* door. There was also a chamber pot, the remnants of her gloves, and the trussing ropes. Not a lengthy inventory.

Pressing her ear to the door, Lydia could hear a soft murmur of conversation. It would seem that the villains were nearby—though the volume of the chortling was muffled, giving the impression that the bounders were not close. Turning her attention to the far wall, Lydia ran her hands across the wood, looking for a board loose enough to pull off—to no avail. Squinting through one of the larger cracks, Lydia tried to see beyond her confines, but brambles and dense shrubbery prevented a long view. Still, she could see the sky; there was a hint of pink. The sun was going down? Already?

Lydia had to have been unconscious for quite a while. She lifted her hand and gingerly touched the goose egg on the side of her head. It was overly tender and the likely cause of the headache that had taken up residence behind her ear. A cool cloth at the base of her neck would have provided some relief, but she was certain that neither Les nor Morley would be accommodating.

Lydia frowned and settled back down on the straw to think. Not as easy a process as it might seem; her brain was decidedly foggy. After a great deal of concentration, she realized there was one other person to consider: the coachman. Was he friend or foe? Jailer or prisoner . . . or had he been pushed from his perch?

Staring at the hole where the rat had disappeared, Lydia wondered if the coachman—what did he say his name was—Mr. Boggs, no, it was longer . . . Mr. Brigmond . . . no, Mr. Burgstaller. Yes, Mr. Burgstaller. She wondered if Mr. Burgstaller was next door—locked in and feeling overwhelmed by the day's events.

Kneeling, Lydia tried to look through the opening in which the rat had disappeared. She was forced to lie down before she could get her eyes low enough to see beyond the wooden barrier. Pausing to allow the dizziness to pass, Lydia breathed deeply through her nose and then squinted through the hole. The room on the other side was similar to the one she occupied, in size and condition. However, it was empty. No straw, no chamber pot, and no Mr. Burgstaller.

Lydia was about to rise when she noticed a great deal of nothing beside the door. In fact, it seemed to be a ribbon of dark, almost as if the door opened into an even darker room.

This presented a possibility. Several plans of escape swamped Lydia's mind in a cascade of "what ifs." Still, all was moot until she was in the room next door.

Sitting up cross-legged—her mother would be mortified—Lydia yanked on a board above the rat hole. A horrible and metallic scream echoed through her cell, and Lydia stopped. She held her breath and waited.

No footsteps. No shouting. No reaction.

This time, when Lydia continued, she tugged in slow increments and wiggled the board as she did. She *was* rewarded for her diligence, for while the wood continued to protest, it was a feeble complaint. After a quarter hour or so, she had loosened four boards and drawn them toward her with enough space to squeeze behind them. Well, she hoped there was enough room, for the boards would budge no farther.

It took a great deal of pushing various body parts, folding others, and contorting the rest to make her way through the opening. She ignored the sound of rending cloth—her skirts were ruined anyway, and it was likely the same could be said about her spencer. At last, Lydia stood on the other side, breathing heavily—in silence. She tiptoed over to the door and was pleased to find that it was ajar, just as she had surmised. The voices were still muffled, and there seemed to be no threat of discovery as yet.

Just as she was about to step forward, a loud, nearby thump forced her to reconsider. Suddenly made of marble, Lydia did not move or breathe.

Another thump and the sound of munching brought understanding, and Lydia's knees threatened to fold in her relief. Taking a deep breath, she touched the wall as if to pat the horse in the next stall and shook her head—amused, temporarily, by her skittishness.

Slowly, using her foot, testing for unseen obstacles, Lydia inched toward the wide barn doors. These, too, had seen better days, pocked and splintered by years of wear and tear. Partially open, the pattern of disturbed dust told Lydia that the doors were fixed open—likely hanging from rusted hinges.

Hidden by the dappled patches of twilight, speckling a derelict cart, Lydia stared and sighed. She had an excellent view where she stood and now knew the answer to one of her "what ifs." She would have to find a less direct escape route. Thugs Les and Morley were acting sentry in the yard just outside the door. And they were not alone. A third man had joined them, and while she couldn't give him a name, the villain looked familiar.

But of poor Mr. Burgstaller, there was no sign.

*R*unning his hands across the rotted wood of the barn wall, Robert searched for a board that might be pried away from the dilapidated building. But Lady Luck, who had been playing hide-and-seek with him all day, had disappeared yet again. The boards did not shift.

Curling his fingers into a fist, Robert gave into his frustration for a moment. He clenched his jaw and silently shouted at the Fates for bringing him so close only to stop him now.

With deliberation, Robert loosened his fingers and began to search the wall again. He had absolutely no intention of failing, not now. Not after coming so close. There was a way in; he would find it, come hell or high water. Then, of course, he would have to get back out . . . with Lydia—even if he had to carry her.

Robert shook away his dread, as he had done all day. Best to focus on her rescue . . . only that. Soon. Soon he would free her. Soon they would head back to Bath—back into the loving arms of her family. That might be doing it up a little too brown, but it served to keep his thoughts from dropping into the treacherous waters of blame.

As a logical creature, Robert knew that his sense of guilt was misplaced. Perhaps it was the uncertainty that sat so heavily on him. The sense of responsibility. He *should* have done something. Over and over he replayed the scene in the coach. What could he have done differently? How could he have protected her?

As soon as he was able, Robert had given chase. The cut on his neck was easy enough to stanch, as it was not deep. It took longer to get the feeling back in his knees. But when it *did* return, he ran, then jogged, and then, as the fatigue set in, he walked.

Three miles down the road he found a farmer willing to sell him a bay mare for the value of his pocket watch.

He rode for miles—following one side road after another until it petered out or a passerby assured him that no coach had come speeding by. Back to the main road and then down the next country lane. And so it went for hours.

Just as exhaustion grabbed Robert by the throat, Fate nodded in his direction. He was passing through a collection of cottages—the number was too small to even call it a hamlet—and there he heard raised voices. It took only a casual inquiry to learn that a farmer had been forced into the ditch by a speeding coach. The man was not best pleased—complaining and explaining in detail the process of dragging a wagon out of the mud.

Sharing his indignation was a tinker, who had seen activity at the old Beyer farm where there was no reason for anyone to be. The house had burned down four years ago, taking most of the family with it. Tales of hauntings kept all but the most stalwart away.

Curious, the tinker had driven into the yard to offer his services. After all, even squatters need to fix their pots. The rude greeting that he suffered was uncalled for. He was just a man plying his trade—just trying to make a living.

Within a quarter hour, Robert found the Beyer farm, tied the mare to a sheltering tree, and slunk through the overgrown shrubbery to spy on the persons who had upset the locals.

Robert squinted at three men sitting outside the dilapidated barn, trying to verify their identity. Only one figure was familiar—the knife-wielding thug from the coach—but that was enough. Robert then circled around to the back.

*L*ydia was exploring the outlying regions of the barn when she heard a strange sound. A strange but somewhat familiar sound—that of complaining old wood. It would seem that someone was pulling at the wallboards in a surreptitious manner.

Why? Who?

Naturally, Lydia's mind was suddenly swamped with theories. The cavalry was coming to her rescue . . . no, curious locals. No, Robert had found the parish constable . . . and a magistrate. Hmm, none of the above, for all would have come through the front door. It could mean only one thing . . . one individual. Well, one of two, if she thought it through properly. Mr. Burgstaller or Robert.

Affable though he was, Mr. Burgstaller was not anyone's idea of a gallant knight—however, Robert most certainly was. Yes, Robert was coming to her rescue. It had to be him.

Lydia was quite taken aback by the sensations that coursed through her person upon that conclusion. Her heart beat faster, and it had not been plodding along to begin with, and she felt light-headed, overcome by excited anticipation.

Her first inclination was to rush toward the sound, but common sense offered another possibility. Might it be a stranger—someone wholly unconnected to this mess? Someone who was there for his own nefarious deeds, like a thief? Well, that made less sense, but she should not jump to any conclusions. Caution was the order of the day. Prudence and caution.

With a slow and calculated approach, Lydia neared the source of the sound—it was not loud, but it was persistent. All of which reinforced the possibility that Robert was the cause. Choosing one of the widest and closest splits in the boards to peek through, Lydia squinted. A waistcoat—albeit a well-made, thoroughly dirty, stained waistcoat. This aspect was not at all helpful. Shifting a little to the side, she found a knothole, pushed out the center, and was rewarded.

"Robert." It was a sigh and a call at the same time. She ignored the lump in her throat and called again.

In an instant, her view was obscured. "Lydia!"

They were eye-to-eye, and neither said anything for a moment or two.

Finally, after an audible gulp, Robert spoke in a whisper. "Are you all right?"

"I've had better days," she said in seriousness, and then realized the absurdity of her words and chuckled. "I'm covered in dirt, cuts, and bruises and sporting a lovely goose egg above my ear. One of my favorite gowns is nothing but a ruin, but other than that, I am fine. And now that you are here, I am better."

"Thank the Lord. I cannot tell you how relieved I am to hear you say so. I have been imagining all sorts . . . well, let's talk about this later."

"Yes, when we don't have to whisper through a wall."

"Indeed."

"So what is the plan?"

"Hmm . . . well, plans are a little lacking at this moment. I had expected to rush in and simply grab you, but there are *three* guards by the door. I procured a thick stick, but three to one . . . well, not good odds. My second idea was to loosen some of these boards and pull you out. I have also acquired a horse. So once out, we can sneak or run, whichever is the most prudent."

"Yes, but the getting-out part seems to be the problem. For, if I am not mistaken, none of the boards on this side of the barn are loose, and the other sides are too close to the villains."

"There does seem to be a decided lack of cooperation on the part of the building. I have, however, noticed something that might offer another possibility. It would require a great deal of trust on your part."

"Oh?" Lydia was almost certain she was not going to like this new possibility.

"Yes. There is a hay door above me. Is there a loft inside?"

"Are you thinking that I should climb a rickety ladder to the loft and then try to escape through the hay door?"

"Just a thought."

"How would I get down?"

"That would be the trust part."

"Ahh. I would jump, and you would catch me." Lydia visualized her descent, skirts every which way, and a very hard landing that might produce a broken body part.

"Yes. Not a brilliant plan. Do you have another?" Robert sounded hopeful.

"Not really. But might I suggest a variation to yours?"

"By all means."

"I will return to my cell and get the rope that the thugs used to tie me up."

"They tied you up?"

"Yes. But don't let it bother you. . . ."

"No?"

"No. Because if they hadn't, then I wouldn't have a rope to lower myself from the hay door. I can use the one they used on my feet; it's thick and long."

"I like that so much better than watching you fling yourself from a high perch."

"Me too. It might take a few minutes as I must return to my original cell—I escaped, you know."

"I didn't. That is quite impressive."

"Thank you. Anyway, I must return to my cell for the rope, climb the ladder, cross the loft to the door . . . et cetera, et cetera. All in silence, of course."

"Of course."

"It might take as much as twenty minutes."

"I promise to wait. Won't wander off . . . pick flowers or party with the thugs."

"Good to know."

"Just warn me before you jump."

"Oh, yes. I will most certainly let you know." With a deep sigh, Lydia headed back to her cell, slowly and quietly.

$\mathcal{R}$obert leaned his forehead against the rough wood of the barn as he listened for Lydia's departure. Nothing, not a sound. It was both relieving and disconcerting at the same time. It left him uncertain once again . . . not knowing where she was, if she was safe. Still, up until some moments ago, Lydia had been hale and hearty. While Robert had not actually seen her, and it was conceivable that she had tossed him a bouncer, he doubted it.

Robert smiled in recollection. It was remarkable. This resilient young lady had been kidnapped and held in a barn for hours against her will. Yet far from being overwhelmed by the whole ordeal, she had escaped from whatever it was that she had called her cell, had been devising a getaway and was, even now, preparing to descend a rope. Miss Lydia Whitfield was rather extraordinary.

Slowly lowering himself to the ground, Robert settled into the tall weeds to wait. Watching the shadows lengthen did nothing to ease his anxiety, especially when they crept up to the barn and scaled the wall. The peak of the roof was half in shadow when the hay door finally opened and something was flung out from within.

Jumping to his feet, Robert reached for the dangling rope to secure it. But it was too short. The bloody thing stopped a good three to four feet above his head. He was going to have to catch her after all.

Arms wide, legs apart, Robert stood directly under the rope, braced and ready. Eyes glued to the door, he barely blinked. He held his breath as he watched Lydia back out of the opening on her knees, hooking one foot and then the other around the rope. Leaning halfway across the threshold on her belly, Lydia pulled her skirts outside. She then slid the rest of her body through the doorway until she reached the tipping point. To go farther, she would have to relinquish her hold on the door frame.

Not surprisingly, Lydia did not move for some minutes. Robert could almost hear her take a calming breath, preparing for the plunge. Her hesitation seemed to last an eon or two, and then she did it; she let go.

Robert grabbed a breath and stiffened in the ready. But Lydia did not drop like a stone; she lowered herself hand over hand, stepping down the twisting and turning rope. Robert refocused on her feet—knots! The length of the rope was covered in knots; Lydia had fashioned herself a ladder of sorts. While the process was excruciatingly slow, it was not the harrowing fall that Robert had envisioned . . . until she came to the end of her rope.

"Um. Robert?" she called down softly. "Did I. Count wrong? Is that. The end?" The cadence of her words was irregular, as if she was trying to talk while panting.

"That's it, I'm afraid," Robert whispered, fairly certain she could hear him.

"Much farther? Can't see."

"Not much farther. I'll catch you, not to fear."

"Just let go? Like that? Rather daunting."

"I can imagine it would be . . . but your choices *are* limited."

"Could climb up."

"Yes, you could."

"Ill-considered."

"Very."

"So one choice. Let go."

"Afraid so."

There was a moment of silence before Lydia spoke again. "Catch me?"

"I will not let you fall. . . . Well, no, that's not true—you *are* going to fall. What I mean is, I will not let that fall cause you an injury."

"I'll land on you."

"Yes."

"Above and beyond the duties of a lawyer's clerk."

"Perhaps it is stretching the definition a little. But it certainly is not above the expectations of a gentleman."

"Gentleman first . . ."

"And a clerk second."

"Quite like that."

"You are dawdling."

"You noticed."

"Indeed. And, not that I wish to hurry you, but your jailers will, at some point, come to check on you, and finding you dangling from a hay door could be rather awkward."

"Very true." Lydia sighed deeply enough for Robert to hear her. "On three, then."

"Excellent, idea."

"One . . . two . . . three."

Lydia arrived in his arms almost before the count was complete. She was not heavy, but the momentum of her descent was such that Robert dropped to the ground to prevent a severe jarring. They landed in a heap all but nose to nose, with Robert underneath. Neither moved for several minutes.

"Are you all right?" she asked.

Robert chuckled softly. "More to the point, are you?" They were both breathing heavily from anxiety and exertion—yes, that was all. He did *not* notice the press of her soft body against his. He was *not* aware that her lips were mere inches . . . so close and—

"I'm in fine fettle, thanks to you."

Her breath puffed gently across his face, and Robert pulled his gaze from Lydia's tantalizing lips to her concerned eyes. "Well, that makes two of us."

Using his shoulders, Lydia pushed up and, unfortunately, off him, sliding to his side. There, she made no attempt to rise. "I'm heartily glad to be on this side of the wall. It was not the most enjoyable of experiences."

"It? The jump, the climb, the cell . . . ?"

"Yes, exactly."

Robert nodded, finding his feet. "Shall we go?" He offered Lydia a hand and pulled her into a standing position. Not quite steady, she leaned on Robert until she regained her balance. They might have stood staring at each other for some moments had it not been for a rustle in the woods that startled them from their stupor.

It was only the wind whistling through the trees, but it served as a reminder. Now was not the time to dillydally. There were villains aplenty on the other side of the barn: villains who would not appreciate their attempt to vacate the premises.

"Follow me," Robert whispered as he fought his way through the shrubbery to the awaiting mare.

Chapter 9

In which an enlightened friendship has its beginnings

The road was barely discernible when Robert finally led Lydia—and the horse, which she had named Fanny—out of the ditch. They had slunk away from the Beyer farm through the bushes, making their way via the trench running alongside what should rightly have been called a lane. Still uncertain of their security on the main road, they chose to endure the mucky ditch, walking for several miles in tense silence. As the distance from the farm increased, their fears of discovery lessened, and yet they found no sanctuary. The few cottages and farms they encountered were shuttered and dark against the night. No refuge to be found—only miles of empty road to Bath.

The moon was not full; in fact, it was barely over half. Still, it provided enough light to allow a faster pace, certainly better than a ditch that was rocky and slippery with moss. At first, Lydia rode Fanny alone—sitting astride with her skirts hitched to her knees in a very unladylike display.

Robert said that he *preferred* to jog alongside. Lydia knew him to be cutting shams—that he was concerned about her modesty. Chivalry and good manners were all well and good in a ballroom. However, being on a lonely road while rushing away from villainous villains was neither the time nor the place for excessive decorum. When it became apparent that maintaining propriety was slowing them down and increasing their danger, Robert relented.

Had circumstances been different, the process of getting Robert seated safely and comfortably behind her would have caused considerable mirth. It was awkward enough mounting from a stump, but near impossible to stay on Fanny's back without holding on to her person. He tried and proceeded to slide off—twice.

"Hold on, Robert. Put your hands on my waist."

"Your waist? But . . . but . . ."

Lydia reached behind her, grabbed his hands, and pulled them around her. "Propriety will have to stand aside for the moment. Just don't think on it."

Robert remained silent for a moment. "That's easier said than done." His voice was strangely husky.

Urging the horse forward, Lydia smiled. She was rather intrigued by the feel of his body pressed so tightly against her; the sensation was quite agreeable—strangely comforting and exciting at the same time. With the extra weight, they couldn't push Fanny into a canter, even with her rest at the barn, but the horse could manage a trot easily enough. And so, at last, they started to make headway.

Just as Lydia was approaching a state of decreased apprehension, she detected a sound. A sound that she had been expecting—but did not *want* to hear. Pounding hooves. Riders—moving fast.

In an instant, Lydia slipped down Fanny's side while Robert slid off the back. He pulled the horse across the road and into the shrubbery while Lydia leaped into the ditch. She found a tall, bushy weed and hunkered behind it, ignoring the smell of rotting vegetation—and other less pleasant odors. Frozen in fear, Lydia waited. It was a long wait, and then all too soon, the riders were upon them.

Three men on horseback.

Lydia recognized the thug called Les immediately, but they thundered past with such speed that she had no time to discern who was with him. The other two figures were a blur, and soon the trio was lost to the dark, and the pounding of iron on gravel faded away. Frowning, Lydia met Robert on the crest of the road. They stared into the night after the riders.

"That was—" Lydia was about to say "odd," but she didn't want to appear ungrateful for going unnoticed.

"Odd," Robert finished for her.

"Yes, exactly." Lydia nodded and then shook her head. "They were not searching for me. Not at all. How extraordinary . . . to go to such lengths to abduct me, then not . . ."

"Perhaps they searched around the farm. Then fled, believing that you would bring the law down on them."

"Yes, I suppose. That makes sense," she agreed absentmindedly as they mounted Fanny again. "But it is rather lackadaisical." This time the closeness of their persons felt natural, and Lydia leaned against him; he did not protest. In fact, he tightened his hold for several glorious moments, and Lydia was entirely distracted. However, sense prevailed. Robert loosened his hold, and Lydia heeled the horse into a quick walk.

"When I think on it, Robert, this whole affair is rather peculiar. I know nothing of kidnapping or kidnappers, but one would assume that once the abductee is secured, one would check on said person every so often. And yet there was no checking—I ran around that barn at my leisure. . . . Well, not really, but you understand what I mean."

"Yes, indeed. If I had a habit of making off with young ladies—not that I would—but if I were a black-hearted villain relying on ransoms, I would not leave a length of rope with a prisoner."

"Rather inept."

"Indeed."

"I don't think we are dealing with experienced kidnappers." Lydia wasn't certain if this realization made her feel better or worse.

"Then with whom are we dealing?"

"I have no idea. Persons in dire need of funds, I suppose."

"That could include the entire population of England," Robert said unhelpfully.

"Except the upper ten thousand."

"Even some of those are hard pressed for blunt."

"True enough. But perhaps we can leave the royal family off the list."

"A safe bet . . . though I have heard that the Pavilion in Brighton is proving to be a heavy burden."

"So you think the Prince Regent arranged to have me kidnapped to pay for his folly?"

Robert laughed, his breath fluttering the loose hairs at the nape of her neck, sending a shiver down her spine. "No. I think it safe to say the Prince Regent is not involved." Then his tone became serious. "I will find out, though, I promise you that. I'm not quite sure how, but I will, even if I have to send to London for a Bow Street Runner."

Noticing the pronoun, Lydia corrected him. "Perhaps *we* can begin with Les."

"Les?"

"Yes, the thug from the coach, the one who tossed you onto the road."

"I didn't know he had acquired a name—one you gave him? It's not very villain-like, you know. Brutus or Attila might be better."

Lydia laughed halfheartedly. "Morley called him Les when we arrived at the farm."

"Ah, I see. Les and Morley. Do they have surnames?"

"I would assume so."

Robert waited, sighed, and then gestured ahead. "I thought I recognized one, the fellow in black with the stubby nose. He carried himself stiffly. Something about him seemed familiar. Was he your driver?"

"*My* coachman? Oh, you mean the one I hired. No, it wasn't Mr. Burgstaller. I wish I knew what had happened to the poor man. I hope he is all right."

"I would say that he is. Les did not slit my throat when he had the opportunity. He tossed me onto the road. Most thugs would kill you as soon as look at you—"

"Met many outlaw types, have you, Robert?"

"Pardon? Oh, I do work at a law firm, you know."

"Yes," Lydia smiled. "You deal in estates and wills. Not criminal law."

"I see you know the difference."

Lydia laughed, twisting her shoulder back to nudge him in an overly familiar manner, and then realized what she had done. "Oh, I apologize most profusely," she said in horror. "I *do* beg your pardon. I don't know what I was thinking. . . . I . . . Miss Melvina's Finishing School for Young Ladies did *not* cover appropriate behavior while escaping from an abduction."

"I am not surprised."

"Still, I am almost certain she would frown upon my behavior this evening. I have called you by your given name twice—"

"Five times, but who is counting?"

"Right. Five times, and now, I have treated you with great familiarity."

"With the familiarity of a friend."

Lydia cocked her head. "Friend?"

"Yes. After all we have been through, I think we can readily agree that our relationship has undergone a change."

"I do feel as if I have known you a great deal longer than a couple of weeks."

"I would agree. So perhaps we might continue as good friends and not worry about the rules of propriety."

"I would like that . . . Robert. Yes, I would like that very much. Though, we can only be this relaxed with each other when no one else is around. My mother would faint dead away to hear me talking in this manner."

"I think Mr. Lynch might object as well. So we shall make a pact—friends at all times, but not obvious in the presence of others."

"Oh, I do like that." Lydia nodded, wishing she could drop into a polite curtsy to do this properly. "Welcome to Lydia Whitfield's social circle, Robert. I will warn you, however, that you are the only gentleman in the ranks until my marriage."

"Thank you, I appreciate the inclusion—Lydia, are you all right?"

Lydia suddenly felt faint, and her ability to sit astride a horse became a bit of a challenge. Breathing deeply, she waited for the world to stop tilting, and it did, eventually. Though her feet were on the ground now, and Fanny was at her back. Robert was still atop the horse, awkwardly leaning down to support her arm. His grip on her elbow was tighter than necessary, but then again, the road did seem to be undulating.

"Are you all right?" Robert asked again, sounding quite concerned.

"Yes, of course," Lydia assured him, though it was not entirely true. Her world had just toppled over. The future, her expectations, plans, hopes, dreams . . . all had dissolved into dust. "I was somewhat overcome by the enormity of what has occurred." She made her voice sound strong and assured, despite feeling anything but.

"I wouldn't think acquiring a male friend would be life-changing." He released his grip and pushed himself off the back of the horse. He moved to be in front of Lydia, arms out, hands hovering near her elbows.

Lydia laughed, although even in her ears it sounded hollow. "No, I was not referring to your friendship. I realized the consequence of this . . . incident—my abduction. I am very glad the invitations for my birthday ball have not yet gone out. That would be most embarrassing."

"Embarrassing? I'm confused."

"My invitations would be unanswered at best, scathing comments at worst. To be in my company . . . no one will associate with me now. To do so would be to condone what I have done."

Robert straightened and dropped his arms back to his sides. "But you have not done anything."

"I have spent the night away without family or a chaperone. A disaster to all polite society."

"It was none of your doing—you were dragged away."

"Immaterial to anyone other than my family. No, I am completely beyond the pale now. A pariah. Any invitation I extend will be ignored or rebuffed for years to come. I can only hope that Ivy will not be painted with the same brush. Perhaps if I go abroad . . . but I do not want to leave Roseberry. Another house, then. Yes, that might serve. I can buy another manor for the family, well away from my taint."

"I think you are overstating it."

"No, I don't think so." Lydia sighed deeply and looked down the road in the direction of Bath. She swallowed the lump in her throat. "Beyond the pale," she repeated.

"I will not say anything about the abduction. It is between us. No one need know—"

"Cora was screaming when the coach pulled away. She will have turned to Mr. Lynch, who will have sent for a constable. And then dearest Mama will have arrived to create a terrible scene. Scandalous gossip will spread like wildfire—growing larger with each telling. Like Pandora's box, the evil will not be contained." Lydia gulped, stared at the starlit sky for a moment, and then continued. "So, you see, no birthday ball and no marriage to Barley . . . Lord Aldershot." It was strange that her last pronouncement did not upset her as much as the first.

"You can speak to Lord Aldershot, assure him that nothing happened."

"Nothing happened?"

"Nothing that would prevent your marriage."

"Appearances mean a great deal to Barley. And as appalling speculation will follow me around for the rest of my days, he will wash his hands of me no matter what did or didn't happen—of that I am certain."

"He will hardly put his happiness aside to bow to the expectations of society."

"He might not if we held each other in deep affection, but such is not the case. While I am fond of Barley—"

"Fond?"

"No, you are right. Fond is too strong. I was resigned to marrying Barley—Robert, stop frowning. It is not such a hum, the boot is quite on the other leg." Spying a large boulder off to the side of the road, Lydia pointed—gestured; ladies don't point. "Do you mind if we rest for a bit?" she asked, plunking down on the rock before he could reply. Fortunately, it had a large surface, and there was room for them both. Fanny did not complain, nibbling instead at the edging grass.

"I have never been a romantic sort, Robert. Always thought it a luxury I could ill afford."

"I beg to differ—your affection for family and friends is very evident."

"I refer not to my capacity to love. *That*, I believe, is intact. However, unlike most young ladies of our society, I have not wasted hours imagining an ideal husband. There was no reason; my father had an agreement with Lord Aldershot, and I have not met anyone who might sway me from his course."

"Not Mr. Chilton?" There was no hiding the amusement in Robert's voice.

"Exactly. There are Mr. Chiltons aplenty in this world, but no . . . who would be the epitome of manly virtue—Sir Lancelot or Adonis? No, Lancelot was not honorable, and Adonis was beautiful to look at but not husband material."

"Are you saying there are no gentlemen of husband material in your vicinity?"

"Exactly. So you see the problem."

"Indeed, you need to get out more. Too sheltered by half."

Lydia laughed. The world was falling down around her, and yet she laughed. Or at least she did for a moment, and then she lapsed into silence . . . with an occasional gulp. She refused to allow the tears to fall. If she did, they might not stop for a very long time.

Robert dug into his breast pocket and pulled out his handkerchief. It looked clean. Well, fairly clean . . . but then it was hard to see in the weak moonlight. Probably just as well. Passing the cloth to Lydia, he fought an overwhelming urge to take her in his arms. He had come to the realization that Lydia was right; not about husbands—he was certain that Lord Aldershot was not her best match. No, Robert's realization was that Lydia was, indeed, facing a changed future—though not necessarily a bleak one.

"I'm quite certain that Mr. Drury will no longer be a problem."

She laughed again, though Robert could tell it was through tears. "Yes, he will be out from under my roof before you can say guilt by association."

"What about your uncle?"

"No, he is being paid by the estate until I'm one and twenty. He'll probably stay, more's the pity." She sighed deeply. "If I had been the son my father wanted, it would not matter—"

"I am glad you are not a man, Lydia. I quite enjoy your company just as it is."

"Thank you, Robert."

He could hear a smile in her tone.

"You will come to visit me, won't you? Even if the world forsakes me."

"Of course. Though I refuse to talk of ribbons and gewgaws to make up for your lack of womanly society."

The idea of offering Lydia his hand, as an alternative to spinsterhood, was on the tip of Robert's tongue. Such a proposal was one that might be expected of any gentleman in circumstances such as these . . . the lack of chaperone circumstances, not the abduction/jumping from a barn circumstances. Still, Robert wasn't certain how Lydia would perceive such an offer. And if he were honest, he wasn't entirely sure how he felt about the idea, either. . . . Though the thought of being riveted to Lydia was by no means abhorrent—quite the opposite.

It was a strange position to be in. Logic allowed that he would one day marry, and yet it was not something that had enticed him: too busy by half—yes, too busy demonstrating his superior qualities as a clerk to secure an apprenticeship. All things in order—career first, marriage second. It wasn't until meeting Miss Lydia Whitfield that Robert began to reflect on when that second step might take place.

While Lydia was a wealthy young woman with an acceptable lineage and an excellent reputation, her marriage prospects were far higher than Robert Newton, third son of the Earl of Wissett. There was no possibility of a romantic association at all. The vast differences in their situations would label him a fortune hunter at best, a kept man at worst, should he put his oar in the water. Even their newly formed friendship was a little untoward, but it had been born on a very unusual day.

And yet, it was not a gentlemanly inclination that was bringing the subject of marriage to the forefront of Robert's mind. No, indeed.

Robert was acutely aware of Lydia's proximity; her lower limbs were mere inches from his. With every breath, she shifted slightly, and they brushed together in a delicious, delicate touch of which he was acutely aware. . . . With a mental shake, Robert concentrated on the hard, cold surface on which they were sitting. Lumpy, uncomfortable . . . rough . . . and, umm, scratchy, inflexible . . .

"Perhaps we might talk of muslin and silk, then."

"Only if required. I am not well versed in—" Robert shifted slightly, trying to put a little distance between them—to allow for clarity of thought—then changed his mind and shifted back. He quite liked the distraction.

"Robert?"

"Yes, Lydia."

"What are we sitting on?"

"A rock?"

"No, indeed. I believe it might be a wall. Are there any headstones behind us? There, what is that shape?"

Robert swiveled and jumped down from what was now apparently a wall. Taking a few hesitant steps, he groped and discovered—a headstone. Off to the left . . . and right . . . there were others. "Yes, it would appear that we are among the dead. But worry not—"

"Oh, that is marvelous. Let me check. I will just skip to the other side of the road." And so saying, Lydia did just that. "Robert, come look."

Puzzled, Robert vaulted over the wall and met her on the far side. As he approached, he could see that she was pointing—gesturing—at some object. Upon closer inspection, he found it to be a mileage marker. Bath was still about six miles distant. It was rather disheartening to his tired, aching muscles.

"Isn't that marvelous." Lydia almost sounded giddy.

"No, actually. I was thinking the opposite. I thought we were a lot closer to Bath than that."

"Not Bath, Robert. Look at the name on the bottom, pointing at the road running alongside the graveyard. I know where we are. Pepney is only two miles in that direction."

Shaking his head, Robert allowed for Lydia's confusion, likely caused by her distress. "But we are not for Pepney; we are for Bath."

"Shelley lives in Pepney at Villers Manor. My good friend Shelley Dunbar-Ross and her new husband, Edward. She will take us in. . . . And Robert, she will help us devise a story. I know she will."

"A story?"

"Yes, something to explain where I have been all day."

"And all night."

"Exactly. Oh come, Robert . . ." Taking his hand, Lydia started across the road, and then she stopped to stare, as if surprised, at the sight of their clasped hands. Lifting her eyes to his, she frowned. A mixture of emotions crossed her face, though none that Robert could identify. He hoped his own sentiments were as enigmatic, for he would not want Lydia to know of his sudden desire to bring their lips together. He swallowed with great difficulty and tried not to lean forward.

After an eon of seconds, she smiled. Better still, she did not relinquish her hold but tugged him off the Bath main road toward some place called Pepney. He grabbed Fanny's reins as they passed or the mare might have been left behind.

$\mathcal{L}$ydia's enthusiasm took her a full minute down the road before recalling the purpose of Fanny. With a laugh, bordering on a giggle, Lydia allowed Robert to help her back up onto the horse's back, where he joined her again. Their proximity was becoming quite natural and—dare she say it—inciting, likely something to do with the firm establishment of their . . . friendship. Yes, the familiarity of friendship.

For some reason, thinking about the change in their relationship made Lydia aware of her appearance. Covered in scratches and dirt, with more hair drifting about her shoulders than in her chignon, no bonnet, and no gloves, she must have looked a veritable hoyden. And yet knowing this did not embarrass Lydia; she knew it didn't matter in the least to Robert.

Male friendship was a splendid and comforting institution—strange that she had had to discover it on her own. One would think that such a boon would be mentioned somewhere along the way. . . . But no, avoidance was more the order of the day. Such a waste. Protecting one's reputation came at a heavy cost.

The ride to Villers Manor was more of a plod than a walk or trot—poor Fanny was feeling the rigors of the day, too. That, coupled with the fact that the moon had decided to play peekaboo behind a collection of clouds, and there were reasons aplenty for the longer-than-expected slog. It made for a slow pace, and Lydia was in danger of nodding off; she did not relish the idea of falling again.

"I have come to a conclusion." Lydia tried to stifle a yawn.

"Have you, indeed?"

"Yes. I have decided that I do not like adventures or surprises. Highly overrated."

Robert's soft chuckle drifted through the dark.

"More of a *mis*adventure, my dear Lydia, and certainly not a surprise, which are generally thought of as pleasant things. No, best label today a shocking misadventure and not rule out surprises altogether."

"My father thought them overrated, too."

"What? Surprises? No, no. Surprises are unexpected guests, a beautiful flower among the rocks, or a woodland trail that opens up to an astonishing vista."

"Lovely when you put it that way, but there are some surprises that are not pleasant in the least." Lydia's thoughts remained fixed on her father. "Hence my lack of appreciation."

"Such as?"

"Losing a loved one too soon."

Her words were met with silence, and Lydia regretted leading their conversation into such deep waters. They were too weary, too overwrought. The nerves too close to the surface for any subject this weighty. "That was thoughtless of me," she whispered, as much to herself as to Robert.

When he spoke, it was clear where her words had taken him—what memories they had dredged up. "I miss him, terribly, you know . . . my brother. And yet, I'm angry, too. I don't understand it really. He is gone. Why am I angry with him? It is unreasonable."

"And normal. My father was not the instrument of his own demise, and yet I blamed him for leaving me for years. It must be harder when you know that, had your brother made other choices, he might still be alive."

"True enough. Lloyd did *not* have to accept the challenge. Even I know dueling is an exercise in stupidity—my *oldest* brother should have known it was dangerous and reckless."

"Pride can lead many of us astray. Such as wearing an orange waistcoat."

As expected, Robert chuckled, but it was halfhearted and did not distract him from the topic of death and duels. "And now, Cassidy has been challenged. I can hardly believe it."

Lydia did not know a Cassidy, and she was uncertain about asking to whom Robert was referring. But a query was not required, for as she considered, Robert continued.

"My good friend, Vincent Cassidy, with his devil-may-care attitude, has now put himself in harm's way." His voice oscillated in such a manner that Lydia was fairly certain that Robert was shaking his head. "He cuts up a lark with the best of them and is often too far in his cups. I suppose it was inevitable that he would cause insult at some point . . . but not inevitable that the insult would lead to a challenge."

"Oh dear. He has been offered a duel?"

"Yes, indeed. And here's the kicker: He knows not by whom or why."

"Really?"

"Unfortunately, yes."

"But, Robert, is that not a *good* happenstance? There is no commitment to an unknown person; the insult must be forgiven."

"Apparently not. I thought the same, but Cassidy feels he must act honorably—show up at the appointed hour. And he will, unless I can discover the offense and smooth over the whole."

"Perhaps he is confident to win?"

"I would think not. His swordplay is no better than mine—which is dismal at best. And as to pistols—let me just say we used to practice together, and we were adept at hitting the broad side of a barn, but nothing else. No, it is his ridiculous sense of duty."

"Oh, Robert, that does not sound good."

"I quite agree."

They plodded on for some minutes, lost in thought, worry, and memories. Finally, they broke out of a copse and rounded what Lydia anticipated to be the last curve in the road before the Villers Manor gates. As expected, the great house was now visible beyond the fields, though half hidden by an avenue of trees down the winding drive. And yet all was not as envisaged. The manor was ablaze with light.

"Well," Lydia sighed. "The good news would be that the Dunbar-Rosses are not abed. We will not have to rouse the house to be let in. The bad news would be that they are entertaining. I did so want to arrive quietly, didn't want to be seen like this. Do you think we could sneak in through the service door?"

"Unless you know the servants well, they will take one look at us and turn us off for vagabonds."

"Oh dear, that is true. I know Trenton, Shelley's butler. She brought him with her from Tipsy, but as to the others . . . no, they would probably not know me."

"Mrs. Dunbar-Ross's butler will be at the front of the house, helping with the guests."

Lydia nodded and turned Fanny toward the drive. "I can't believe I'm suggesting this, but I will hide in the bushes while you speak to Trenton. If you use my name, he might be persuaded to inform Shelley that I am here or let us in through the servants' door. What do you think?"

"I agree that you should stay to the shadows and that we should approach the front door. As to what and how I will persuade Trenton or Mrs. Dunbar-Ross remains to be seen."

"Excellent. You can use your lawyer's clerk countenance."

"Not sure that I have an official aspect about me at present."

Lydia sighed in agreement. As they approached the manor, the light shining through the windows helped illuminate their mucky glory. Though she couldn't see Robert behind her, she knew him to look nothing like a respectable clerk or even a gentleman, for that matter. The dried blood on his neck was the most damning, giving him a thuggish aspect. And she did not look like the respectable Miss Lydia Whitfield of Roseberry Hall if the ruination of her skirts were anything to go by. Even poor Fanny was spattered with mud.

Tired and hungry and, now that she thought about it, cold . . . yes, chilled, right to the bone, Lydia longed for a glowing fire, a warm drink, safety, and comfort. She did not want to wait behind this bush, this . . . boxwood. She wanted to march through the front door and collapse in the drawing room.

But she had no choice. If she was going to protect her

reputation, she had to abide while Robert tried to persuade a complete stranger to trust him. Then, Lydia smiled.

All would be well. Robert could charm anyone . . . including Shelley Dunbar-Ross, the most forthright of Miss Melvina's young ladies. Yes, any minute she would be—

Lydia frowned. What was that noise? It sounded like a shriek emanating from the front door. She immediately stood, lifted her skirts, and ran.

Robert needed her.

Chapter 10

In which a conspiracy of silence is formed
at the end of a most unusual day

The scene Lydia beheld on the threshold of Villers Manor was not what she had expected, though she hardly knew what to think. The shriek, for it was indeed a shrill involuntary cry, was not being issued by Trenton, or a housemaid . . . or even Robert, for that matter. The horrible sound was being produced by a blond female person hanging around Robert's neck as they stood in the doorway.

Affronted by the vulgar use of her friend, Lydia marched up the steps and grabbed the arm of said person—and then stopped as soon as the lady lifted her head. "Cora? What? What are you doing here?"

"Lydia!"

Lydia stepped back to retain her balance as Cora threw

herself at her. The shriek became a shout and then a laugh, and suddenly Lydia was bouncing. Cora proceeded to hop up and down for some minutes, which would have been acceptable had she not been holding on to Lydia at the time.

"I can't believe it. You are here. I thought you killed," Cora repeated at least twice before Lydia brought the jumping to a halt with a laugh of her own.

"Cora, dear. I am exhausted and confused, and you are not helping one iota."

"Of course, forgive me. Come in. You must sit." And with those words, Cora pulled Lydia past the threshold and Trenton, who had been holding the door open with a mild expression of interested disinterest.

Villers Manor was not much older than Roseberry Hall, perhaps a few decades at most, and it, too, wore its Tudor heritage with pride. Though the high stone walls of the entrance were now lined with dark wood panels, a huge traditional fireplace with a pair of stacked andirons occupied one end of the hall while a heavily carved staircase sat at the other. In a nod to comfort, a fringed Persian carpet covered the gray slate floor.

Once inside, Lydia's gaze fell upon a dissimilar couple waiting near the staircase. Shelley had one hand to her lips and the other tightly clasped by her broad-shouldered husband. Her expression raced from dazed to euphoria and settled somewhere near jubilant. Shelley Dunbar-Ross was of a diminutive stature, but bound within her petite frame was a huge heart and ample emotions that were seldom hidden or reined in. One always knew where one stood with Shelley; prevarication was an art she had never perfected.

With a quick squeeze, Shelley dropped Edward's hand and stepped forward to hug Lydia—without any bouncing. Finally, leaning away, Shelley held Lydia at arm's length. She smiled and then grinned. "You don't look your best."

"I have had an *unusual* day."

"Yes, of that there is no doubt."

"You, on the other hand, are a marvel." Lydia was not doing it up too brown; Shelley was dressed in an exquisite gown of apricot silk and Belgian lace. With amber at her neck and feathers in her thick auburn hair, she looked very different from the girl who had walked up the aisle a couple of months ago. "Marriage must agree with you."

Shelley turned a flattering shade of pink and glanced over her shoulder to her husband. "I highly recommend the institution."

Edward Dunbar-Ross looked startled, and then a slow smile spread across his face. While the tall gentleman was focused on his wife, Lydia had the opportunity to observe that wedded bliss had done the groom no harm, either. Lydia, who had previously thought Edward merely passable in countenance, was quite prepared to reassess the gentleman's appearance. His dark hair was longer and without the former rigid styling; his eyes suggested a gentleness that hitherto was missing, and his shoulders, always broad and straight, were relaxed. Yes, there was something to be said about a love match; both parties were quite content.

"Do you have company?" Lydia interrupted their penetrating stare that was growing overlong and addressed the overabundance of candles. "We thought with all the lights . . . at this time of night . . . Are you entertaining?"

"Yes, indeed. My good friend Lydia Whitfield has just arrived. We have been looking forward to her company all evening." Shelley turned to her butler. "Trenton, could you ask Cook for some chocolate and cakes? I don't imagine she has gone to bed yet what with all this fuss. We will have a tray in the drawing room—"

"I can't sit on your furniture in this condition," Lydia interrupted.

Ignoring her, Shelley continued. "And have Mrs. Salinger prepare two more rooms as quickly as possible. Tell Vernon to take care of the horse, and that should be it. We will see to ourselves for the remainder of the night. Thank you and the staff for accommodating our frenzy of activity. As you can see, it was a tempest in a teapot."

Hooking her elbow through Lydia's, Shelley led the procession up the stairs and into the drawing room. After the introductions, nothing further was said until the door was firmly shut and they were alone—all five of them.

"Forget chocolate," Edward said, striding over to a small table by the French doors. "What say you to a brandy, Newton. I certainly need one—you must need one doubly so."

Robert joined him by the window, lifting his hand to take the offered glass. He hesitated. "I'm not fit for company, I'm afraid."

"Nonsense." Edward placed the glass in Robert's dirty hand and gestured for him to take a place by the fire.

It was a good-sized room, with two seating arrangements. At the far end sat a collection of chairs near the French doors, which could be thrown open as soon as the word *sultry* was uttered. In the deeper parts of the room, a pair of settees offered the comfort of thick cushions near the enthusiastic fire.

Naturally, Lydia chose the settee nearest the fire, directly opposite her new friend; the dark brown brocade might hide any smudges from her dirty skirts, and it was as close to Robert as she could devise without causing comment. While the need to remain in chummy proximity was somewhat baffling, Lydia was neither prepared to fight the urge nor try to fathom its meaning.

Until the chocolate arrived, the conversation was frivolous. Questions were no deeper than what was the horse's name and when was the last time they had eaten. Even after Trenton had deposited a tray full of goodies and a hot silver pot onto the side table near the fireplace, Lydia and Robert were allowed only a few sips and nibbles before the whole of their story was demanded.

Not wishing to alarm the company, they told the tale baldly. Emotions and fears were kept to a minimum, and yet the expressions of those listening made it clear that they were aware of their existence.

"If Robert hadn't secured us a horse, we would still be miles away," Lydia concluded with a tired smile. She looked from face to face, expecting some sort of remark, but was met with silence. She looked to Robert with her brow folded.

"We shall have to return to surnames, Miss Whitfield, now that we are back in the circle of civilized society."

"Did I use your first name, Mr. Newton? Oh dear, I do apologize . . . to you and the company."

"Very natural, I would assume." Shelley patted Lydia's knee. "Especially under such circumstances, but perhaps best not repeated. I don't believe your mother would be so accepting."

"Yes, quite right." Lydia sighed. "Poor Mama, she must be frantic with worry."

"I can send one of our grooms to Roseberry in the morning, if you like." Edward stared at the liquid in his glass as he spoke, swirling it one direction and then the other. "That will allow you to return at your leisure. Though you need not be overly concerned. Mrs. Whitfield does not know that you were missing."

"Excuse me? How could she not?"

"Your mama didn't make it into Bath, Lydia." Cora's expression indicated a sense of exasperation. "None of them did."

"I don't understand. Was there an accident? Are they all right?"

"It would seem that forcing five into the family coach put them so out of sorts they turned around within ten minutes of starting off." Cora sighed.

"How do you know this?" Lydia watched Cora turn to Edward as if about to ask something, but she hesitated.

"Cora, best explain to Lydia and Mr. Newton what happened—from the beginning." Shelley nodded and looked encouraging.

"Yes, that would be best. But I will apologize to you ahead of time, Mr. Newton, for I'm afraid your employer, Mr. Lynch, is not an admirable character in my tale."

Lydia heard Robert take a slow, deep breath, pause, and then let it out in a meaningful sigh. "What has he done now?"

"It wasn't so much what he did, as what he didn't do," Cora explained, her eyes flaring with unexpressed anger. "When I ran into his office seeking help, Mr. Lynch did not believe anything I told him. Not who I was, why I was there, and certainly not that you, Lydia, and Mr. Newton had been taken. He called me utterly insulting names—never have I been so affronted. And then, he asked me to leave. Declared that Mr. Newton wasn't in the office because it was Sunday."

"But it's Thursday." Robert looked at the clock on the mantel. "Or at least it was."

"Yes, but apparently Mr. Lynch thought I was cutting shams about everything, including the day of the week. I was beside myself with worry but had to remain calm; Mr. Lynch threatened to have me tossed into the asylum. Finally, I simply insisted on staying in the outer office, knowing help would arrive in the form of your mother and Lord Aldershot. I waited for hours . . . but neither arrived."

"Not even Barley?" Lydia stared at Cora with incredulity.

"No, I'm afraid not. Eventually, I sent a boy for a constable, but without Mr. Lynch's support, I was branded a liar again."

"Oh, Cora, I am so very sorry. What a horrid day you have had." Lydia swallowed with difficulty and then blinked in surprise when her friend started to chuckle.

"Lydia, my dear, *you* had a horrid day. I merely had the worry about it." Cora paused to give Lydia a significant look and then continued. "I didn't want to leave the office. It was foolish nonsense, I know. It wasn't as if you were going to miraculously return—unscathed. I eventually realized that I needed to find someone who did know me, who would listen, and who would do the utmost to render me . . . or rather, you . . . assistance. I hired a carriage and sped here to Villers Manor as fast as I could.

"Edward thought it best to inform your uncle and solicit his opinion on how to proceed; after all, he—Mr. Kemble—is your guardian. Edward rode over to Roseberry to do just that. . . . But when he arrived, the family would not accept callers." She looked to Edward, as if expecting him to take up the story, and he did.

"Shelley had impressed upon me the need to speak with your uncle—and none other. Particularly not your mother." He glanced at his wife for confirmation.

"I was fairly certain that your mother's reaction would hinder rather than help us in our search," Shelley explained with candor.

Lydia tried not to wince.

"I spoke to your butler, Shodster I believe is his name," Edward continued. "And assured him of the dire nature of this need. He imparted the circumstances of the ladies' return and informed me that Mr. Kemble was with a gentleman referred to as the Major. I tried to track them down, going from his . . . the Major's rooms in Spelding . . . to the nearest drinking establishments—of which there are three. But to no avail. I returned to Bath unsuccessful and thoroughly exasperated."

Lydia refrained from commenting on the drinking habits of her uncle but shook her head in solidarity—in regard to Edward's exasperation and bluntness.

"But before heading back to Pepney, I sent a message by way of the night coach to London. I imagine a Bow Street Runner will arrive here in a few days to help us find you." He lifted his mouth into a ghost of a smile that held no levity or pleasure.

"I am heartened to know that my mother is not frantic with concern, but . . ." Lydia paused. She was rather disconcerted by her family's lack of interest in her whereabouts. Did they value her so little—not that she wanted them to be anxious . . . but to have not noticed her absence?

"Perhaps they assumed that you and Cora undertook an impromptu jaunt to visit me." Shelley must have seen the furrow of Lydia's brow. "After all, we have not seen one another in a couple of months."

"True, that is a possibility. And I should not question Providence's wisdom—better that my disappearance went undetected, my reputation untarnished. All is well, and as it should be. But don't you find it peculiar that Barley, Lord Aldershot, did not arrive for our appointment, either?" Lydia turned to Robert for her answer.

"Indeed." He met her gaze and mirrored her frown. "Too smoky by half, if you ask me. It will be interesting to hear why."

He glanced toward Edward. "Good to know about the Runner. He should be of great assistance catching the villains."

Edward nodded. "I will send him to you as soon as he arrives." Then, a true smile spread across his face. "And now, perhaps we should let you two retire; you look done to death."

Lydia nodded and glanced over her shoulder to the door. It seemed so far away. . . . And then there would be stairs to negotiate, the process of undressing, and a bed to climb. The settee was comfortable; perhaps she would stay there. And as Lydia contemplated the whys and wherefores of sleeping in a drawing room, she recalled that there was one last subject that had to be addressed before her brain could rest. "What of how I arrived here? We should present a unified story if we want it to pass muster with all the gossips."

"Whatever do you mean, dearest friend?" Shelley offered Lydia her hands. "You arrived with Cora just after five. We had a wonderful roast beef dinner, with chowder to start. You commented most favorably on the custard and plum pudding." She hauled Lydia to her feet. "Though I am heartily sorry that the wine slipped and ruined your pretty gown. Something will be found for you to wear in the morning, after you are well rested."

Lydia smiled her thanks, too tired to articulate the words, and followed Shelley and Cora out of the drawing room and its comfortable settee.

Robert watched Lydia ascending the stairs ahead of him. Though he could barely put one foot in front of the other, he was at the ready should she lose her balance, trip, or simply drop from exhaustion. Overseeing her well-being had been his purpose for so many hours; he couldn't let go—not yet.

It was almost miraculous the way the end of the day had unfolded—in complete contrast to the beginning . . . middle. Whatever. His mind was so befogged by fatigue; he could hardly form an articulate thought.

Upon reaching the second floor, the party split up along gender lines. Edward guided Robert down the corridor to the right, while the ladies veered to the left. He hadn't gone much more than a few paces when a soft voice called him back.

"Rob—Mr. Newton, might I have a word?"

Robert glanced over his shoulder. Lydia's worried expression cut through his fatigue, and he immediately swiveled, returning to her side in a trice.

"Is all well?" he asked in a half whisper, glancing about to see that her friends, while still nearby, were being discreet in their distance—allowing them a semiprivate conversation.

"Yes, oh yes, of course. No, I just . . . well, I doubt I will have another chance to thank you. . . . And even if I do, I think it best to express myself earlier rather than later. . . . Because I would hate to think that you did not know . . ."

Robert smiled and felt an unexpected tightness in the vicinity of his heart. There was nothing that he wished more than to pull Lydia into his arms, hold her for an eon or two, kiss the top of her leaf-encrusted hair—or better yet, her luscious lips—and assure her that their friendship was forged and strong and that nothing—such as an unexpressed thank-you—would ever cause a rift between them. Because he did know how honored he was to be her friend. "I do know," he said simply. They stared at each other for several minutes, until a small smile grew and transformed Lydia's face.

Breath taken by the change, Robert wondered how Mr. Lynch had ever considered this beauty anything other than . . . beautiful. And how Lord Aldershot could not know that his soon-to-be betrothed was fascinating, intelligent, and brave. The man should be thanking his lucky stars that Oliver Whitfield had chosen him to be Lydia's life mate.

Perhaps it was fatigue or the stress of the day that pushed Robert beyond his usual calm, but as he returned her smile with one of his own, a surprising realization leaped to the forefront of his mind. Robert was disheartened—indeed, quite melancholy. With the return of her exemplary reputation, Lydia was once again beyond his reach. There would be no stepping into the role of a suitor, whether he wanted to or not. It was no longer a choice. A deep, abiding friendship was the best he could hope for, and he would treasure it. The thought that it could have been more would have to be tamped tightly into some recess of his mind—and forgotten.

He bowed, watched Lydia stifle a yawn with a delicate hand, and turned back toward Edward Dunbar-Ross, somewhat confused by the grin on the fellow's lips.

"Something I should know about?" he asked the master of Villers Manor.

"No, not at all." But the grin did not disappear until Robert closed the door of his chamber. The vision of the man's toothy maw was soon replaced by the recollection of a brighter, prettier smile that Robert, despite his best intentions, took with him into the world of dreams.

The day was well started when Lydia opened her eyes and groaned. She ached all over, no exaggeration, no melodrama. Lydia truly did ache all over.

"Good morning, miss. I've been nursing a bath for you to step into as soon as yer wantin' it."

Lydia lifted her head and blinked at the person with the unnecessarily cheerful tone. "Pardon?" she said with intelligence.

Glancing around, she took in what her tired eyes had bypassed the night before. She was ensconced in a comfortable room, cozy despite its generous size. The color palette was a restful shade of green, accented with creams in furnishings and crisp white bed linens. Or rather, the bed linens *were* white—they were now also painted with various blobs and smears, exactly the same hue as dirt, blood, and grass. Lydia cringed and hoped the stains could be boiled away.

"A bath, miss? Or I can bring you some breakfast first, if you prefer."

"No, a bath would be lovely. Thank you . . . ?"

"Jill, miss. And I brought you a gown from Mrs. Dunbar-Ross. It come from Paris—that's in France, you know. Shame you fell off your horse and ruined your own lovely gown . . . and then a wine stain . . . and being as how you decided to stay over with no plan to do so, previouslike," the cheery Jill continued in a rush. "You didn't have a change of clothes. Just one of those things, miss. Just one of those things," she repeated.

Lydia smiled, recognizing the tale that would now be bandied about as the truth about her visit in Pepney. She fought to sit up and, after having done so, was surprised that it did not make matters worse—though neither did it make matters better. The aches would likely accompany her everywhere for a day or two.

After the long bath, which involved a great deal of scrubbing, Lydia enjoyed a welcome breakfast and finally felt ready to face the morning. Jill helped her don the Paris gown, fastening the delicate buttons down the back while Lydia stood before the full-length mirror. Staring with surprise—the pleasant kind—Lydia wondered at the style and fit of the pale lilac dress. The waist was a little lower than she was used to, the sleeves smocked delicately to the elbows, and the skirts gathered into an artful pleat on each hip. More of an afternoon dress than a day dress, the style was elegant and inspired, but most important: it fit like a glove.

This was as great a wonder as any, for Shelley and she were not of a size. Lydia was decidedly taller and had expected to be showing an uncomfortable amount of ankle in a borrowed gown.

But, no . . . she turned to the side to take in the full effect. No, the length was perfect. She wondered what Robert would think about the transformation—from vagabond to lady. Would he notice how well the color set off her eyes?

"Don't you look comely, miss. Mrs. Dunbar-Ross knew what she was about."

"Yes, well, umm. Thank you." Lydia straightened, embarrassed about being caught preening. "My other clothes, is there anything salvageable among them?"

"'Fraid not, miss. They was quite done for."

Lydia nodded but sighed inwardly. She had quite liked that spencer; it had matched the ribbon on her bonnet. . . . Oh, yes, the bonnet was gone, too. Well, it hardly mattered, after all.

When presentable, Lydia found her way to the ground floor in search of her friends, especially her newest friend. There was no doubt that her attachment to her lawyer's clerk was the product of a shared experience, a shared nerve-racking experience. Relying on each other had brought them closer than would ever be expected on such a short acquaintance, but rather than feel a sense of discomfort, Lydia was . . . well, excited—in a calm, dignified way, of course—with the thought of seeing Robert.

It came as a bit of a shock to find Shelley and Cora alone in the dining room enjoying their luncheon. The sun had already reached its zenith and was now on its way across the western half of the sky.

"Why did you not wake me?" Lydia asked as she approached the table and then blinked in amazement.

Cora, too, was dressed in more elegance than was required at this time of day. Her gown was a subtle shade of blue silk accented with sapphire trimmings. The style and fit were excessively flattering. Cora had a fuller figure than Shelley, and the bodice of a borrowed gown should have been challenging the seams. But it wasn't.

Lydia grinned, realizing the answer. Shelley had thought of her friends while she was on her wedding trip. She had bought these beautiful dresses specifically for them in Paris.

"Might it have something to do with your arrival last night in a completely exhausted state?" Shelley replied. "Let me see, oh, yes, wasn't there something about an unexpected visit to a farm?"

"No, I don't believe so. I spent the day in Bath, didn't I? And then joined you for an exemplary meal last eve. Though I must ask, how did I fall from my horse when I was seated inside a carriage?"

"Whatever do you mean, Lydia dear? Are you forgetting that you left your carriage in Bath and rented a horse by the name of Fanny?"

"I exchanged a comfortable, though small, coach for a bay mare?"

"Yes, indeed, you wanted a breath of fresh air . . . and your solicitor's clerk felt an unquenchable need for exercise. He walked beside you—you and Cora . . . on the mare."

Lydia laughed, thankful that the whole was over. Well, not entirely. They still had to catch the culprits and see justice done—but at least she need not be concerned about ruination.

Pulling out a chair across from Cora, Lydia waved away the offer of food from Trenton. She had only just finished her morning repast. "Speaking of my solicitor's clerk, where might Mr. Newton be?" Her question was met with an exchange of glances between Cora and Shelley, grins, and a vast amount of silence.

"Now, girls. Don't start."

"You seemed quite taken with Mr. Newton, Lydia." Shelley stated in a deliberately casual tone. Cora watched with what seemed to be excessive interest, absentmindedly nibbling on her baked sole.

"Naturally."

"Yes, naturally, as he is a handsome young man who has heroic tendencies . . . and thinks very highly of you."

"No. I meant, naturally I am taken with a person with whom I spent a great deal of company while evading danger. I would be taken with an ancient mariner or bedraggled hag in like circumstances."

Cora and Shelley exchanged glances yet again. "What do you think?" Cora asked Shelley. "It sounds like humbug to me."

Shelley nodded. "I think a bedraggled hag might not have warranted this much interest."

"What interest? I merely asked where Mr. Newton might be and have received no answer, I might add."

Shelley turned back to Lydia with a laugh. "Too true. Mr. Robert Newton has returned to Bath. Edward took him this morning. He was loath to go. Felt himself torn—wanted to see you safely escorted to Roseberry first—but it would seem there was a pressing issue with a gentleman by the name of Cassidy. He also mentioned Mr. Lynch, though I wasn't sure in what context. Anyway, Mr. Newton, once assured by Edward that he and at least two footmen had every intention of accompanying you to—no, don't protest. There is no question of your journeying out on your own. No, Lydia, close your mouth. I will brook no disagreement on this. Where was I? Oh, yes, having been reassured—several times—Mr. Newton quit Villers Manor and set off for Bath. I expect Edward back at any moment. . . . He will not wish to miss luncheon. Are you sure you do not want to try the sole?"

Lydia shook her head and sighed. She had so wanted Robert to see her in this new gown, but she had forgotten about the dire circumstances of Mr. Cassidy. Of course Robert had to go. Her hero had to be heroic. Off to save his friend, leaving her in Villers Manor, protected by the Dunbar-Rosses. It was a logical conclusion to their misadventure . . . but somehow it felt deflating . . . unfinished.

Shaking such selfish thoughts from her foolish brain, Lydia thanked Shelley for the beautiful gown, verifying that it was, indeed, a gift. One bought a month or so earlier as a souvenir in Paris.

Lydia smiled as Shelley launched into a full description of the vibrant city and tried not to be distracted by thoughts of brown caring eyes. And yet the sense of incompletion and disappointment did not go away. She had so wanted to implant a new vision in Robert's mind: one of his friend Lydia, the elegant young lady in a Parisian gown, and not Lydia, the disheveled and thoroughly rumpled creature falling out of the Beyer barn.

Chapter 11

In which Mr. Newton rushes hither and yon while Miss Whitfield is inundated with doubt

"I'm afraid most of the family is still abed, Mr. Newton." Cassidy's, or rather Lord Tremont's, sour-faced butler stood in the doorway, blocking the threshold as best he could.

Robert had no time for the antics of disobliging servants whose perception of dignity superseded all else. "Not to worry, Cranford, I do not plan to disturb *most* of the family." He stepped past the man and into the generous hall of the three-story town house. The design was not *that* dissimilar to his own—though this one, of course, was much larger—and, as a consequence, Robert knew that he would not have too much trouble finding the bedrooms with or without Cranford's help. "I'm just here to see Cassidy."

He started toward the stairs as if he knew exactly where Cassidy slept, fairly certain that his bravado would carry the day—or rather the moment. Robert doubted Cranford would allow him to open the wrong bedroom door in his search. Intervention was imminent.

Robert had been heartily disappointed, upon arriving at his place on Boliden Street, to find . . . rather, to *not* find . . . Vincent Cassidy within. They had a lot to discuss and a limited amount of time to fashion a miracle.

Longdon had informed him that Cassidy had found it difficult to comply to Robert's simple request—that of staying in residence until Robert's return—despite Longdon's excellent suggestions of reading, billiards, or solitaire. But Robert had left Cassidy high and dry for too long; he finally left.

At that point in his narration, Longdon had looked at Robert in such a way as to indicate that Longdon, too, wondered where Robert had been—but it was the type of implied question that could be ignored, if necessary. And it was necessary.

As it was still early in society terms, Robert planned to drag Cassidy from his bed—fill him with fortifying victuals, ply him with questions, and drag him about town looking for the answers. They had to learn as much as possible about the night his friend was challenged.

"Newton?" asked an incredulous voice.

Robert turned to glance down from the first-floor landing, where he had raced to. Below him, fully attired . . . looking alert and quite wide awake . . . was Vincent Cassidy. Robert was momentarily at a loss for words, though he swiveled, marching back to the ground floor.

"What are you doing here?" he finally asked when they were both on the same level.

"Me?" Cassidy's baffled expression broke into a grin. "As it happens, I live here."

"Yes, but I thought you were going to stay at Boliden Street until I returned."

"If you had taken less than a day, I would have. Rather bad form to leave me twiddling my thumbs for an entire night."

"Believe me, it was unintentional."

"I do believe you. I spoke to Mr. Lynch." These words were uttered in such a serious manner that Robert entertained a sense of foreboding.

"Oh?" he said as lightly as he could.

Cassidy made matters worse by looking over his shoulder at the glowering countenance of Cranford and then gesturing to a door in the corner.

It proved to be a study, albeit a small one, with just enough room for a desk and two chairs. The air was thick, as if it had not been aired, or used, in some time. Though there was, of course, no dust to speak of, not even on the mantel clock that showed it to be ten minutes before nine.

"What gets you up at such an early hour?" Robert asked, stalling. Girding himself for the questions about Mr. Lynch's instability. But Cassidy surprised him.

Dropping into one of the chairs next to the unlit fireplace, his friend approached a different and even more sensitive subject. "Were you seized yesterday?"

"Seized?" Robert's astonishment was not feigned. He had not expected the need to explain his absence. Playing for the time needed to organize his thoughts, Robert made a show of choosing his seating. Eventually he leaned against the windowsill; it gave him a higher vantage point. "Seized?" he asked again.

"Yes. That was the word Mr. Lynch used. Although it was used with great derision and mockery. I thought he was funning me, but . . . oh, have I put the cart before the horse? You are wearing a puzzled expression."

"You are making little sense."

"Let me explain."

"Please do." Robert sighed, giving up his vantage point in favor of the chair. His aches needed to be appeased.

"When I awoke—which, I grant you, was late afternoon—I was not in the mood to sit around waiting for you to finish your clerking duties. Really, Newton, leaving me idle for so long. Longdon kept trying to feed me. And I did not have the stomach for it."

"Feeling better now?"

"Yes, indeed, thank you. . . . Don't distract me." Cassidy mugged a snarl and then continued. "Mr. Lynch was still at your office, despite the late hour. He was rather confused—you might have to look into that, my friend. Lawks, where was I?"

"Late hour."

"Oh, yes, Mr. Lynch said he was working late to make up for the time lost while dealing with an addlepated hussy. She—the hussy—claimed that you and a young lady had been forced into a coach and rushed away. Complete nonsense, of course. Or so I thought . . . except that I could not find you anywhere. Believe you me, I looked—I looked well into the night. That is, in fact, why I am up at this ungodly hour—to continue my search . . . for you."

Robert stared for some minutes at the carpet, recalling the strength of their friendship, thinking about the newest member of that circle. "This has to be between us," Robert said finally, with a tone earnest enough to secure Cassidy's undivided attention.

"Without saying," his friend said.

Robert told Cassidy the whole. Well, not the entire whole, for he didn't use names, avoided mentioning Lydia's exemplary qualities, and skipped the change in their relationship. So, actually, it was only a part . . . and as a consequence, not long in the telling.

"Well, your day was far more interesting than I had imagined." Cassidy nodded to himself. "If one can use that word."

"*Interesting*? No, I think I would use *harrowing* instead."

"*Harrowing* might be too strong. Shall we agree on *curious*?"

"*Curious*, it is."

"Now that that is settled, I will say that I had not anticipated such a curious day for you. I imagined that you had latched on to a pretty miss and been so thoroughly distracted that you had forgotten about me." He snorted a laugh. "I was right in a way, wasn't I?"

Robert shook his head in a stiff jerk and ignored the rejoinder—and the reference to a pretty miss. "If that were true, you would not have been searching for me."

"I'd like to sit here and pretend that my search started with concern, but in reality it was driven by the need to ring a fine peal over you. I was thoroughly piqued. Thought you had left me high and dry. Should have known better." Cassidy glanced out the window into the gray featureless sky, shrugged to an inner thought, and then turned back to Robert. "What are your plans?"

"You."

"Me?"

"Yes, I believe we have to make arrangements to cancel a duel."

"But what of your lady?"

"Lydia?"

"Is that her name?"

"Just a figure of speech."

Cassidy laughed outright. "Of course, that makes perfect sense."

Robert rubbed at his face, trying to rearrange his thoughts. "The miss is now with family and friends, protected and soon to be returned to her home. I will find the villain behind this dirty deed soon enough, and he will pay . . . but first, your duel."

Growing serious again, Cassidy swallowed. "Thought I might visit a rifle club. Get in some practice."

"Don't be foolish. You cannot learn to be a crack shot in less than a week. You would be better served by practicing a heartfelt apology."

"For what? I know not what I did."

"Practice anyway," Robert said unreasonably.

They arranged to meet at Cassidy's club, Lewis's, where they might talk to Peterson, the only witness of this foolish business that Cassidy could recall. Until then, Robert had to see Mr. Lynch to arrange for a few days away from the firm. If need be, he would take a leave; there was really no choice.

And as Robert rushed hither and yon, he found his thoughts constantly wandering to the subject of Miss Lydia Whitfield. Would that these thoughts were of a useful nature, listing possible ways in which to investigate or puzzling out who might be worked upon for answers about her abduction. Those would, at least, be worthy avenues of thought.

No, indeed. His befogged brain had the audacity to be distracted by recollections of her tinkling laugh, her gentle touch, and her intelligent eyes. When called to task, said brain acquiesced, refocusing on how enticing was the sweet smell of lavender, even when overlaid by an odor of stale hay. It really wasn't very helpful.

$\mathcal{L}$ydia arrived at Roseberry with pomp and ceremony. Or at least that was the only decent name that she could conceive for the helter-skelter squeals, disjointed conversation, and angry tones. The concoction would soon give her a headache.

As it was, Edward *and* Shelley had accompanied Cora and Lydia to Roseberry Hall in their large travel coach. Edward was obliged, having promised Robert to do so; though he stated that he would have done so regardless and with great enthusiasm even had he not been duty-bound.

Lydia was not certain of this eagerness, as Edward had fallen asleep, leaning against his wife's shoulder, before they had even seen the last of the church spires of Bath. Shelley, on the other hand, could not be doubted on her keenness to stay in her friends' company. When the time had come for Lydia and Cora to prepare for their journey, Shelley had only just started to describe the Louvre. She still had to talk about the splendid shopping, spectacular nightlife, and the journey home through Calais. Nothing could be done but continue their conversation in the coach. . . . Perhaps it was no surprise that Edward had fallen asleep.

When Shelley had reached the end of her many tales, Cora took up the subject of Mr. Granger; the girls spent a good half hour discussing the whys and wherefores of the gentleman's possible betrothal. In the end, Shelley thought that she would be the best one to engage in a correspondence to ascertain the validity of the rumor.

"There are advantages to being an *old* married lady," Lydia teased.

But other than shared laughter, a few teasing remarks, and an odd comment or two, Lydia was unusually pensive. She knew her friends believed this silence was caused by the events of the previous day, and while that was partially true, Lydia was not as distracted by the abduction as much as by the person abducted with her. Try as she might, Lydia could not stop thinking of a handsome young clerk—not in the will-he-be-able-to-discover-the-villain sense but in the engaging-manner-and-attractive-countenance sense. It was rather disconcerting to find that most comments by her friends—on completely unrelated subjects—could, without intent, grab her thoughts and shoot them back to Robert Newton.

A ride down the fine streets of Paris led to recollections of a long ride down the dusty country road. A sumptuous meal in a restaurant near the Seine reminded Lydia of their supper at Roseberry. Stranger still was that when Cora talked of Mr. Granger with significant affection, Lydia thought of Robert. She was hard pressed to understand that association. Perhaps it was that both gentlemen possessed brown eyes.

However, once through the gates of her estate, Lydia had no choice but to think and deal with an entirely different subject. Her family members—their censure and criticism. There would be no avoiding it. They would not be best pleased that Lydia had done something so untoward as to leave without them and then stay away on an unplanned visit. She would have to be vigilant in her conversation, instilling just the right amount of ennui to discourage questions.

The idea that Lydia would do something of a spontaneous nature was so absurd that she was certain there would be an excessive amount of doubt. She was right, but not in the manner she expected.

Mama couldn't believe that the Dunbar-Rosses had ridden all that way with her puss, just to see her safely home. Yes, they were the most considerate of couples. Aunt Freya could not believe that Lydia had thought nothing of depriving Elaine of her outing. This harping was whispered in Lydia's ear even as the others were greeted with great aplomb and offers of refreshment.

Ivy couldn't believe that Shelley had brought Lydia and Cora gowns from Paris . . . and not brought one for her. Elaine could not believe that Lydia was so forgetful as to leave her bonnet behind in Pepney, while laughing in such a manner as to contradict her own words. And Tessa couldn't believe that Lydia hadn't missed her. So Lydia assured the girl that she had. Uncle Arthur was not present to cast doubt or complain at any length; Lydia had not missed him at all.

Feeling that the worst of it was over, Lydia waited and watched as the company traipsed up to the drawing room for the proffered refreshment before the Dunbar-Rosses returned to the road. She intended to speak to Shodster, to make sure all the mail and any messages passed through her first over the next week. She had no idea how the villains had intended to call for their ransom, but a threatening note was a possibility. It might have been sent on its way before her escape. If so, it could provide a clue or two—and it needed to stay out of the wrong hands . . . any but hers.

However, when Lydia turned, she found the great hall held three persons, not two.

"Mama? Did you not want to see to your company?" Lydia sighed, knowing she was about to get an earful.

As expected, Lydia's mother squared her shoulders, pursed her lips for some moments, and then glared before opening her mouth to speak. "That was inconsiderate of you, Lydia. I would not think it possible. It was quite untoward—you disappeared. And before you ask, yes, I received the knowledge of your return this morning but not until this morning. Why was I not apprised of this jaunt, this surprise visit yesterday? It is not like you, Lydia. Too impulsive by far. What really happened?"

Lydia caught her breath, wishing that she could explain. Had her father been alive, she would have run to him and shared the burden. Would her mother be able to help without complicating the situation even more with histrionics? Lydia lifted her lips into a halfhearted smile. Perhaps she might tell the one parent she had left.

"I thought there might have been an accident. That you were lying dead on the road."

"No, Mama. Nothing like that."

"Nothing short of death or injury is excusable, Lydia. I was that worried. And you are not dead and as best I can tell not injured. Although . . . is that a scratch on your chin?"

"Not injured or dead, Mama." Lydia ignored the chin query. "I had a bit of an adventure—" She wanted to start slowly, a calm pace to allow her mother to digest the information in small pieces. But rather than create an awareness that she was about to impart what had happened, the words fanned her mother's indignation.

"An adventure? Lydia Whitfield, I believe even your father would have been disappointed in you today. I was ready to have a fit. Can you imagine? And had I suffered an apoplexy, it would have been on your shoulders." Before Lydia could say another word, her mother took hold of her skirts, lifting them high and her chin higher. "I hope you are satisfied." She stalked to the stairs and climbed them with exaggerated grace. She did not look down.

Standing and staring after her mother for some minutes, Lydia swallowed her disappointment. Why was it that she and her mother never seemed to understand each other? There was no doubt that her mother wished to know what had occurred, and Lydia had wanted to explain. And yet they had not found a manner to answer either of these wishes.

Perhaps this was the better way. Her mother was annoyed; however long that lasted, it was a familiar reaction, easier to deal with—a normal situation. Yes, an inconsiderate daughter would not overly tax her nerves—an abducted daughter who had escaped certain ruin was an entirely different concern.

"Might I suggest, miss, that you inform your mother that Mr. Dunbar-Ross did come by last eve?" Shodster had soundlessly approached to allow a soft conversation—though still at a respectable distance. "She need not know there was no message. You could imply that I didn't think the news worthy of disturbing her rest."

Lydia sighed. "I appreciate your offer, Shodster. But I would not see you in discord with Mama. I am well used to her frustration. It will pass soon enough." Then turning to face her butler, Lydia noticed a gray tinge to his coloring and deep circles under his eyes. "Are you all right, Shodster? You do not look up to snuff."

Shodster was not a young man, though likely a decade away from retirement, of medium height and build and an unremarkable appearance—other than styling his silver hair in a way that it winged out over his ears. He was quiet and calm, a trusted and reliable man who had been with the family since before Lydia was born.

"Yes, Miss Whitfield, I am fine. Though I did have some difficulty sleeping last night. My own fault, as I stayed up past the usual hour, waiting for Mr. Kemble's return." Likely seeing Lydia's brow folding, he hurried on. "I was fairly certain that something was amiss. Expected Mr. Kemble to explain but . . . when he did return, he was in no state to elucidate. Until Mr. Dunbar-Ross's message this morning, I thought you might be . . . in difficulty."

It was Shodster's attempt to underplay his disquiet that Lydia found most touching. Her mother had not been the only one troubled by her absence. "Thank you, Shodster, for your concern. I was in some *difficulty*, as you surmised. However, with Mr. Newton's help, I was able to escape."

"Escape?" Shodster swallowed visibly.

"Yes, there was an abduction yesterday. I know that sounds excessive, but I know not what else to call it—seized, taken, nabbed . . . they all smack of melodrama—"

"Seized? Are you all right, Miss Whitfield?" His gray tinge was now suffused with red. "Are you hurt?"

Reaching out, Lydia lightly placed her hand on Shodster's arm. "Please, do not fret. It's fine. I'm fine. Do not be concerned. I spent most of the night riding—trying to get back to Bath. And then we discovered that Villers Manor was nearby. I must say, I will be heartily glad to resume my routine tomorrow." Lydia knew her conversation to be disjointed, but she was somewhat taken aback by the intensity of Shodster's reaction. "Might you consider resting until dinnertime, to recoup some of your energies?"

"Not with guests in the house, miss."

"No, of course not. Silly suggestion." She frowned, trying to recall what it was that she required of her butler. "Oh, yes. Might I ask that all mail or messages go through me first, Shodster, for . . . let us say, a week or more?"

"Of course, Miss Whitfield."

"Thank you." Lydia turned and then pivoted back, realizing that their discussion was not quite complete. "Pardon?"

"Mr. Newton? Your solicitor's clerk? He was the one who came to your aid?"

"Yes, Mr. Lynch's apprentice-in-waiting." Lydia heard the pride in her voice, though she was not entirely certain whence it was derived. "He helped me escape and accompanied me to Pepney."

"Impressive. A fine young man."

Lydia laughed. "Indeed." He was most certainly both impressive and a *fine* young man.

Lydia's mind wandered over the face and figure of her new friend, appreciating the way Mother Nature had formed him. Appreciation for his lips had to be added to his other exceptional attributes—a new discovery. She had found them quite fascinating as they had stared at each other in the half-light of the moon, to the point that she had even wondered what they might feel like pressed . . .

"Indeed," she said again, trying to hide her distraction. "Mr. Lynch could not have found a better apprentice."

Heading up the stairs to join the others in the drawing room, Lydia hesitated on the first step. Had Shodster made a parting remark? No, she must have been mistaken. It had sounded like "a better man than Aldershot will ever be."

Lydia glanced over her shoulder to see Shodster heading toward the back of the house. There, she was mistaken. Her butler had said no such thing.

Unfortunately, that meant the critical comment had come from the less than helpful voice in her head.

Chapter 12

*In which a carriage should not have been ordered and
an apology has unseen consequences*

Despite occupying three floors, Lewis's was not a large
gentleman's club. Certainly not anything that would
rival Brooks's or White's in London. Still, its address could not
have been in a better part of Bath, close to the river and—more
important—within a stone's throw of two gambling dens should
any gentleman prefer much higher stakes. The labyrinth of
rooms was comfortable and suited to those of a young and foolish
nature; Cassidy was well known there.

Robert had arrived later than expected—by several unfortunate hours. His meeting with Mr. Lynch had not gone as anticipated. There was plenty of dithering and wringing of hands, but
not of the confused kind. That in and of itself was part of the
problem. Mr. Lynch was clearheaded and rife with anxiety when

Robert crossed the threshold of the law office. The planned excuses could not survive the scrutiny of a coherent Mr. Lynch.

"Only this morning, this morning," Mr. Lynch said after a remarkably effusive greeting. "Only then did I recognize the name of Miss Whitfield's friend. Oh, I have been beside myself, quite beside myself." He shook his head and pointed to the chair in front of his desk for Robert to rest his weary bones. "I began to think that I had made a mistake, that Miss Shipley had the right of it. Said you were made off with . . . in a coach—seized, seized!" He lifted a quizzing glass to his eye, squinting at Robert. "Thought it might be true, after all. Especially when you did not arrive as usual and no message as to why you were not here on time." He paused, giving Robert the opportunity to explain.

Robert stared at his employer, trying to decide how best to handle this situation. While there was no doubt that Mr. Lynch was declining in acuity, it was not all the time and in varied degrees, depending on the day. Anxiety seemed to be his worst enemy. Robert had noticed it before. Perhaps now was not the time to offer Mr. Lynch a full account of his *curious* adventure, not when the gentleman would be required to manage all their cases for the next few days.

The truth was rather fret-worthy.

"Yes, Miss Shipley was correct in part," Robert said slowly, thinking his way through the maze of pitfalls. "The horses bolted and . . . the driver was flung from his perch. We were well out of Bath before they could be brought to a halt. Miss Whitfield suggested that we detour to Pepney . . . as it was closer—where she had friends. Mr. Dunbar-Ross drove me back this morning; Miss Whitfield stayed a little longer to visit." Robert bobbed his head with finality and sighed in relief. He had found an acceptable story within the bones of the truth.

Robert's relief was mirrored in Mr. Lynch. The old gentleman's smile erased his furrowed brow and squinty eyes. He scratched, absentmindedly, across his bald pate and huffed a breath; it was almost a snort. "Knew it, knew it. Capital. Well done, Mr. Newton. Though I don't envy you Miss Whitfield's company. Poor little thing must have been scared witless."

The words to disabuse Mr. Lynch of this ridiculous notion were on the tip of his tongue, but Robert stayed his comment and nodded yet again. He then launched into his need of a few days respite. The excuse of family obligations was flimsy, and Robert was certain that Mr. Lynch knew it to be a pretext. Still, pretending that all was on the up and up meant that the man was under no obligation to do anything.

After dashing off some letters and compiling various contracts for signatures, Robert set off for Lewis's. But not before he had inscribed, *As agreed, will be back in a few days*, on a piece of paper and placed it in the center of his desk. It was a nod to Mr. Lynch's ever-vacillating awareness, should he forget their arrangement. Robert had purposefully left off a date—there was a possibility that it would take longer.

Lewis's was not overly busy, as it was still afternoon when Robert arrived—albeit late afternoon. The first sitting room, with large, comfortable wingback chairs, was almost empty, and the second likewise. However, the gaming tables of the third room were half full, and that is where Robert found Cassidy surrounded by friends and IOUs, ironically referred to as vowels, and deep into whist. As he approached the card table, there was a great guffaw of laughter and several thumps on the back shared among them.

Robert paused, observing the easy comfort of the men, their colorful waistcoats, overly styled hair, and unrestrained mannerisms: idle young gentlemen of Bath's upper society. They had no obligations and no responsibility. Not long ago, Robert had resented the fact that he could not stay within their ranks—for he knew them all well. They had been at Eton together. But, like Cassidy, each of these pups was a firstborn. Their futures were secure—fortunes and estates were a given, though in varying degrees. Cassidy alone looked forward to a title as well.

When Robert had been forced to choose a profession, he had done so by eliminating those of no interest, such as a career in the church or the army. In the end, the law was all that was even mildly intriguing. Not an auspicious beginning. And yet the more Robert learned about the law, the less he yearned to be back with his fellows. He found that he had a talent for the complicated terminology and a great ability to memorize. Robert's day had form and function; what he did affected people's lives. In short, he quite enjoyed being a solicitor's clerk and greatly looked forward to his apprenticeship. Something he never expected.

In fact, something that he rarely, if ever, articulated, either.

And would not have done so at this point in his life had he not walked into Lewis's and seen what might have been. The tableau before him was . . . well, for want of a better word, boring.

"Smiling to yourself, Newton? Not a good sign. Been around Mr. Lynch too long, I'd say." Cassidy, it seemed, had broken away from the group while Robert had been woolgathering. "And, to top it off, you are late again."

"Not for the same reason."

"I certainly hope not. But be that as it may, I have good news." Gesturing toward the gamers, Cassidy brought another friend into the fold. "It just so happens that Byng, here, has a complete recollection of the night in question."

"Excellent. We have a name, then."

"Except that."

"Ah, not quite everything, then." Robert glanced toward Byng, nodding a greeting. The sandy-haired fellow was flying his colors in a rich red shade of discomfort. Robert looked back at Cassidy and wondered at his friend's giddy smile. "Rather important missing detail, don't you think?"

"Perhaps, but we *can* learn to whom I must go hat in hand easily enough. It seems that we were down the street at The Gammon." His grin grew as he casually mentioned one of the most notorious of the gambling Hells in Bath. "More to the point, I have discovered my offense. It truly was a misunderstanding, and I have been fashioning an apology. What say you to: I did not mean to cast aspersions upon your honor. I have no doubt of your ability to cover your vowels and am quite prepared to say as much officially—such as placing an apology in the newspaper. Or what about this: I apologize most profoundly for our misunderstanding. I was too much in my cups to attend my tone of voice. There was no mockery intended, nor doubt on my part that—"

"Might I hear what occurred before we choose an apology?"

"What occurred?"

"Yes, what happened, Cassidy?"

"Oh yes . . . well." Looking around, Cassidy swept his arm back toward the second sitting room. "Come, let us make use of the fire." And so saying, he crossed the threshold and plunked down on an overly stuffed chair near the glowing embers.

Robert joined his friend; Byng trailed behind as if unsure of his participation.

"Is something wrong, Byng?" Robert chose a seat farther from the fire in a position that allowed him to study both his fellows at the same time.

"I'm not certain that an apology will be accepted. The umbrage seemed contrived—as if the man wanted to take offense. In fact . . . if I remember correctly, all Cassidy asked was if *he*—whoever he is—was sure he wanted to increase his debt. The man's losses were significant already; Cassidy held most of his vowels—poor brute was having a run of bad luck. Here . . . wait, what about those vowels. His name would be on them—his signature at least."

"Lord Rennoll," offered a new voice, and they all looked up.

Another of their comrades, by the name of Peterson, stood

above them, leaning against the back of the unoccupied chair in the group. His countenance was serious, no hint of his usual devil-may-care attitude.

"You're not likely to get around Lord Rennoll. He's a crack shot who likes to show off—actually *enjoys* the high stakes. He's winged a couple of opponents so far—with nary a scratch on himself to show for it. Just a matter of time before he . . . well, I wouldn't want to test his odds."

"But . . . I didn't insult him. The cards were against him; I simply asked if he was sure he wanted to continue. Meant to be helpful, not insulting." Cassidy swallowed visibly and turned to Robert. "What should I do?"

"Return his IOUs."

Shocked silence reverberated around the room. Robert clenched his jaw to retain a serious bearing in face of the gaping, fishlike expressions of his friends. He was well aware that he had just suggested committing the most extreme of blunders. But it was a possible solution and, therefore, should be addressed.

"Return his vowels? That would be an even greater insult," Cassidy eventually huffed. "Might as well measure me for the undertaker right now; he'd shoot me on the spot."

"He can't. That would be murder."

"Justifiable, if you ask me," Byng said disobligingly.

Robert thought of the many tomes lining the walls of the law firm that would disagree, but he kept that knowledge to himself. The issue had nothing to do with legalities.

"How can you even suggest such a thing? Nothing's more

important than a debt of honor to a gentleman." Cassidy's indignation continued to climb.

"Oh, I don't know, I've found that money can smooth over many a disagreement."

"You have been in the company of the entirely wrong people, Newton. Perhaps the lower ranks would see nothing untoward in such a suggestion—but really, it is outside of enough. I'd rather participate in the duel."

"As you might have to."

Cassidy snapped his mouth shut, swallowed, and then returned to his original question. "What should I do?"

"Well, you are back to fashioning the best apology you can devise. Better than the ones you were suggesting earlier. Less grinning and more humble pie. But you will not have to do it on your own; I'll come with you. If your apology doesn't do the job, I'll discuss the legal ramifications with Lord Rennoll. After all, dueling is illegal. Worry not, this duel will never take place."

Robert spoke with extreme confidence. If all else failed, he had every intention of locking up Cassidy on the fateful day of the duel. He knew of a barn well suited to that very purpose.

$\mathcal{S}$eated at her escritoire, finally alone in the morning room, Lydia sealed a long letter to Shelley. With all that had transpired the day before, they had not had an opportunity to discuss the particulars of the ball arrangements. Shelley had offered to help, but without instructions, her friend would be stymied.

Lydia would post the letter in Spelding herself if she thought she could slip away without Cora's being aware of her intent. While Lydia greatly enjoyed Cora's company and was pleased to find her friend buoyant and at ease once again, she was less than pleased with the other results of their *adventure*.

Cora had taken it upon herself to accompany Lydia anywhere and everywhere beyond the confines of the manor. That had included Lydia's lovely solitary walk just after luncheon, which had been neither lovely, due to the rain, nor solitary, due to Cora's presence. Worse still, Lydia was now peeking around corners in anticipation of seeing Les or Morley peeking back. Left to her own devices, Lydia would have put the whole incident behind her, but returning to the subject continually was a bit wearing: whispered recollections at breakfast, speculation on the culprit in a quiet conversation in the drawing room . . . and then throughout her daily promenade. If this continued, Lydia would soon be shrieking in utter frustration—with the delicacy and grace insisted upon by Miss Melvina, of course.

Still, if Lydia was fair, the *adventure* had been but two days previous, and Cora was only being protective. It might take as much as a week before the high emotions faded completely . . . for all three of them. Lydia counted Robert in this select group. And as she allowed her mind to drift in his direction, yet again, Lydia became aware of a commotion just beyond the door of the morning room. Standing in anticipation, she was unexpectedly disappointed when Shodster announced Barley.

"Oh," she said with great intelligence. She dipped her curtsy slower than was her norm, giving her time to hide her reaction. When she lifted her eyes to those of the gentleman who would one day be her husband, she was startled by his looks. Not that his glare and hard-set mouth were terribly unusual; she had seen that glower before. Nor was his confrontational stance extraordinary, either. She had known Barley a long time.

No, it was the color of his hair, for rather than a rich brown, as she had thought previously, it seemed muddy. And his nose . . . why had she never noticed how very sharp and unappealing it was? And his manner of dress was . . . overly elegant, his waistcoat an unnecessarily bright red. Strange that she had not noticed these proclivities before.

"There you are, Barley," she said, blinking away her distracting thoughts. Waving toward the settee near the fireplace, Lydia crossed the room. But when she perched on the edge of her seat, Barley had still not moved.

"What are you doing here?" he demanded.

"That is a strange question since this is my home and where I live."

"Why were you not in Bath?"

Lydia rose, feeling the tension in the room increasing still further. And while she might not understand its underlying cause, she would not be put to disadvantage. "I might ask the same of you."

"What are you on about? You were not there, and Mr. Lynch

was certain that you were not expected. We had no appointment. I rode all the way to town and back in the rain—as you insisted—and for what? Nothing. I am greatly disturbed by your lack of consideration. What would it have taken for you to let me know that *your* plans had changed? We are neighbors, after all."

"This seems like a lot of thunder for something that is two days old. I was in Bath, *Lord Aldershot*, as arranged. It was you who failed to show. And why is of great interest to me."

"You are the most ridiculous of young women, Lydia, but I would never have expected such blatant prevarication. I was most decidedly there. In Bath. To discuss our marriage contract. At one. Precisely. You were *not*."

"Today? Of course not. It is Saturday—the twenty-ninth."

"Indeed. All day, as is the norm." The tones of mockery and derision were excessive.

Pursing her lips for a moment, Lydia breathed through her nose, trying to gain control of her pique—extreme pique . . . fully warranted, deserved, and . . . and proper pique!

"Our appointment in Bath," Lydia said in slow deliberate tones—as if dealing with an idiot! "With the lawyer to discuss and sign our marriage contract was arranged for Thursday the twenty-seventh. At one, precisely."

"You said Saturday."

"No, I did not." Lydia continued to stare at Barley, not backing down one iota.

Perhaps it was the clipped manner in which these words were spoken or perhaps it was the glare that accompanied them, it hardly mattered, for there was something in her words or look that took Barley aback. He shook his head in a sharp, jerky motion, and then his shoulders relaxed, and he sighed.

"Oh, Lydia, what am I to do? I was certain our meeting was today. I ordered a new carriage on the strength of it. I am in an awkward position now."

"Counting your chickens before they are hatched?" Lydia, a great advocate of the adage "forgive and forget," found that she was not yet ready to forgive when there had been no apology. And forgetting was equally difficult—being called ridiculous greatly rankled. She was absolutely certain that Robert would never describe her in such a manner.

"'Fraid so. Can you write Lynch and arrange another appointment—soon?"

An unequivocal no was on the tip of her tongue when Lydia realized that Barley was still falling in with *her* plans. . . . And yet she was not as relieved as one might expect. "I will see what I can do."

"Excellent. Yes. That will be fine. The carriage maker does not need to see the glint of my money yet, does he? Oh, wait until you see it, Lydia. The seat is so high I'll need a ladder to climb onto it. Oh, yes, and I might need a little more blunt than we discussed on the signing of the contract. Can't have such a bang-up curricle being pulled by a mismatched set. No, indeed."

Barley was certainly warming to the idea of using her money. "Curricle? You ordered a curricle?" Lydia sighed and wondered if Robert had ever felt the need to kick up a lark or drive a *ridiculous* carriage. Looking away, lest Barley see the look of disapproval in her eyes, Lydia spied the letter for Shelley on her writing desk.

"Do you have your carriage?" It being a miserable day, the odds were fairly high that he had not come on horseback; she scarcely waited for his nod before continuing. "Might I get a ride with you to Spelding? I was hoping to get a letter for Mrs. Dunbar-Ross in the post today. A ride there and back would save me some time and trouble." It would also prevent Cora from skipping the girls' lessons to accompany her.

"No, I think not, Lydia. I *am* off to Spelding but plan to tarry at the rectory. Reverend Caudle is fashioning his sermon for Easter next week and has need of my opinion. I might be there for some time and would not have you wait. It would cause Mrs. Caudle grief to be so put upon. I am rather surprised that you would not better consider her feelings."

Lydia tipped her head and stared at her gallant, who was not in the least gallant. "I did not invite myself to the Caudles, Barley. I merely . . . Never mind, I will give it to Shodster. He'll arrange for the letter to go out on the morrow."

One day more would not make the least difference. In fact, there had been no need to ask Barley for his assistance at all. She simply wondered if he would be willing to go out of his way for her. A test of sorts, for want of a better word.

"Yes, indeed. Problem solved." Barley nodded his farewell and without further comment closed the door behind him.

Yes, an impulsive test. Which he had failed miserably.

$\mathscr{I}$t took the better part of three nights to run Lord Rennoll to ground. The problem was not in locating his residence—though a new arrival from London, the man was well known throughout Bath. The difficulty rose from the fact that the gentleman was seldom at his rented town house and rarely at the same gaming den two nights in a row. Bath had diversions aplenty for titled bachelors, even for those of such advanced years as four and thirty, and Lord Rennoll took advantage of them all.

In the end, Robert resorted to leaving a card and an appointment request with the man's butler. There was no mention of the subject to be discussed, and as such, Robert was fairly certain he would return at the arranged time to find Lord Rennoll at home. Curiosity was a marvelous tool.

Unfortunately, obstinacy was not.

Neither Robert nor Cassidy made it past the front hall.

"Well, that went well," Cassidy said with no little sarcasm as they returned to the street. He donned his top hat, which had literally been in his hand in preparation to eat humble pie.

Robert pivoted, staring first at the closed door framed by decorative beige pillars, and then lifted his gaze to the first floor. The full-length window, running the entire width of the town house, was partially concealed by a balcony, but there was no mistaking the face staring back down.

"Is that him?" Robert pointed with his chin.

Cassidy followed his friend's gaze. "Indeed." And then, in an ill-considered move, Cassidy swept his hat back off his head and bowed—far too slowly and far too deeply. The mockery was evident; the face in the window disappeared.

"Now why did you do that? I was going to work on him. We still have two days."

"Lord Rennoll is not about to cancel our duel. He greatly enjoys the bragging rights of his success. If we learned nothing else in our traipsing about town, we learned that."

Robert hated to admit it, but Cassidy was right. The man was spoiling for a fight. So it was back to his contingency plan; he would tie Cassidy up to prevent him from participating. Robert would have to send Longdon out for a length of rope.

Chapter 13

In which Mr. Newton is caught
woolgathering . . . twice, and Miss Whitfield
has an odd encounter in Spelding

The next morning found Robert mulling over the future of his friend—with fervent hopes and plans to extend that friendship into old age. He had just pushed away his breakfast plate, unable to face the kippers and toast that were now stone cold, when he heard the loud bang of the front-door knocker. Glancing at the clock on the mantel, Robert observed that a reasonably civil hour had only just been attained, and he frowned.

An unexpected visitor before midday did not bode well.

Rising, he reached the morning room door just as Longdon stepped into the hall. His butler lifted a questioning brow.

"Yes, I am in if there is need for me to be," Robert answered the unexpressed query. "I leave it to your discretion."

Longdon gave him a long-suffering look. "Of course, sir. That goes without saying." Straightening, he adopted the stiff stance and superior look required before pulling the door open. The conversation was brief, and though Longdon did close the door without ushering anyone in, he approached Robert with a card on his tray.

Ignoring the disapproving click of Longdon's tongue, Robert lifted the card to read.

BURT WARNER

Principal Officer of Bow Street

LONDON

"Excellent," Robert said to no one in particular. He met Longdon's stare with a nod and curled his lips in an attempted smile. However, the effort was wasted as Longdon's expression grew even more dour. "Did you leave the poor man standing outside?"

"Sent him downstairs to the service entrance, sir. Where he should have gone in the first place."

"Ah, yes, of course. Well, when he knocks again, could you see him to my study?"

"You know that this person is a Runner, sir. A person who dabbles in criminal elements."

"More than dabbles, I would hope. Yes, Longdon. The study, please."

"Very good, sir. Far be it for me to suggest that the back hall might be more appropriate for someone of his ilk."

"I'm pleased to know that you are not going to suggest such a thing."

Robert pivoted and climbed the stairs, almost glad to put his worries of the duel aside temporarily. It was a sign of his distress that talking about a kidnapping would be a relief.

Burt Warner was a tall, angular man in the fortyish range with a stern countenance and a sparse head of hair—although bald would have been an overstatement. He wore the typical blue overcoat with brass buttons and top hat of his office, and his manner was not in the least affable.

"Been given the runaround." Mr. Warner tapped his top hat against his thigh in impatience. "Sent here, there, and everywhere."

"Come by way of Pepney and Villers Manor, I assume." Robert had stood when the Runner entered the study, and he remained on his feet. There was nothing about Mr. Warner that made one inclined to offer the gentleman a seat; it might imply a weakness. . . . One would never want to insult this man.

"Indeed, and though I was told that I might see you first, I had it in mind to visit your Mr. Lynch. Didn't have much to say for himself."

Robert stilled, wondering how he was going to explain the Runner's purpose to Mr. Lynch. Inquiries didn't fit with the scenario that Robert had devised.

"Told me to return at another time; he was that busy. Decided to go back this afternoon at one—"

"Precisely?" Robert asked, relief making him foolish. He was favored with a withering look. "I beg your pardon." He cleared his throat and banished the smile from his face. "I believe that I can answer your questions. No need to disturb Mr. Lynch."

"Hmm. Yes, well, thought it best to speak to the people in that there area at the same time as the snatch. Find out if anyone saw the two characters who made off with you and Miss Whitfield."

"There was a third man as well."

"Hmm, indeed, Morley, but not until the farm. I'll get to that later."

"Are you going to visit the Beyer farm?" Robert thought about his burning need to throw Cassidy into a secure cell somewhere around dawn tomorrow. The farm was really too far away—the wine cellar of his town house would have to do.

"Pardon?" Robert realized that his internal thoughts had overshadowed Mr. Warner's dialogue.

The Runner stopped midsentence, fixed Robert with a steely look—which made him squirm like a schoolboy—and rocked back on his heels. "Something wrong?"

"Distracted is all."

"Abduction and violence not of interest, Mr. Newton? You must live an exciting life. Thought you were a clerk."

Robert clenched his jaw briefly before he spoke—clearly and without any hesitation. "I am a lawyer's clerk, Mr. Warner, and while it might not be the most exciting of careers to some, I feel it is worthwhile and immensely satisfying. Miss Whitfield's abduction is of grave concern to me; however, at present I am greatly distracted by a difficult situation involving a friend."

"A difficult legal situation?"

"Why do you ask that?" Robert said quickly—too quickly

if one used the smug look on Mr. Warner's face as a barometer. With a swallow of discomfort, Robert offered the man a weak smile.

"You *are* a lawyer's clerk, as you said, Mr. Newton. Stands to reason that a friend might come to you on a legal issue."

"Oh, yes, right. Exactly." But it was too late, the Runner was aware that something was decidedly amiss.

With brows raised, the Runner stopped rocking on his heels and leaned toward Robert. It was a very predatory stance.

Robert swallowed yet again.

"Has a *friend* of yours gotten into difficulty? Is *he* involved in Miss Whitfield's abduction?"

"No, no. Of course not. One has nothing to do with the other." Robert reassured the Runner as best he could, leaning away, trying not to feel intimidated. "His situation is more immediate—his danger is imminent—whereas Lydia's danger has passed." Robert cringed upon hearing Lydia's first name slip out, and he shook his head in disbelief.

Mr. Warner chose to ignore the *faux pas*, for Robert was certain that the slip had not gone unnoticed. "Would this danger involve a dawn meeting?"

"That is a leap of logic that I do not understand."

"Come now," Mr. Warner said in a bonhomie sort of way. He straightened and began to rock back and forth on his heels again. "You society pups are not original. No surprises in your high spirits. Been getting into scrapes in the same way for years:

gambling, riding neck-or-nothing, chasing a bit of muslin. None of these would call for the use of the word *dangerous*."

"I misspoke."

"Think not, young sir. I believe that you, being a clerk and all, are very careful with words. No, don't think dipping too deep could be called dangerous, or even drawing someone's cork. Pockets to let is more of a waste, what with all your blunt, and, well, the petticoat line is a whole lot of trouble—but, again, not dangerous. No, if I were a betting man—and I'm not—I would say your friend might be facing a pistol at dawn. That is not only dangerous, it is illegal."

"Of course it is." Robert turned to the window and scrubbed at his face before resting his forehead on the cold glass. He had to decide if Rennoll was a menace to avoid . . . or stop.

"It's a practice that requires luck and skill. Wouldn't want to count on either, if it were me."

"Indeed. Is that all you need to begin your investigation? I will not feel any security for Miss Whitfield until the criminals are found. It was no happenstance. The thugs were waiting, knew her name and nature. It was planned—"

"I'll do my best, Mr. Newton. And the sooner I get started the better. Give me a day or two here, and then I'll need to speak to the young lady in question."

Robert lifted his head with a start and a smile. "Oh, of course. I shall drive to Roseberry Hall with you, to initiate the introduction."

"A letter would suffice."

"No, no," Robert turned. "With all that has occurred, a stranger requesting an interview might be somewhat disconcerting. I wouldn't want Miss Whitfield to feel any misgivings." Though Robert was certain Lydia would take it all in stride—not nonplussed in the least—he still felt an overwhelming urge to see her, to smell her soft lavender scent, and to watch the light in her eyes sparkle as she laughed. . . . "Pardon?" Robert realized there was a great deal of silence emanating from the other side of the room. He flushed in discomfort; he had been caught woolgathering for the second time in their short meeting.

"Distracted again?" asked the Runner. "Not by the same thing, I'm thinking."

Robert had never observed before that a silly smile pasted onto a person of a serious character could look quite out of place—as if the lifted cheeks caused pain.

"No, indeed. A very different subject."

"Not dangerous, I'm thinking."

"Indeed not." Robert would almost welcome the return to their discussion about dueling. "So then, we are settled in regard to your investigation. You have enough to start with?" Robert heard the repetition of his words and flinched.

"Yes, I believe I have it all straight. Still, I must warn you, and this will likely come as no surprise, there is a good chance that I will not discover who is behind this foul deed. We don't always succeed."

"Yes, I understand. It is what I expected, though I do hope that this will not be one of those cases."

The Bow Street Runner's shrug was not in the least reassuring.

𝒟ydia tripped and would have taken a tumble had she not been holding Hugh's hand.

"Are you all right, miss?" he asked, helping her into the carriage.

Frustrated by her clumsiness, Lydia settled beside Cora and then turned to stare at the offending step. "Yes, yes. Splendid. Thank you," she replied absentmindedly.

"Are you sure?" It was Cora's turn to fret needlessly.

When Lydia turned, exasperated by the fussing, she met a confused rather than worried expression. "Why? Do I not look fine?"

Glancing from Lydia's face to her chartreuse spencer, Cora nodded. "More than fine, more than splendid. That is a very flattering color for you, Lydia my dear. Fine, indeed." And then she paused. "But you are a mite . . . how shall I put it? Um—distracted. It is such an odd state for you."

"Yes, I suppose so." Lydia lapsed into silence for a moment, uncomfortable with the idea of revealing that her thoughts had been focused on the breadth of Robert's shoulders and not the placement of the carriage's step. "Yes, well," she said, giving her head a shake, "onward and outward, a fun day to be had."

Sitting back, Lydia offered a wink to both Ivy and Tessa, who were seated facing them. "Shall we go?" Pleased with the girls' grins and giggles, Lydia called up to Mr. Hodge as soon as she felt the dip of Hugh stepping up onto the back of the carriage.

It was a fairly short and uneventful drive into Spelding and not much of a substitute for Bath, yet both the young young ladies and older young ladies of their party were quite excited about the outing. Lydia had had a few days to settle back into her routine; she had reclaimed her equilibrium and found that, despite all that had transpired in the past week, life had returned to such a state of normalcy that one could almost wonder if the harrowing events of her abduction had really taken place.

No, that wasn't entirely true. There was one significant change.

Cora's spirited character had returned, along with a pretty blush on her cheek, colorful ribbons at her waist, and light conversation on her tongue. Lydia attributed this upturn to eager anticipation of a letter from Shelley . . . or Mr. Granger, rather than setting aside the terrors of their Bath excursion. It hardly mattered whence the euphoria came.

Cousin Elaine and Aunt Freya were still being thoroughly uncivil to her, departing any room as soon as Lydia entered. Her company—in her own house—was apparently too much to bear. It was one part humorous and three parts pathetic. Unfortunately, that in and of itself was not a rare occurrence. A transgression of this magnitude was perceived at least once a month. Their pique would undoubtedly increase when they learned that their hoity-toity attitude had contributed to a missed opportunity to venture afar. Their disappointment would likely be reshaped into disapproval and laid at Lydia's feet.

Lydia had offered her mother an olive branch in the form of a solicitation to join the shopping excursion, but dearest Mama had claimed the need to finish the invitations. She alluded to her tireless efforts to complete the chore, ignoring the fact that Lydia had done all but a handful.

Yes, indeed. All was back to normal.

Spelding was a good-sized village working its way up to a market town. As such, it had several shops, two hostelries, a smithy, and three pubs. It was a pretty place; the buildings were predominantly redbrick with white trim and the occasional black door. Flower boxes had been set in place under the mullioned windows, though it was too early for planting. Still, the common in the center was greening up nicely, and there were a fair number of persons milling about.

Mr. Hodge set the company down at the west end of the village and would wait upon their pleasure at the east end. Hugh, in his stylish green livery, followed—as requested by Cora—ostensibly to carry parcels, but Lydia knew it to be more for her protection than the need to remain unburdened.

The girls skipped ahead, pretending they were interested in their surroundings when, in fact, Lydia knew them to be directing their steps to the milliner. Ivy and Tessa had been offered new bonnets, and they could barely contain their excitement. Cora, who would usually walk to the inside of the road, made a very

pointed maneuver to the right. Lydia shrugged, and they continued, as was their norm, discussing arrangements for the ball as
they meandered.

Stepping over a puddle left from the rains of the day before,
Lydia was rather disconcerted to find Cora, once again, placing
Lydia next to the buildings in a definitive move. Shifting aside
when ladies or families passed going the other direction, Cora
jumped in front of Lydia if any person of the male persuasion
approached, singly or in a group. The scowl that accompanied
the move was endearing and comical—although how it could
be both, Lydia was not entirely sure, but it was.

"You are being a goose, dearest friend. You need not fear the
inhabitants of Spelding on my behalf. I am quite safe." She spoke
in a soft tone so that her words would not carry to the girls ahead
or Hugh behind.

"I know you think so, Lydia. But I am not so certain. We do
not know the reason you were taken or the persons involved, and
until we do, there is no such thing as too much caution."

Lydia laughed and hooked her arm through Cora's, stepping
forward and pulling her along. "This was an impromptu jaunt.
The villain or villains could not know that I was to Spelding
today, and as I am seldom here, they would hardly await me with
nefarious plans."

"Visiting Bath is an event even more rare, and yet that is where
it happened."

"True enough, but it was a *planned* outing and had been part
of my schedule for over two weeks. Plenty of time for thugs,

deviants, and generally unscrupulous persons to . . . to . . . Cora?" Lydia stopped midstep and stared at the far distance without seeing it. "Did you hear what I just said?" She turned toward her friend, who was nodding slowly, her expression troubled.

"Oh dear. I did, indeed."

"The entire parish would not be curious about my schedule. News that I was to visit Bath would hardly be bandied about. No, in truth . . . just the inhabitants of Roseberry Hall and Wilder Hill Manor would have had any interest . . . though, not excessively. It is possible that news spilled out a little farther. A casual comment here or there . . ." Recalling the shadows and the sensation of being watched, Lydia considered for a moment and then veered toward another possibility. "Or a question asked here or there. Hmm. I wonder if I should ask Shodster to speak to the staff? Ask if there has been anyone querying my comings and goings. That might be a productive avenue of investigation."

Glancing behind, Cora frowned. "We are holding up others and receiving some very impertinent looks," she explained as she pulled Lydia forward. "You are forgetting someone. There was someone else who knew about your Bath appointment, someone who likes to comment on your punctuality and lives in Bath . . . where there are far more unscrupulous persons."

"Are there? Why do you say so?"

"Numbers if nothing else. A city has a larger population— that alone . . . oh, Lydia, stop teasing. You know to whom I am referring."

Lydia fought to maintain a solemn expression and finally

capitulated, allowing her mouth to curve into a grin. "You speak of Mr. Robert Newton."

"I do, indeed. And though it is clear that you esteem the young man—"

"I have said no such thing!"

"Really, Lydia. What is there not to like? A handsome, intelligent gentleman who admires you—"

"You are exaggerating."

"No, indeed not. Mr. Newton has not disguised his protective nature in your regard. He thinks very highly of you . . . in a professional manner, of course."

"Of course."

"But what if it's a ruse? What if he is after your money?"

Lydia laughed; she couldn't help it. Of all the people she knew, Robert Newton was the least sinister she could imagine. "I think there would be easier ways to ensure a big purse than making away with me. Besides, you are forgetting that he suffered at my side."

"What if he set it up to garner your admiration? Woo you away from Lord Aldershot?"

"That would be a very strange way to woo." It was also odd that the mention of Barley knotted her belly in an unpleasant manner.

"Yes, but everyone knows you are destined to marry Lord Aldershot. And . . . were you not seized *before* the papers were signed?"

"Cora dear, Robert has not made any advances," she said,

stifling a sigh. "He has not shown any interest in me other than in friendship."

"But—"

"I was in Mr. Newton's company for an extended period of time, and I believe that I had the opportunity to assess his character, with fair accuracy, during our *adventure*. I can, quite confidently, say that I trust him."

"Really?"

Lydia noted the change of her friend's voice and glanced over to see that Cora was grinning. "Oh, Cora, now you are funning me! Were you hoping for a disclosure?"

"How can you say so!" The tone of indignation was perfect: the straightened shoulders, the glimmer of hurt in her eyes. . . . However, Cora could not control her dimples. "Bother," she said, resigning to a giggle. "I would so like for you to find a love match, such as I have found in Mr. Granger. There is nothing that can match the giddy euphoria of true affection."

Lydia nodded, finding it easy enough to put euphoria and Robert in the same sentence. She squeezed her friend's arm and then turned her gaze back to the road ahead. "Oh Lud."

Standing not four paces from them was Mr. Ian Chilton in all his foppish glory. He was engaged in an animated conversation with a woman that involved sweeping arm movements and a bobbing head. At any moment, he might turn and see Lydia. Then she would be done for; Mr. Chilton would attempt to latch himself onto their party, and if he succeeded, all enjoyment of the excursion would be gone.

Shushing Cora, Lydia maneuvered to the side, planning to quietly step around the couple. Unfortunately, the conversation wrapped up as they were passing, and the dandy turned his head, seeing Lydia immediately. As soon as their eyes met, Lydia was forced to halt, albeit briefly. It would be the height of bad manners to walk on without some acknowledgment—she might get away with it at Roseberry but not in the village.

"Miss Whitfield . . . oh my, what a surprise. Excellent, excellent. Well met. Here you are in Spelding. You seldom visit. Aren't we blessed." Blinking, the affected gentleman stared at Lydia with his mouth partially open. He grabbed a deep breath . . . let it out, opened his mouth as if to speak, and then closed it again.

Lydia nodded and was about to continue on her way when Mr. Chilton pivoted and hurried off in the opposite direction.

With a frown, Lydia stared after him.

"That was odd," said Cora. "The man seemed quite nonplussed to see you. Your jaunts to the village are not *that* irregular."

"No, indeed. He seemed more befuddled than his norm—verging on perplexed. I wonder . . ." Lydia looked to the ground for a moment, trying to understand what had just transpired.

"Wonder what, Lydia?"

"Umm. Oh, yes. I wondered if Mr. Chilton knew I was going into Bath last week . . . at one, precisely."

The sun had yet to slip above the horizon when Robert and Cassidy climbed Daisy Hill in silence. The mist, swirling in and around the trees, gave the meadow an eerie, haunting quality. The air was heavy with the smell of freshly turned earth—newly formed mole mounds dotted the incline. The dueling arena seemed deserted, but Robert knew better; he squinted into the gray, looking for any telltale shadows.

"There," he whispered to Cassidy, and pointed ahead to a spot, slightly off to the right.

Robert assumed Cassidy had nodded, for there was no verbal response, simply a redirection of their path. Some moments later, two figures resolved and grew larger as they approached.

Finally, Robert and Cassidy halted not ten feet from the easily insulted man and his second. There was a sardonic look to Rennoll's smile, and he leaned forward as if eager, an unseemly glint of excitement in his stare. Not a pleasant sight. The man was overly thin, not unlike the skeletal appearance of an opium eater; his fine clothes hung awkwardly.

"So you have come, after all. Quite expected you to turn tail. Your inability to shoot straight is quite well known. Should I have my second stand behind a tree?" He laughed as if his words were a jest.

Robert felt his ire rise, but he knew the man to be goading Cassidy, to make him careless—ruin his aim . . . what aim he had. Robert said nothing. It had been agreed that Cassidy would take the lead.

"I am here because I said I would be. My honor is intact; it is yours that is in question." Cassidy sounded calm despite his nervousness.

"I would challenge you for those words alone were we not already here for your previous insult."

"There was no previous insult. You simply manipulated the situation so that it seemed that way. . . . And I was too drunk at the time to realize."

"Not only did you cast aspersions on my financial situation, you did so in front of others."

"If I had apologized in public, would you have withdrawn your challenge?"

Lord Rennoll laughed in an ugly staccato. "No, not likely." Then he straightened his shoulders and stretched as if bored of the whole enterprise. The fevered shine of his eyes hinted otherwise. "Come now, let's have done with this. I have plans to celebrate. Where is . . . interesting, you did not bring a physician. You are ill-prepared, my friend—not even dueling pistols. Worry not. I am equipped. Harold, if you please."

The indistinct figure who had been standing off to the side stepped forward. He was a squat bulldog of a man made broader by his billowing greatcoat. In a showy flourish, the man presented the case to Cassidy, opened it, and indicated the two pistols nestled in blue velvet.

Robert heard Cassidy take a deep but shaky breath.

"Steady," he whispered, hoping that Cassidy could hold the course—that they could put a stop to Rennoll's treacherous method of grandstanding.

"Yes, listen to your second." Lord Rennoll laughed. "You need a steady hand to see this through. Oh, have I mentioned that you are not the first to turn and face me?" He paused dramatically. "I have yet to lose."

"It's the dawn of a new day." Robert snorted with derision.

A confused expression flashed across Rennoll's smarmy countenance. It was quickly quashed, and the light of manic enjoyment returned. Still, the glow was not quite as bright—muted by a whisper of concern.

Robert smiled.

Chapter 14

In which an anonymous mole affects a duel and
Miss Whitfield experiences a strange sort of tingling

Robert stared at Lord Rennoll, aware that Cassidy had not moved—not to look into the pistol box and certainly not to gesture which of the offending weapons was supposed to seal his fate. Rennoll's smirk made it clear what he thought of the delay.

And then, as they had agreed, Cassidy stepped back, feigning confusion. "I'm not sure. . . . I can't decide. What think you, Newton?"

Robert leaned forward as if to judge the contents of the box. Deferring to a second was not unusual. Checking and loading the weapon was his responsibility, so garnering his opinion would be advisable.

"It is difficult to say." Robert heard the stiffness in his tone and altered it, trying to match it with his trivial words. "This one has a scratch, and that one looks dirty—probably used too often." He sighed dramatically. "No, they will not do. I don't like either for you. We will have to go with swords." He noted that the sky was lightening and knew that the increased visibility would be to their service.

"Swords?" Now it was Rennoll's turn to sound stiff. "I think not. Pistols at dawn. Swords are from a bygone era."

"Really? There are fencing academies aplenty that would likely disagree. Still, if the blades are not here, the point is moot. Boxing—perhaps you might bash each other about for a bit. Call it a draw, and then we can all have a drink at the pub. Though it is a little early for whiskey, ale would be fine. So . . . well, what say you?"

"I say this is nonsense! Stand ready! This is a duel, not a garden party!" The roar of Rennoll's words echoed throughout the meadow, followed by an unfortunate silence.

Unfortunate, for in that stillness a twig snapped.

Rennoll, however, had worked himself into a grand pique. So intent with his own concerns, he had failed to understand the significance of a snapped twig in what was supposed to be a soulless copse.

"Pick your pistol and mark your line," Rennoll barked. He pointed at the box, gesturing Harold forward. Robert didn't deign to look down.

"No, I think not. I have a different solution to this . . . disagreement."

Sensing that he was losing the upper hand, Rennoll frowned,

leaning back ever so slightly. "This is not a disagreement, boy. This is a duel." He glanced at Cassidy and then back to Robert.

"Not in my eyes. You see, if this were a duel, I would have to report it to the authorities."

"You would have to do no such thing. Where is your sense of honor?"

"Which honor—my honor as a gentleman or my honor as a lawyer?" Robert wasn't going to dilute the point by mentioning that he was not *yet* a lawyer, but an apprentice . . . in-waiting.

Both Rennoll and Harold swallowed audibly and looked around.

"Let me tell you a tale. It's not overlong. Simply told, it's about a baron with an excellent shooting ability who likes to feign insult and challenge young bucks to a duel. Only the baron knows the *why* of his actions. However—and this is the crux of the matter—when a certain young lawyer looked into the matter, he discovered that the baron had participated in three duels with increasingly serious injury to the offending principal. In short, it was just a matter of time before the baron's shot would be fatal. So you see, honor dictated his actions. The baron could not be allowed to continue unchecked."

Harold took Robert's meaning faster than Rennoll, thrusting the box into the man's hands and rushing into the woods. A resounding thud offered a clue to the results of that folly.

And then at last, the signal Robert had been waiting for, though not the whistle he expected but a disembodied voice. "Nab him, sir."

Blinking in surprise, Rennoll stared at Robert. Robert stared back, allowing a slow rise at the corner of his mouth in what could be mistaken for a smile . . . but one of satisfaction, not pleasure. A catalog of emotions flitted across Rennoll's face: puzzlement, discomfort, concern, and then, finally, realization.

Rennoll threw the open box at Robert's head, turned tail, and ran. As he dodged the flying pistols, Robert's grab was off-kilter and a split second too late; his fingers closed on air. Rennoll raced across the meadow in a great lopping stride.

A carriage, visible now in the early light of day, sat waiting on the far side of the clearing. The baron's escape was assured should Robert not bring him down. Surprised by the man's speed, Robert chased after the miscreant with an ever-increasing gait until he was hard on the man's heels. Cassidy, as evidenced by his labored breathing, was hard on *Robert's* heels, shouting out a needless warning. "The carriage. Robert. Don't. Let—"

Rennoll went down, tripped up by a mole mound. Jumping to prevent his own spill, Robert heard a grunt as the heel of his Hessian landed on the man's butt. Stumbling, Robert fell forward, but he rolled just as he made contact with the ground and regained his feet in a trice. Turning back, he joined Cassidy, who had somehow managed to avoid the heap of tripping gentlemen. They watched Rennoll struggle to stand, ready to grab him if he succeeded.

Winded, Lord Rennoll sneered and labored into a sitting position, trying to gain his feet. But his energies were spent; he could only pant and bluster. "I am a baron of the realm, and I will not be interfered with." He spat this out as if it were a threat of some sort. "I have had enough. I am leaving."

His words were hollow. No sooner had he spoken than the sound of carriage wheels on gravel reached them. The jingle of equipage, the snap of a whip, and the shout of a driver put paid to Rennoll's hopes. His ride had just departed.

"Worry not," Robert said with great satisfaction between his gulps for air. "Another coach. Will be here presently. One that will take you. To court." He glanced across the clearing, watching a party of three men emerge from the woods. One held his arms in front of him, walking awkwardly—as if his wrists were tied together.

Looking down at the expression of dismay on Lord Rennoll's face, Robert smiled. "I would like to offer you an introduction," he said while placing a restraining hand on Rennoll's shoulder to prevent him from rising.

A figure in a dark blue coat with brass buttons stepped ahead of the others, quickly closing the distance.

"To Mr. Burt Warner, Principal Officer of Bow Street."

*L*ydia glanced into the shrubbery and then up and down the road before stepping off the Roseberry estate. Surprised by this overly cautious impulse, she gave her head a shake at the foolishness that *other* people had instilled in her. One: This was far from a bustling, traffic-infested lane, most often deserted and, therefore, needed no excessive caution when crossing. Two: There were no tree trunks large enough to hide behind, no suspicious shadows, no strange sounds, no villains peeking out from the bushes. Really! Thank the heavens no one else in the family was privy to the abduction secret—the angst of Cora and Shodster was enough, for they had infected her!

Fighting for the peace and calm that was the usual result of her daily constitutional, Lydia focused on more relaxing thoughts. There was one subject in particular that usually brought with it a smile, perhaps a chuckle or two, in recollected dialogues. That subject, of course, was Robert Newton.

It was odd, but Lydia seemed to be counting the days since she had last seen him: six or seven depending on where one started counting. Was their arrival after midnight considered the same day or the day after? Well, it hardly mattered. The most important fact was that Lydia missed her new friend, and she was devising a perfectly rational reason to contact him. None would see anything untoward about a young lady contacting her solicitor's clerk.

Writing and then rewriting the words in her head, Lydia tried to compose the letter, something that might entice Robert Newton to Roseberry. Should she ask about the duel? Perhaps add a comment in regard to her suspicions about Mr. Chilton. Might she ask for information on the progress of the investigation and his presence for reassurance? No, that smacked of weakness, and she needed no reassurance—just his company.

They were friends, that was true enough. . . . And friends should not belabor their words. But this was a newfound relationship, and Lydia did not want to infringe nor did she want to contribute to any misinterpretation of her intent. She certainly did not want Robert to believe that there was anything other than friendship between them . . . yes, friendship.

Indeed, it was normal to miss one's friends. Did she not miss Shelley? Of course! Although Lydia could not recall missing Shelley in a wistful manner, laden with undefined hopes. Yes, it was all very disconcerting.

Looking up, Lydia realized that she had stopped walking . . . and that she was still many paces from the Roseberry gate. Tarrying would not be wise; Cora had not objected—overly—to Lydia's solitary constitutional, but Shodster had made his feelings known. She could envisage the entire household being roused should she be later than expected. And as she hurried toward the gate, Lydia heard the clopping of hooves and the rattle of wheels on the very road that she had declared deserted not moments earlier.

Turning with great interest, Lydia saw an open carriage approaching from the direction of Bath. There were three persons of the male persuasion in the small phaeton, two on the driver's bench and one other in the back. The hood was folded, allowing them the full advantage of the warm spring sun, the fresh breeze, and, more important, Lydia's scrutiny.

Standing to the side, she felt no alarm . . . or disinterest, for there was something quite familiar in the figure of the driver. Even before she had identified him, Lydia's heart quickened, and she held her breath, waiting for confirmation. Fortunately, it was mere seconds before she could verify that, yes, indeed, the driver was none other than her very own Robert Newton. She was so very pleased to see him.

Swallowing, taking a deep breath, and smoothing down her skirts—which needed no such reproof—Lydia tried to understand why she had suddenly acquired a jittery energy. She had come to no conclusion when the carriage pulled up in front of her.

"Well met, Miss Whitfield," Robert said, making no disguise of his pleasure.

Lydia returned his grin, appreciating the deep pools of his expressive eyes. She wondered if something had transpired, noting a slight hint of excitement. But now was not the time to ask, as he was in the process of introducing her to . . . "I beg your pardon, I was distracted—you were saying?"

Robert paused, lifted his brows, and then began again. "This is Mr. Burt Warner of Bow Street."

Lydia pulled her eyes from Robert and glanced at the thin man beside him. She had little time to take his measure—and understand the reason for his smirk—when the introductions continued to the person taking up most of the backseat.

"Mr. David Selleck, recently of Menthe—just this side of Shaftesbury. He has been a land agent for the better part of fifteen years."

Surprise, of the pleasant sort, had Lydia assessing Mr. Selleck more closely. The man wasn't rotund but broad; his shoulders were substantial and his girth proportional. Well dressed, but by no means stylish, Mr. Selleck exuded an affable air, though not overly jolly. His manner, if one can assess character by something as minimal as a nod, was pleasant, interested, and approachable. Yes, Robert had brought her a possible replacement for Mr. Drury. She should not have been surprised.

"Are you on your own?" Robert frowned, swiveling in his seat to look around. "I wouldn't have thought that advisable."

Lydia laughed lightly. "My daily constitutional, Mr. Newton. I'm hardly in need of an escort."

His expression was pained, as if he wished to argue the point. "Can we take you up to the house?" He glanced over his shoulder to the somewhat diminutive space left on the backseat.

As much as Lydia might find Mr. Selleck an agreeable sort and looked forward to getting to know him, she preferred not to increase their acquaintance by bouncing up the road on his lap. "That would defeat the purpose of a constitutional, don't you think? I should be along soon enough. By the time Shodster has set you up in the study with a bit of refreshment to satiate you after your journey, I will be there."

Robert did not look pacified; he shook his head and passed the reins to Mr. Warner. "The stables are to the back to the house," he said as he jumped to the ground. "I'll be there presently."

Mr. Warner merely nodded and flicked the reins, leaving Robert and Lydia staring after the diminishing carriage. Neither said anything for some minutes, staring at the empty road—as if watching a parade. Lydia wasn't sure what had brought on this stillness, discomfort or companionship. It proved to be the latter.

"Lydia, my dear friend, I am so glad to see you." Robert

turned, taking both her hands in his. "It has been a month of Sundays since we last met."

Lydia laughed, or rather tried to. She knew him to be funning; his tone was light and frivolous, but she was finding it difficult to form words. "One . . . Sunday, actually."

Staring at their clasped hands, Lydia was experiencing the most disquieting sensations: a tingling that began at her toes and rose all the way to every hair on her head—stopping only to intensify where their gloved hands met. Heat and shivers and excitement all mingled, coursing through her like a raging river. And her breath was puffy—as if she had run some distance. Stranger still was that all these contrary sensations were agreeable—very agreeable.

Had Lydia not known better, she might have taken these wonderful, exhilarating sensations as a sign that Mr. Robert Newton had imposed upon her. And as the thought that this was impossible surfaced from the floodwaters of her emotions, it brought with it another possibility—in complete disagreement with its companion. She was, indeed, deeply attracted to Robert. Deeply.

Now, she was in shock.

Was it true? And if it was, did that change everything or nothing? And what of the sensations themselves? Did they disappear over time or intensify? Was this what great poetry described as love? Or was her imagination running amok? Would she ever feel these heady emotions when Barley held her hands and looked confused—as Robert was doing now?

"Lydia? Lydia, are you well? Your color is very high." He slid his hands up to her elbows to support her weight.

"Fine," she squeaked, barely aware that she had stepped closer.

"Are you certain? There seems to be something terribly wrong."

"No, no. Nothing wrong." Lydia breathed in his scent and considered wrapping her arms around his neck. Perhaps he would kiss her. What a most improper, delicious thought. No, the term *imprudent* might be a better descriptor. After all, the marriage contract was not yet signed. Barley could hardly object to something that took place—

"Lydia?" Robert truly sounded concerned.

Lydia sighed and leaned back—placing herself at a disappointing, respectable distance. "Worry not, my friend. I was merely deep in thought."

A small smile played at the side of his mouth, and the frown disappeared. "What about?"

"The marriage contract."

"Oh." Robert's mouth curved back down. "I see."

"I was wondering about the possibility of putting off the signing. If Mr. Selleck is a good match for Roseberry Hall, I would no longer need Barley's support to replace Mr. Drury."

Barley had not been keen on an early betrothal anyway; he thought it best to wait. It would seem as if she were catering to his needs . . . and give her more time to understand what she was experiencing, and its significance. She would deal with the over-zealous ordering of a curricle later.

"True." Robert's smile was back. It was very nearly a grin.

"We shall have to see, of course, after the interview." Lydia tried to instill a tone of authority.

"Indeed." Stepping to the side, Robert offered her his elbow.

Lydia crooked her arm through his. Normally, she would place her other hand atop her own, but this time she allowed it to rest on Robert's forearm. It was an experiment. She wanted to see if the warmth and agreeable sensations dissipated.

They didn't. In fact, they seemed to multiply. Delicious.

It was a lovely walk to the manor.

*R*obert said very little during Lydia's interview with Mr. Warner. They wanted the meeting to be as succinct as possible so as not to arouse any interest within the family. It was conducted in the morning room, while Mr. Selleck waited in the study. Shodster had been sent to find Uncle Arthur—slowly—allowing for a good half-hour conversation.

As expected, there was little for Lydia to add when describing the *curious adventure*; however, she did have comments and questions regarding Mr. Chilton.

"He seemed very surprised to see me in town and very flustered. To the point that he didn't even wait for me to greet him. Do you not find that odd? Especially when the man has tried to be nothing other than a clinging burr for the better part of two months."

It was no surprise that Lydia was handling the interview with great aplomb. Her comments and questions were concise and well considered; her intelligence was far from hidden. It was good to see, for Robert had been rather unnerved by Lydia's initial reaction to his arrival, and he had wondered, briefly, if she had had an upset.

He had been quite prepared to thrash whoever had caused her dismay, but she had denied such an event and chatted and laughed with him all the way to the manor. For a few moments, he feared that Lydia had seen through him . . . realized that she affected him quite profoundly. But no, she regained her equilibrium in jig time and—other than the occasional squeeze—behaved as if nothing was amiss.

They did not hasten after the carriage but took their leisure and pleasure in each other's company. Good friends could do that without causing any discomfort. The duel was discussed, which seemed to warrant those occasional squeezes. Lydia did little other than listen, harrumphing and scowling at the appropriate moments, but it set him at ease.

And now he stood by the low-burning fire, watching his lovely Lydia . . . ah, no . . . his charming friend, conduct the interview with Mr. Warner. Her movements were graceful even as she gestured with her words, and Robert tried not to notice the flattering cut of her gown. . . . Or that the rising color in her cheeks gave her a very becoming glow. When she glanced his way, Robert nodded and smiled back, though he was not paying any heed to the conversation. Lydia had it well in hand.

"Don't you agree?"

"Indeed," Robert answered without thought, and then sharply shook his head. "I beg your pardon. You were saying?"

"That Mr. Warner is a thorough investigator, and despite his doubts, I believe he will succeed in ferreting out our master criminal." She stared up at him from the settee, looking quite at ease.

"Master criminal?"

"Yes, Les and Morley could hardly be accused of the cleverness needed for such a planned endeavor."

"Yes . . . no . . ." With a frown, Robert scanned the room. "Indeed, a master . . . Where *is* Mr. Warner?"

Lydia laughed, a delightful carillon. "Robert, my dear friend, you were woolgathering. I thought as much; your expression was rather blank."

"Was it?" Robert was very glad to know that he did not look the lovesick calf he felt.

"Yes, most definitely."

"And Mr. Warner?"

"He is off to Spelding. Hugh is to take him, where he intends to hire a horse and proceed in his investigation. Yes, I have great confidence in his abilities."

"Excellent. Then shall we see to Mr. Selleck?"

Lydia rose and approached Robert in a smooth swaying stride that left him dry mouthed.

"Can you stay?"

"Pardon?" Robert cringed at the high pitch of his voice. He

cleared his throat and tried again, this time in a bass. "What do you mean?"

Lydia stopped a few paces from him and stared into his eyes. "Might I persuade you to stay until tomorrow? Dine with me . . . and the family? Or are you obligated to return right away?"

"I can stay. Nothing would give me greater pleasure," Robert reassured her, keeping his tone light to disguise the deep truth of his words.

"Wonderful! I am delighted," Lydia said, sounding as if she really was.

Lydia accompanied Robert down the corridor into the great hall and there stopped abruptly. People were cluttering up her entrance. No, not people. Ladies. Three ladies, to be precise—in lovely dresses, somewhat finer than necessary for the afternoon. They were all turned toward the wall, staring at a painting as if they were collectors appreciating the artistry of an undiscovered masterpiece. It was artifice, of course. The painting was that of the Melrose Abbey ruin in Scotland and had been in place . . . well, for as long as Lydia could remember. And the ladies were none other than her mother, aunt, and cousin, trying to appear occupied while waiting for Robert.

Smiling at the antics, Lydia noted the heaving chests. It was not to be wondered at; the transformation from ordinary to impressive had been accomplished in a very short half hour.

Mama was the first to turn and feign surprise. "Lydia, my dear child, you have brought us a guest."

As expected, Robert bowed to each lady in turn as they dipped in acknowledgment.

"So good to see you again, Mr. Newton." Elaine stepped closer, tipping her head to the side. Lydia couldn't be certain, but she thought her cousin batted her eyelashes.

Robert seemed oblivious to the simpering, and Lydia felt a twinge of sympathy for Elaine. But no more than a twinge. The emotion might have been fully realized had Lydia thought that Elaine truly cared for Robert. However, Lydia could determine no starstruck glimmer in Elaine's eyes, no listening with rapt interest to what he was saying, and no desire to know his character. Robert represented security, not love, to Elaine.

It was not what Lydia would wish for him. Robert Newton deserved love.

"I'm afraid I must take Mr. Newton away, Mama. Mr. Selleck is waiting for us in the study."

"Mr. Selleck?" Lydia's mother frowned and glanced in the general direction of that room as if she could see through the west wall.

"Yes. Mr. Newton has brought us a candidate to replace Mr. Drury—"

"Oh dear, your uncle will not like that idea," Aunt Freya interrupted. She swallowed convulsively. "He will be most upset . . . when he awakes."

The heavy silence that followed her pronouncement likely

held a different meaning for each. Embarrassment, possibly, for Aunt Freya and Cousin Elaine, who liked to pretend that Uncle was not overindulgent with the Roseberry liquor cabinet. Perhaps discomfort for Mama, who never enjoyed her brother's sullen moods. Likely disinterest for Robert, who knew Uncle only in this upset state. And frustration for Lydia, who wanted to resolve the land-agent problem as quickly as possible.

"Might you join us, then, Mama? If Uncle is incapacitated and cannot participate in the interview, might you not give us your opinion?"

The logic was clear. Lydia could not make the decision on her own: she was quite capable, but she did not have the authority. Robert could represent Mr. Lynch. And in a pinch . . . without examining the whole too closely, Mama could represent the second part of the trusteeship—her uncle. Yes, that would work.

"Me?" A slow smile spread across Mama's face. "You would like my opinion?"

Lydia blinked at the tone and stared at her mother in surprise. Mama was pleased. So pleased, in fact, that she had forgotten that she had been giving her daughter the cold shoulder for the better part of a week. She stepped forward, touching Lydia's arm as if to gain her attention.

"Yes, Lydia dear, let's meet this Mr. Selleck."

"Joan." Aunt Freya's voice held a warning of some sort.

"No, Freya. I will not be stopped. Lydia would like my opinion." Lifting her chin, then straightening her shoulders, Mama took Lydia's arm, pulling her toward the study. "There was a time when your father, too, thought to gain my estimation. And I must say I served him well. Yes, indeed. He said so, many a time. I remember in our younger days . . ."

Glancing over her shoulder, Lydia met Robert's gaze and smiled. She was gladdened by her mother's transformation, and he seemed to understand that. He winked and followed them into the study.

Chapter 15

*In which a catalog, dry as week-old toast,
is given high praise*

"Zawks! I will not have it!" Kemble's voice blasted across the dinner table as he slammed his hand down.

The company shrugged—well, near enough. No one reacted. There was no shocked exclamation, no reproof for the vulgar language, and no cajoling. This was clearly not the first time the man had sought to assert his will. Though one had to observe that the effort was less than successful. Perhaps if Mrs. Kemble was not afflicted with a sick headache and unable to join them, she might have infected the family with *her* faintheartedness. . . . But she *was* so afflicted and, therefore, unable to spread her contagion.

"It is done, Arthur. Mr. Drury left hours ago, and Mr. Selleck is getting himself settled in as we speak. I'm sure once you have met him, you will find him a great improvement. He has been a land agent for fifteen years—five in Heper and ten in Menthe." Mrs. Whitfield lifted her glass to her lips and took a deep drink of ratafia. She glanced at Lydia, offering her a smile. "I found him quite knowledgeable."

"Then why is he not still working, this wonder, this great savior who promises to transform Roseberry into a moneymaker?"

"He promised no such thing, Uncle. Perhaps you are confusing Mr. Selleck with Mr. Drury." Lydia, sitting directly across from Robert, did not appear to be upset by her uncle's mood, either. "As to his availability: We are to be thankful that the heir of his late employer arrived with his own steward, making Mr. Selleck redundant. And that Mr. Newton's brother heard about the travesty."

"Might have known. We have you to thank, do we?" Kemble turned the full force of his pique on Robert, scowling and pointing. He was rather like an overexcited basset hound—all bark, no bite . . . and droopy ears.

Robert bowed in acknowledgment as if the accusation had been an expression of gratitude. "In part, sir. My brother sent Mr. Selleck to me for consideration for the post—"

"A post that was not empty."

"It was empty, sir, even if there was a person standing there."

"Don't be insulting."

"I have never considered truth to be an insult. Mr. Drury was a placeholder, little else. He did not know the job and would have been the ruination of Roseberry Hall." Robert glanced across to

Lydia and was rewarded with a broad grin, though he was not entirely sure why she saw levity in his words.

"That is a gross exaggeration!" Kemble demanded the return of Robert's attention.

"No. Indeed, it is not." He stared the man down, until Kemble dropped his eyes to his plate, grumbling under his breath.

Robert didn't bother to listen.

"Are you going to stay for a few days and celebrate Easter with us, Mr. Newton?" Elaine asked breathlessly, leaning against his arm. "We could go for a walk after church . . . down by the river—just the two of us." She laughed—rather shrilly—for no apparent reason. "And I can have Cook make your favorite dessert for Easter dinner. . . . What is your favorite dessert?"

Robert was forced to turn, yet again, toward Miss Kemble, who was seated directly to his right. "No, I'm afraid not. I must return to my duties at the firm. I have neglected—"

"Aha! A lackluster, are you?" Kemble slammed his hand down on the table again—to the same mild effect.

"A lackluster?" Robert wondered how generously the man had poured his . . . third glass of wine.

"Lazy, ne'er-do-well. You won't amount to much, young man!"

Opening his mouth to rebut such an unwarranted attack, Robert found that he was not the first in line.

"Uncle. That is totally uncalled for. Not only is Mr. Newton a credit to his profession, he is a worthy gentleman about to make his mark in the world. I will *not* have you speak like that to my solicitor's clerk and will thank you to keep your derision to yourself." Lydia glared with undisguised animosity; spots of an angry blush colored her pretty cheeks.

Before the man could continue his ridiculous tirade, Mrs. Whitfield interrupted. "Come now, let us have a civil discourse. Cora, how are the girls' studies coming along? . . . Oh, and I must tell you how much I admire your shawl, my dear. Yes, yes, such a pretty shade of . . . what would I call that . . . let me see. Pink. Yes. Lovely. Did I ever tell you about the pink gown I wore to the Upper Rooms when I was a bride?"

And so it was that Mrs. Whitfield proceeded to manage the entire dinner conversation. A question here, a tale—a long tale—there, all sprinkled with cheerful comments and jovial observations. In no time at all, the caustic beginning of the meal disappeared, and it resolved into an amiable, relaxed repast involving lots of smiles and laughter. Even Elaine's overt attempts to secure Robert's attention faded with the distractions.

Robert found that he could ease back in his chair and simply observe. He had to be careful, of course, doling out his nods to *all* the ladies in the company as he agreed with whatever the topic was in discussion. He was certain that no one could discern his favoritism.

Although he did catch Mrs. Whitfield watching him on occasion, with an enigmatic smile twitching the corners of her mouth.

In the study, Lydia sat curled up in a chair by the fire. Normally, she would have chosen the other end of the room to relax with a

book in her lap, but this position had the advantage of overlooking the front drive. It was a lovely aspect in most respects. Even
in the rain—which had kept her from her constitutional—the
view included three tulip beds and a lovely collection of shrubs. . . .
But it was lacking. The drive was empty; Robert's phaeton was
gone. And it had been gone for a whole day. Yes, almost twenty-
four hours.

It might not have been such a tragedy had Lydia known when
she might see him again, but there were no plans to . . . meet . . .
to visit . . . no, to consult. Yes, that was it. There were no plans
to consult within the foreseeable future—nothing scheduled. It
might be next week, next month, or next year.

Lydia considered—very briefly—the idea of another round of
marriage-contract discussions. At least that would provide a means
to see *him* . . . Robert. Robert Newton, her very good friend
and solicitor apprentice in-waiting. But somehow the thought
of rehashing the various clauses that would tie her to Barley
was unappealing. In fact, she was rather glad she had decided to
postpone the engagement.

She had no doubt that it would take place eventually, just as she
had no doubt that this odd feeling of loss would disappear . . .
sometime . . . one day. She was not a romantic type; she was the
responsible, do-the-right-thing-for-the-estate type. Barley had
been her father's choice, and Papa had been a man of great knowledge and understanding. Hard at times, yes. But for a purpose.
The purpose of securing Roseberry Hall a worthy lineage—a
noble lineage.

Lydia sighed and then frowned as she listened to the echo of the words in her head. *Securing a worthy lineage.* Would Papa have chosen Barley as her husband had he known that Mr. Robert Newton, third son of the Earl of Wissett, would enter their lives?

Robert did not come with a title or vast lands, but his ancient lineage could put Barley's to shame. Would that have been enough to satisfy her father?

And then, out of nowhere, arrived a terrible query. Could she be happy with her father's choice now—now that she knew Robert?

Before Lydia had a chance to form an answer, a movement outside the window caught her eye. For a moment, the briefest of moments, Lydia brightened with the thought that Robert had returned. There was no logic in that thought, and yet it blossomed and grew until the movement resolved into a figure—not a phaeton, a figure with skirts and a Paris-style umbrella.

Blinking back her disappointment, Lydia swallowed and lowered her feet to the floor. It wouldn't do to greet a guest while sitting on her legs. For while the other ladies of the house were ensconced in the drawing room as usual, Lydia knew that this person would be seeking her out.

Mavis Caudle was coming for a visit.

"Make yourself comfortable." Lydia gestured toward the chair placed opposite. She had decided not to move into the morning room, as Miss Caudle was a self-proclaimed book addict. It hardly made sense to rush to another room only to lead the girl back to the library.

Miss Caudle placed the books that she had in hand on the table between them, then sat as directed. "Thank you for the loan. I do hope your butler informed you that I had visited. . . . I think it was, yes, a couple of weeks ago. Amazing how quickly time can pass."

"Of course." The girl's comment was a nod to convention rather than logic—had Lydia not asked Shodster to avail the library to a Miss Caudle whenever she might appear, Mavis would not have made it past the front door. And having allowed her access, Shodster would have been very remiss in his duties to not report Miss Caudle's call. "I apologize for not being here. I believe I was taking my daily constitutional."

"Yes, indeed. I was quite afraid that I had made the same mistake today. My timing is not the best."

Lydia smiled, wondering if while Miss Caudle was interested in her library, she was not interested in forging a friendship. That would be a shame. "Are you chilled from the damp? I can have tea sent in."

"That is kind of you, but I really can't stay. I only stepped out for a moment. Papa is in full Easter passion—intense and focused—and in a bit of a dither. He seems to think today's sermon was lacking and the one planned for Easter not quite adequate, although I think it rather fine. I noticed *Hazlitt's Sermons* when I was here last, and I wondered if he might find inspiration within its pages, if you do not mind my borrowing yet another book?"

"Borrow away." Lydia was somewhat startled when, upon receiving this permission, Miss Caudle immediately stood and headed to a bookcase on the far side of the room. Lydia opened her mouth to continue the conversation, but it would have required raising her voice. Something a lady would never consider. Well, she might consider but never actually do.

Instead, Lydia waited for her visitor to return to her seat and occupied herself by perusing the titles that Miss Caudle had taken away a couple of weeks earlier. While one looked to be an entertaining read, being the anecdotal tale of the author's journey through Tuscany, the other, *Debrett's Peerage and Baronetage*, looked to be as dry as week-old toast.

"A fascinating read," Miss Caudle said, unknowingly contradicting Lydia's thoughts.

She sat once again, though on the edge of her seat, as if already in mind to leave. "I find it so comforting to know one's roots, don't you?"

Lydia frowned at the book in her hands. It was a list—a catalog, as it were—of the British peerage. The Whitfields would not be honored with a page. She laughed, noticed Miss Caudle's dour expression, and turned it into a cough. "Yes, indeed," she said eventually. "Our family would not be in the annals of Debrett's, though we can trace our family history to the sixteenth—"

"We are," Miss Caudle interrupted with a bright smile, seemingly unaware of her *faux pas*. She reached over and plucked the book from Lydia's hands. Flipping it open and with a quick and practiced move, she found what she was looking for. She passed it back to Lydia, stabbing her finger against the page. "See!" There was no disguising her pride.

Lydia nodded as she read. "CAUDLE OF BENSLEY CASTLE. Earl of Bensley: Darren Caudle, born June 9, 1750; Issue Henry, born January 24, 1785; Malcolm, born October 15, 1788." Lydia did her best to stifle a sigh. "Oh, most excellent. So you are of the Bensley Caudles . . . the Earl is your grandfather?"

Miss Caudle smiled indulgently. "No, indeed not. My father is the Earl of Bensley's grandson; second son of a second son. The earl is my great-grandfather. "

"Well, isn't that lovely for you," Lydia said, knowing that she was meant to be impressed.

"Yes, it is very gratifying to see it written in black and white. It helps others understand your position in society, too . . . you know, to be recognized as a member of the upper peerage."

Lydia bit her tongue, so as not to point out that Miss Caudle's side of the family had not carried a title for three generations. . . . But that would have been unkind. It seemed to matter to poor Mavis.

"I was so desirous to show Lord Aldershot. He had been impressed enough to offer the Reverend a living. I wanted him to know that his trust had not been abused."

"Ah," said Lydia thoughtfully, remembering a discussion of the living some time ago. It was shared between the two estates and required a consensus. Lydia had left the decision of that appointment to her mother and Barley. "You wanted to borrow this book so that you could impress Lord Aldershot?"

"Yes, indeed." And then Mavis blinked, swallowed, and smiled in a most unnatural manner. "You do not mind?"

Lydia returned her smile of a kind. "Of course not." She waited for a knot to form in her belly . . . an angry tension to tighten her fists . . . hmm, perhaps a grumpy rejoinder to form in her mind. A vulgar expression to hover on her lips?

Nothing formed or hovered. She was not riled; she was not jealous. This pretty, young lady, likely her own age, was setting her cap at the man who was meant to be her husband, and yet Lydia felt nothing. Except, maybe, a flutter of something that almost felt like hope.

Glancing at the large, darkening portrait over the fireplace, Lydia scowled. What would her father think?

"Fortunate, indeed."

Lydia looked back at Miss Caudle, aware that she had made a comment but not sure of its direction. "Fortunate?"

"Oh, yes. For he . . . Lord Aldershot . . . is a most astute and personable gentleman. It must be gratifying to know that your futures are tied together. That security alone . . ." Her words petered off as she stared at Lydia's frown, misinterpreting. "It is general knowledge, is it not? Lord Aldershot spoke of your upcoming announcement quite freely."

"Did he?"

"Yes, he had planned an outing with our family a week or so ago. I believe we were going to visit a local mill, but he was forced to cancel and rush off to Bath. At your behest, I thought, to sign the contracts."

Miss Caudle was certainly well informed. "Nothing is yet settled."

"Oh, oh dear. I believe I have said more than I ought."

"No, indeed. You simply wish to understand the dynamics of the great houses on which the Reverend relies for his living. I would wish the same in your position." And then Lydia had an idea, a perfectly splendid idea. "There is no obligation on either side as yet—an expectation, it is true, but no more than that. Time will tell."

Miss Caudle flushed, looked down at the carpet for a moment, and then lifted her eyes to meet Lydia's once again. There was a cast of determination in her stare.

Lydia smiled—perhaps more broadly than was polite, but she was pleased—almost to the point of elation. Her father could hardly rise from the grave if Barley chose a different bride. And if dear Papa did object, he would have to go where the fault lay; he would have to haunt Wilder Hill.

Yes, a splendid idea.

Though she might need to offer the couple a generous bride gift to nudge Barley in the right direction.

The note, when it came, was deceptively demure: a white folded piece of paper, sealed with red wax without a crest or identification marker. It lay benignly on Shodster's silver tray—presented to her with the rest of the post while Lydia sat at her desk in the morning room.

In fact, when Lydia first saw it, she put it aside. She pulled out the bills to be directed to Mrs. Buttle, the letter from Great-Aunt Charlotte for her mother, and the *Lady's Magazine* for Elaine. It wasn't that Lydia was not paying attention, nor was she being cavalier—for she had been expecting some sort of consequence for her *curious adventure*. Though, as each day had passed, she had thought it less likely.

If anything, she was distracted.

She had just completed the remainder of the invitations—the ones allocated to her mother. They had to go out right away if she was going to know the number of those attending her ball. Shelley was doing her best to help with the arrangements, but until the responses came in, they were at a standstill. At least the question of where they were staying in Bath had been settled; Shelley had hired a town house on their behalf.

Piling the outgoing invitations on Shodster's tray, Lydia watched him depart before turning to the innocent-looking piece of paper. With a sigh of relief, she broke the seal and began to read, stifling a yelp as she did so. It was just as well that she had the morning room to herself.

Looking down at the neat, florid script, Lydia read the note a second time. It didn't seem real; it couldn't be real!

Miss Whitfield.

>*You are not half as clever as you think you are!*
>*It is known that you spent an entire night away from*

good company! No chaperone, no parent, no guardian to protect your reputation.

A whisper in the right ears will see you labeled a harlot; the doors of polite society will be slammed in your face. Ruination and censure will be your companion for the rest of your days.

Unless an investment of four hundred pounds is left behind the Havisham grave marker at St. Mary's in Bankend. Then, and only then, will the whispers be silenced.

The future is up to you.

You have three days.

Lydia laughed; it was a weak sort of gurgle that didn't sound like amusement even to her ears. She didn't know which part of this threat upset her the most. The idea that someone would stoop so low; the thought of trying to secure such a large sum in three days; or that this rotter thought her weak enough to succumb to villainous blackmail.

Marching across the room, Lydia stood before the fire, her arm partially extended. And there it stayed while she examined the whole.

Was this then the true purpose of her abduction? A source of income—for Lydia was fairly certain that once paid, other notes of its ilk would arrive on a regular basis. That could account for the ease of her escape and the lack of a ransom demand.

Or was the note a byproduct of her *curious adventure*? Few knew of the episode, but it took only one immoral character to see an opportunity in her calamitous day. Could the author be found before the havoc of rumors was wreaked upon them? She did have the services of a Bow Street Runner near at hand. And she did not doubt that the blackmail would end only with the writer's apprehension.

Lydia stepped back from the fire, lowering the paper away from the heat.

Best preserve the letter for Mr. Warner to see in person. She would send Jeremy to Spelding on an errand of some sort and include a request, a return visit from the Principal Officer of Bow Street.

With a smile born of satisfaction, Lydia reached for the bell-pull.

This person, this villain, would rue the day he or she tried to take on Lydia Mary Whitfield. She ignored the niggling thought that it could also be the ruination of her life . . . and all those around her.

"*An* empty threat." Cora selected two playing cards. "Fret not. Fifteen two, fifteen four . . . and a pair for six. I think that is all I have." She moved her pegs in the cribbage board and then glanced up at Lydia.

"I am trying not to be affected, but . . ." She allowed the sentence to trail off. Trying not to fret was proving to be difficult.

Enough time had passed for Lydia's temper to lessen, and as it dissolved, disquiet filled the void.

A ruined reputation would affect the entire household. Society would look askance at *all* the ladies of Roseberry should news of Lydia's disappearance be made known. Worthy marriage prospects for Elaine, Ivy, and Tessa would vanish on the strength of Lydia's immoral influence.

She sighed, far deeper than she meant to, and offered Cora a weak smile to compensate. "Mr. Warner said much the same thing, although he used a lot more words."

Cora laughed and then looked around uncomfortably.

Lydia, too, glanced at the other occupants of the drawing room and was pleased that none had been disturbed. Mama dozed in her favorite chair, and Elaine and Aunt Freya were in deep conversation over a magazine article that declared ruffles passé. The girls had long since gone to bed, and Uncle . . . well, Lydia did not know where he had taken himself off to, but then, neither did she care.

"He said the rumors could be quashed. The incident passed unnoticed to begin with, and to dredge it up after a fortnight seems rather desperate." Lydia shook her head, unintentionally causing the candles to flicker in the wafting air. "He intimated that ladies were so talented at prevarication that we would have no problem staring anyone down. I don't think there is a gender requirement for hedging, do you?"

"Most definitely not—oh, the kitty is yours, I believe." Cora pushed the four cards in Lydia's direction. "Still, if stonewalling is to be our tactic, there are many routes to take. We could react in great surprise, or incredulity. Oh, no, the truth. Yes, that should be our avenue. 'You cannot be serious; I was with Miss Whitfield in Bath. What did she do, leave me screaming on the side of the road?'" Cora grinned. "Oh, yes, I could have great fun with that."

Lydia blinked at her friend's words, surprised by her teasing tone. She was fairly certain Cora's levity was meant to set the tone between them—establish that they were placed well enough in society that they could ignore such plebeian discourses. Lydia hoped it was true.

Glancing down at her cards, Lydia showed Cora her pair and then passed them back to be shuffled. "There is one person who might be abjectly affected by the rumors."

"Lord Aldershot."

"Yes. True or not, he will be upset that my name should be bandied about. Poor man."

"Perhaps you should tell him."

"I might have to, but for now I will wait to see how this plays out." Lydia glanced up to see that Cora was watching her with a troubled expression—though that might have been a trick of the low light.

"Are you sure that is the way you want to play it?"

Lydia frowned down at her cards and then, realizing that her friend was not referring to the game, looked back to Cora. "You don't agree?"

"Well, it is not for me to say," she said, "but I think that a husband should be someone with whom you can share all your worries and concerns. Someone whom you can support but who can also support you."

"Ah, but you are talking about a romantic marriage. One that involves heady emotions and a great deal of leaning." Lydia was surprised by the passing thought that the words, which she had spouted on more than one occasion, sounded . . . well, more appealing than they had before.

"It's mutual leaning, Lydia. Sharing and caring and . . . euphoria."

"Yes, so you say, but is that reality or a temporary state that fades over time?"

"I would certainly hope the former, but my experience is not vast. All I can truly speak about is the joy of affection . . . and the pain of separation."

"Oh, Cora. I am a selfish creature. I have not asked how you are doing. I'm sure we will hear from Shelley soon about Mr. Granger."

Cora nodded. "Yes, it shouldn't be long now." She smiled wistfully.

Lydia picked up her cards, placing two facedown in the middle of the table. Her thoughts returned to Barley and their last discussion—a discussion about his new curricle, a need for horses, and that *blasted* marriage contract. She had yet to inform Barley about her . . . their new timetable. He might not be as pleased as he would have been a few weeks ago—before he had started spending her money.

What to do? A quandary without a doubt. And one that deserved careful consideration.

Unfortunately, that night, when she put her mind to the whole, Lydia made a most disconcerting discovery. Her reluctance to speak to Barley was born from the fact that she did not want to postpone their engagement; she wanted to cancel it entirely. Mavis Caudle came to mind as a peace offering between them, but would Barley wish to marry a young lady with an excellent lineage but no dowry? And what should come first, the break or the encouragement?

Lydia spent most of the night tossing and turning, wondering what the family, and more important, what her father, would think of such a turn of events. Was she right to change her plans for the future based on a few heady emotions when looking into a handsome young man's eyes? Was it the discovery that a romantic inclination could find a home in her person, after all, or was her reluctance to marry Barley a result of her feelings for Robert, and for him alone? Was she being charmed by romance, or Robert?

Equally important: How did Robert feel about her?

If she broke with Barley and Robert's affections didn't amount to more than friendship, would she regret tossing her father's wishes aside? There would be no going back. It might lead to strained relations between the estates . . . for the rest of their days.

There seemed to be no answers—only an ocean of questions.

Exhausted, after hours of sleeplessness and no conclusions,

Lydia turned her thoughts away from Barley and the prospect of their engagement. She chose one subject that she knew would bring contentment—one that, when examined on its own, brought a smile to her lips and serenity to her heart.

That subject was the charming Mr. Robert Newton, his laughter, his wit, his broad shoulders, and his fascinating eyes . . . and with that she fell asleep.

Chapter 16

*In which a nonexistent dustup sends Mr. Newton
rushing back to Roseberry*

*W*ithout any evidence of charm, Mr. Robert Newton jumped to his feet. "What?" he shouted, acute surprise adding to the volume of his word. He shook the letter in front of him as if in doing so he were shaking the author . . . or rather the subject of which the author spoke.

"Yes, hmm. What?" Mr. Lynch's voice drifted in from the other room. The door between their offices stood open to the firm's entry.

Robert leaned across the threshold, nodded to the startled gentleman who sat at Robert's *former* desk, and called back to his mentor. "Nothing to worry about, Mr. Lynch." Then, looking down at the paper still in his hands, he added, "Though I must return to Roseberry Hall for a few days; there has been another dustup." Though not a true definition of the circumstances outlined in the letter, Robert was not about to offer a clearer explanation.

"Very good," the old man called back cheerfully.

Robert was fairly certain Mr. Lynch had not heard him properly.

Turning back to his desk, Robert nodded with satisfaction. Yes, he could, indeed, leave the firm without fear of its falling apart. Over the past ten days, Robert had worked hard to clear his desk of all pending files, preparing to begin his apprenticeship. He had taken over the spare office and hired a new clerk. Rather than grab a young man intent on a career in the law, Robert had secured the services of a retired lieutenant who had helped keep a general in order.

The end of the Napoleonic Wars had seen many a good man sell out of the army. Robert had taken full advantage of that glut, interviewing upward of twenty former soldiers. Mr. Cargoff was proving to be a most excellent choice.

Picking up the few allotted files that required signatures, Robert dropped them in front of Mr. Cargoff. He reviewed them quickly with the gentleman, asking that he make a few inquiries, as well as obtain the necessary signatures. He left the firm confident that all was in hand—much more confident than he had been on his departure before Cassidy's duel.

It was too late in the day to start off immediately, though a quick stop at Templeton Stables assured him a horse first thing in the morning. Robert rushed home to pack. This time he included a dress coat in his satchel. He would see to this nonsense and

remain at Roseberry until he was convinced of Lydia's safety. . . .
And he would be dressed appropriately for dinner while doing so.

The morning dawned gray and damp. As the journey continued, it became grayer and damper until, at the time of his arrival at Roseberry Hall, Robert was caught in a torrential downpour. After Hugh had taken away Robert's satchel and sodden greatcoat, Shodster led him to the morning room, where the family was still at breakfast.

While Robert appreciated the gesture, this acknowledgment of his intimacy with the family, he was acutely aware of his bedraggled state—and that he could not explain the true purpose of his arrival in front of everyone. A quick glance told him that Lydia was safe and sound—though grinning somewhat broadly—so he proceeded to ignore her.

"Mr. Newton, what a pleasure. I hope you are well?" Mrs. Whitfield gestured for a chair to be added to the table as she spoke.

A niche was found for him next to Miss Elaine, who seemed to be suffering her usual eye affliction—batting and blinking—while leaning in closer and closer until Robert feared she might tumble from her chair. Robert did his best to keep his gaze away from Lydia—he would *not* be distracted by her loveliness; he would *not* be distracted by her bright smile; he would *not* be distracted away from his anger and frustration. No, she would feel the full force of his temper as soon as they were alone . . . as long as he didn't look at her.

"So nice to see you again." Mrs. Kemble waved at her daughter. "Get Mr. Newton something to eat, Elaine. He must be fairly starving after his journey."

"Oh, you poor thing." Miss Kemble touched his arm. "You must have suffered dreadfully. I will be your savior." She jumped up and began piling a plate with eggs, ham, kippers, and toast from the sideboard.

"To what do we owe this *great* honor?" The query was made with noticeable derision.

Robert was prepared for both the condescension—from Mr. Kemble—and the question, but he waited for Elaine to pass him the plate before answering. He nodded a thank-you and lifted his fork. "There are a few clauses that need to be reviewed in the contract our firm is drawing up on Miss Whitfield's behalf." He instilled an official ring to his words; there would be a general assumption that he was speaking about the private business of the marriage contract. Theoretically, Lydia's uncle should have been present for these discussions. . . . Or at the very least her mother, but neither showed any interest.

Directing the conversation away from the hazardous subject, Robert inquired about Mr. Selleck and the estate. Mrs. Whitfield was most accommodating in her replies, finding these topics led her into recollections of previous crops, alfresco summer meals by the lake, a pretty new rose planted by the head gardener, and

Mrs. Foster's journey to Paris. There wasn't a clear path to the last subject, but Robert did his best to look attentive and refrained from asking who Mrs. Foster might be. Elaine giggled throughout her aunt's soliloquy, hovering at his elbow to replenish his tea—before it was done—and offering him any number of foodstuffs that he did not want.

Through it all, Robert maintained a mildly interested expression, hid his tension with an occasional smile and light repartee, and avoided looking directly at Lydia. Though he did watch her from the corner of his eye.

The short meal was interminable—a good three-quarters of an hour. But when, at last, the ladies pushed away from the table, Robert rose with them. As the remnants of their meal had to be cleared, Lydia suggested that they adjourn to the study.

Robert met her gaze, nodded, and then looked away as quickly as was politic.

He meant to offer the first volley as soon as they crossed the threshold into the study, but Lydia won that battle.

She pivoted before they had taken two steps and leaned toward him. "All right, out with it." Her voice didn't have its usual dulcet quality. "Why are you here in truth, and why are you so out of temper with me?"

"As both are rooted in the same muck, perhaps you can guess." He tried not to notice that her person—leaning in such a delicious manner—was in very close proximity.

"No, indeed, I cannot."

"Might it have to do with your appointment with Mr. Warner this morning?"

Lydia shook her head and, unfortunately, leaned back on her heels. "Does it? Do you know something that I don't? Mr. Warner sent a note requesting an appointment, but as to the subject of our meeting, I assumed it had to do with my abduction. . . . Doesn't it?"

"I believe he will be discussing his findings, yes. He informed me of the meeting . . . thought that I would be interested as well. Which I am! But he also made mention of *another* subject. One of which I had not heard before. He used the word *blackmail*."

Then, to Robert's great surprise, Lydia laughed. "Oh, so that is what has put you into a huff."

"This is not a huff—it is frustration, if one has to give it a name—or concern, or alarm. No matter what you call it, I was very troubled to learn that you had suffered another affront and deigned not to inform me. I am your friend as well as your solicitor's apprentice, and yet you didn't trust me—"

"Robert, Robert."

"—you did not have the de—"

"Robert. Trust was not the issue."

"Then what was? For I cannot fathom any reason not to include me in this latest . . . this . . . See what you have done? I cannot find my words!"

Stepping closer, Lydia laid her hands across his forearms, tilting her chin up. Robert swallowed with great difficulty as she stared into his eyes. He knew she was saying something, but he couldn't hear her above the noise of his hammering heart and the buzz in his ears. Then, she stopped talking and leaned infinitesimally closer still.

Robert could now feel her warm breath caressing his face. He could smell sweet lavender soap and feel the heat of her body as it pressed against his.

"Right?"

Robert blinked and lifted his cheeks. "Pardon," he croaked, trying not to watch her lips.

"How could I have done otherwise?" she asked. "We all hoped that the threat was toothless and decided to regard it as such. Not needing to fret meant there was also no need to drag you away from the city, either . . . as much as I would have loved the excuse—" She stopped, frowned, and then continued. "Had you known of the letter, you would have jumped on a horse and madly rushed to Roseberry, arriving soaking wet and in a lather, only to find that all was well—just as you did. Do I not know you, my friend? Was I not right?"

Swallowing—or rather trying to swallow—Robert stared and remained silent. It seemed his safest route. He was all too aware that his anger was driven by fear, not frustration. Until he saw her, in the flesh, safe and sound, his mind had conjured up any number of disasters. He wanted nothing more than to claim her as his own, so that he could keep her protected and thriving and . . . if that miserable sot who was going to marry her did not honor her as he should . . .

Robert shook his head, realizing that his thoughts were all over the place and that Lydia was talking again and yet all he wanted to do was kiss her. Kiss her and pull her into his arms. Yes, they could stay that way. Just toss food, no need for more, no need to go anywhere. Just there. Stay. Yes. Indeed. He would kiss her.

"Robert?" she whispered, and, if he could not be mistaken, she lifted her mouth toward his. Inviting. Waiting.

It was both fortunate and unfortunate that at that precise moment there was a knock at the door. They sprang apart so quickly that when Lydia acknowledged the disruption, they were once again standing at a respectable distance. Robert could see she was breathing heavily, as was he. And her complexion was rather high, in a most becoming manner. But other than that, there was no indication of the intense emotions of mere seconds ago.

Still . . . as Mr. Warner entered, he looked back and forth between them. And his frown dissolved into a grin.

Sitting on the edge of the settee, Lydia found it hard to concentrate on the discussion despite the seriousness of the topic. Her eyes kept wandering over to Robert, who was seated across from her—but not with rapt attention to his words. No, she found that her focus vacillated between his shoulders, his eyes, and, dare she say it, his lips. She was fairly certain that Robert had been about to kiss her just before Mr. Warner arrived—to spoil the moment.

Why would he do it?

Robert, not Mr. Warner.

Why would a gentleman want to kiss a lady unless there was an attachment? The implication was enormous, life-changing. . . . Or was it? Might a gentleman wish to kiss a lady without any sense of obligation? She had heard of these types of arrangements. Granted, only in breathy whispers while meandering the corridors of Miss Melvina's finishing school, but to know, nonetheless, that they existed filled Lydia with insecurity and doubts. Emotions that would usually be ascribed to Elaine, and yet . . . she was using them in reference to—

"Not Chilton," Mr. Warner said with such finality that it pulled Lydia out of her reverie. He had rebuffed her offer of a chair and was standing before them.

"Not Chilton?" Lydia repeated.

"Indeed," Mr. Warner agreed as though unaware that Lydia had only just joined the conversation. "His discomfort that you observed in Spelding had nothing to do with your abduction. He was not shocked to see you because he thought you to be secured in a barn on the other side of Bath. No, his discomfort was derived from your witnessing his association with a Mrs. Flanders."

"Who?"

"It would seem that, in interest of self-preservation and in desperate need of funds, Mr. Ian Chilton has not put all his eggs in one basket. He is courting a wealthy widow as well, by the name of Mrs. Flanders—the lady in the flowery bonnet. The sense of guilt at being *caught* brought Chilton to stammer, blush, and rush away."

"Oh," Robert and Lydia said at the same time. They shared a glance and a chuckle, and then they looked back at Mr. Warner to see him wearing an odd expression.

"Yes. Well. Shall I continue?"

Robert nodded, and Lydia found herself doing the same—it almost brought the fit of giggles back.

"Your hired driver, Mr. Burgstaller, has been found. He suffered a broken ankle when he was tossed from the coach and is still being nursed by the family that found him on the side of the road. This I learned from his brother, who lamented the terrible loss of the vehicle—it was the man's livelihood, after all."

"Oh dear, I shall have to send him some funds to compensate."

"Admirable, Miss Whitfield, but not necessary. The man's coach was insured, and the brother thought I was there to assess the loss. There was a fair amount of exaggeration in his account."

Glancing back at the notebook he held in his hand, Warner nodded to some inner thought and then flipped a page. "Ah, yes. Mr. Kemble and Mr. Drury. There was an agreement between the men that they would share the profits of a successful yield rather than put the money back into the estate as is expected." He nodded at Robert. "Drury is an out-and-out thief, whereas your uncle, I believe, is merely in want of funds. His tenants vacated his own estate last autumn because of a leaky roof, and he has done nothing to resolve that situation—thereby making it worse still. I can find no connection between him and the abduction."

With a nod, the man snapped his book shut and turned to face Lydia. "As I told you before starting my investigations, success is not always assured. I am pleased that I can offer you the answers to some of your queries, as I have just outlined. But I find I cannot answer the most important question: Who was behind your kidnapping? Once known, we would understand why.

"However, I could find no helpful witnesses near the farm where you were held. No clues were left behind and no trails to follow. In short, there is nothing more I can do. And as such, I will be returning to Bath on the next coach. I want to make sure Lord Rennoll is suitably situated."

"Oh," Lydia said with great wit. She frowned. "Well, do you have any theories, any possible suspects?"

"No. I don't point a finger unless I have proof. That would be irresponsible."

While Lydia agreed in principle, the whole exercise left her quite dissatisfied. She had, despite his warnings, expected the Runner to solve the mystery. "And the attempt at blackmail?"

"What exactly was in the letter?" Robert asked in a strained voice.

Mr. Warner explained succinctly, concluding with a shrug. "I could continue to watch the graveyard, but it is closing on a week since you were meant to leave the money . . . and there has been nary a whisper of scandal. It is possible that the blackmail was not a true threat but a device meant to cause fear and upset."

"The author cannot know Lydia—umm, Miss Whitfield—very well then, can he?"

The Runner nodded. "Indeed."

But Lydia was not convinced. "No one. No one visited the graveyard."

"St. Mary's in Bankend is more of a chapel than a church. The Reverend only comes once a month. Sends the congregation down the road to Spelding most Sundays. The groundskeeper said the place could go for weeks without a visitor. Quiet. Quiet as a grave."

Lydia blinked, surprised by the Runner's attempt at levity.

"His words not mine," Mr. Warner clarified.

Lydia nodded and then frowned. "Not a true threat?" she repeated the Runner's earlier comment. "That does not make sense. What if I had awoken one morning in a state of idiocy and quietly placed the money in the graveyard? Would it still be sitting there now?"

"I can't say. Perhaps the church was being watched. It's at the end of a lonely road. Your blackmailer might have been waiting in the shrubbery."

Lydia was reminded of the odd shadows on the grounds of Roseberry and shuddered. "But you don't think so."

"We don't really know enough to decide one way or the other, Miss Whitfield."

"But there has been no repercussion for my disobedience. Not a whisper against me."

"There might have been no attempt to carry out the threat,

or it could be that your standing in Spelding is beyond reproach—the rumor was started but given no credence."

"So we don't know the *who* behind this blackmail or if the person is in cahoots with the kidnapper. . . . Or if they are one and the same."

"Exactly."

"Clear as mud," Robert added.

"Exactly."

Lydia did her best not to chunter until Robert left the room to see Mr. Warner off. When he returned, she was still staring out the window, her jaw tight and her thoughts dark and angry.

"I'm rather put out, Robert."

"Yes, I can see that."

"There is a possibility that I will never know the who or why of this whole mess. That very idea makes me angry!"

"Yes, I can see that, too."

"I don't want to look over my shoulder for the rest of my days . . . or question the purpose of those around me. There has to be an answer."

"Yes, there is, and we will find it, I am almost certain. But it would seem that we must wait for the time being . . . though not likely to the end of your days."

Lydia glanced up, about to admonish him for his inappropriate teasing, but the words never left her mouth. Instead, she stared, eyes widening as she watched him cross the room, each step bringing him closer and closer. Her breath caught, and all thoughts of villains and blackmail disappeared into a fog of tingling sensations.

And then—

There was another knock on the door.

Shodster had brought the post, and in it a letter from Shelley.

"*I* will stay until your departure and then accompany you to Bath." It was a statement, not a question. Robert stood beside the mantel, an unreadable expression on his face.

"No, this is too fast. You cannot do it. I cannot do it." Mama shook her head with so much enthusiasm that Lydia thought her mother might do herself an injury.

"Please, Mama. You know I rarely ask for your help. I am desperate."

After scrubbing at the folds above her nose, her mother took a deep breath. She looked sightless at the far side of the library and then back to Lydia. "Rare, my dear? You *never* ask for my help. That alone tells me how important this is to you."

"I asked for your advice just last week. . . . Or was it the week before? Mr. Selleck—remember?"

"Indeed, I do. But my role was to support your decision—"

"And you did an excellent job, I must say."

"Yes. Thank you. I did, didn't I? However, what you are asking now is more along the lines of moving heaven and earth."

It was Lydia's turn to scrub at her face and sigh . . . a little too soon, because an idea had come to mind as she did so. Lifting her head, she glanced at Robert and then returned her gaze to her mother. "We don't need to move the entire household . . . no. It would be better if we didn't . . . yes. There is no room for the necessities of seven ladies—and one gentleman—in a single travel coach and a family landau. Indeed, it makes perfect sense to accomplish the resettlement in two lots. You and I and Cora in the first group . . . the others to follow whenever they can gather their bits and pieces."

"But Cora will be needed to see to the girls."

"The whole point of leaving three weeks early is to distract Cora, Mama. We have to think of a plausible reason for her to join us while leaving Ivy and Tessa with Aunt Freya."

"Yes, yes, of course . . . but four days, Lydia? We must leave in four days? Can you not tell me why?"

Lydia glanced toward Robert, observing his changed expression—unreadable was now stony.

Poor Robert. He must have been acquainted with the inconsistent emotions of young ladies; he did have two sisters, after all. Still, the change had been so abrupt that it had left him speechless. One moment they were drawing ever closer in a charged and heady atmosphere, the next Lydia was in his arms—crying. It wasn't something either had expected.

Robert had held her as she explained and allowed a few tears to dribble off her chin. He made all the appropriate *tut-tut* and *tsk* noises and then sent Shodster in search of her mother. It had been his idea to transplant the Whitfields and Kembles to Bath immediately—the town house had already been secured and an early arrival would take only a little renegotiation.

"Experience has taught me that this kind of pain cannot be lessened by anything but time. So it is best to help time pass quickly," he said. "Distraction. What could be more diverting than a change from a quiet country life to the bustling streets and entertainments of the city?"

Lydia thought it sound advice—and tried, very hard, not to find joy in the thought that they would also be closer together. . . . They would be able to see each other more often. No, she would not think those thoughts. They were disloyal to her friend. No, she would put them away and concentrate on Cora. Poor Cora.

"I have to give Cora some disturbing news, Mama. She has been waiting to hear . . ."

"About a gentleman?"

"Yes, I'm afraid so."

"Oh dear, oh dear. Is she about to be heartbroken?"

"Yes, I'm afraid so."

"Oh, no. Nothing worse. Dear. Dear. The poor, poor girl. Hmm. Yes. No, we can't have that. I . . . yes, let me see. Yes, there has been some confusion in regard to your birthday ball. . . . We have to complete the arrangements; it is only three weeks away, you know. . . . And you need Cora to help you decide on a gown—yes, my advice is old-fashioned and our taste is at odds. Yes, well, who would not believe that one? And . . . let me see. Yes, we do not want to inconvenience everyone. There, that should be enough; those will be our excuses. The girls will quite enjoy a week or two away from their lessons. And now, I must go. Hurry, hurry. I have to be ready to leave in four days. Goodness."

With that, Mama rushed to the door but turned back before she opened it. "How would you like me to act, Lydia? Play ignorant or offer sympathy?"

"Sympathy can sometimes make it harder to be strong."

"Yes, all too true." Mama turned and left the room, nodding as she disappeared.

Lydia glanced at Robert. He, too, was nodding but not for the same reason.

"There is a romantic tendency in your family, after all. Your mother is quite understanding."

Lydia smiled weakly, despite the sadness that was weighing her down. "Yes, indeed." She refrained from mentioning that she was not at all devoid of romantic thoughts and emotions as she had once supposed. . . . Best to let that one alone for now.

Instead, Lydia squeezed his forearm and left the library in search of Cora. She had a duty to perform, a terrible duty. She had to tell her friend that the love of her life was not going to be calling at Roseberry Hall. Gloria had spoken true. Mr. Lorne Granger was engaged to be married; the wedding would take place at Michaelmas.

Chapter 17

In which Bath provides more than its share of distractions

Robert had caught a whiff of subterfuge in Lydia's account of Miss Shipley and Mr. Granger—not as described by Lydia but in the underlying tale. Something was not all on the up and up, and he had every intention of learning the truth behind this tragic story of unrequited love. And so it was that Robert could be found standing in front of Cassidy's Circus town house, having arrived the day before in Bath with Lydia, Miss Shipley, and Mrs. Whitfield.

Cassidy had had fair warning—Robert had sent a note announcing his intention to visit from Roseberry four days earlier. As it was a working day, Robert had already stopped by the firm to question Mr. Lynch about various procedures and to speak to Mr. Cargoff. It was nearing eleven. All this meant that Cassidy should be up and waiting for him as soon as Robert presented himself at the front door . . . and made it past Cranford.

"Mr. Vincent Cassidy is not at home," Cranford intoned, as if greatly burdened by such news. The butler saw no need to accommodate Cassidy or his fellows.

Robert nodded, ignoring the customary fiction. "Excellent. I will wait in the drawing room." He didn't bother to secure an agreement but set his feet on the path to the stairs and the aforementioned room—where his friend was, indeed, at home.

"You do know that Cranford is getting more and more difficult, don't you?" Robert shook his head as he crossed over to where Cassidy was seated by the fire.

"Told you to shove off?"

"No. Just that you were not here."

Cassidy laughed. "The man must like you. Sees most of my friends as ne'er-do-wells and slams the door in their faces."

"After telling them to shove off?"

"Exactly." Pointing to the seat opposite, Cassidy yawned. "So why, pray tell, did I have to rise so early?"

"It's almost eleven."

"Yes, but in order to be ready, I had to be up by the ungodly hour of nine."

"Unforgivable."

"I think so."

"Well, I have a favor to ask of you."

"You got me up early to ask a favor. I know I owe you—but,

really, I would have been in a much more receptive mood had you waited until . . . say seven this evening."

"Perhaps, but this favor involves intrigue, betrayal, feminine wiles, and a healthy dose of acting the man-about-town."

"I am a man-about-town; acting would not be required there."

"Good to know. . . . And so, the favor."

"You have my interest. Tell me more."

Robert smiled and shifted forward on his seat.

Cassidy did the same.

"Let me give you a little background first."

Cassidy smiled. "As you wish."

Sitting in the ground-floor parlor of their rented town house, Lydia stared out the front window onto the bustling thoroughfare of Great Pulteney Street. The midafternoon hour meant that most of the drays and wagons, laden with goods bound for the Bath markets, had long since given way to the stylish carriages and coaches of the newly arrived gentry and the sedan chairs of those well versed in Bath's narrow streets and steep hills.

The Whitfields were not the only family to vacate the rural environs in spring and make their way into the lovely spa town to enjoy the city's entertainments. The general atmosphere was one of exuberance and conviviality as friends and acquaintances reestablished their ties after the deadly quiet of winter.

Smiling as she watched the social niceties being enacted on

the other side of the glass, Lydia hoped that the pleasant ambience would work its magic on Cora. Three days prior, they had settled into their town house, a place of generous living spaces inside, though no garden to speak of. It was indistinguishable from the other tawny-colored buildings in the row, and yet there was comfort in that conformity. Fitting in without having to make any effort.

Planning to partake in the many upcoming events, Mama had already signed in with the Master of Ceremonies of both the Upper and Lower Rooms. Lydia was quite ready to venture out. In fact, she was greatly looking forward to the first planned excursion.

With a glance to the clock on the mantel, Lydia snorted a laugh. There was no one to hear such an unladylike sound, as Lydia was . . . well, early. Bonnet firmly affixed, coat buttoned, and gloves smoothed back from the tips of her fingers, she sat on the edge of her seat waiting. She could be waiting a good quarter hour, for the note had stated three o'clock and Robert could be relied on for his punctuality. He could be relied on for many, many things. Punctuality was merely one of them.

Turning her eyes back to the window, Lydia frowned, wondering if there was some sort of underlying purpose to his invitation. Robert had stated that he would enjoy escorting her and Cora around Harrison's Walk—a popular promenade on the other side of the River Avon. It was the underscoring of Cora's name that led Lydia to believe that Robert had an ulterior motive. It might be something as simple as following through on his advice to keep Cora busy . . . but she thought not.

"Sorry, I'm late."

Lydia jumped at the sound of Cora's voice and then greeted her friend with a smile.

"Mr. Newton will not be here for a few minutes. Sit, sit." She waved toward a settee placed catercorner from the window while assessing Cora's expression—grim—and her choice of ensemble—grimmer. Gray with an accent of black: neither did Cora's complexion any favors. But it was not the outward expression of Cora's grief that bothered Lydia the most; it was the lifeless look to Cora's eyes and the passive line of her mouth. It hurt to see her friend in so much pain.

Lydia was about to blame the wonders of romance and eschew all such emotions . . . when she realized that she could no longer walk that path. What were her feelings toward Robert if not romantic? It was becoming more and more difficult to reconcile herself to the possibility of a life without that strange thing called love.

She turned back to the window.

Before Lydia could delve much further into the confusing workings of the human psyche, a figure appeared, strolling from the direction of the Pulteney Bridge. Lydia smiled and stared . . . and then frowned.

It would seem that Robert was not alone. Another gentleman walked at his side. While coloring and hairstyle were similar, the newcomer was taller and thinner, without the broad shoulders that Lydia so admired.

"Ah, there is Mr. Newton," Cora said with a long-suffering sigh.

"Yes." Lydia rose, even though Hugh had yet to open the front door. She was feeling rather twitchy—excited to see Robert, but afraid . . . very afraid . . . that he had overstepped. She sincerely hoped, prayed, begged the Fates that he had not brought this gentleman to meet Cora. It was too soon. Much too soon.

The murmur of voices in the grand entrance brought Lydia to a standstill. She took a deep breath, plastered a benign smile on her face, and prepared to be introduced.

It was quickly and smoothly done. Little fanfare and, fortunately, the stranger did not single Cora out for special attention. If he did bow a little lower than necessary and stare with deep consideration, it was in regard to Lydia, not Cora.

Lydia did her best not to show any undue interest in Mr. Cassidy, but it was difficult when she knew his circumstances. The way his gaze kept alternating between Robert and her made Lydia think that Cassidy might be aware of hers as well. The idea did not make her uncomfortable, quite the opposite. It was as if a sentinel had been added to their company.

"Harrison's Walk has become the place to be seen in Bath," Mr. Cassidy explained. "Newton wouldn't know that, of course. He has had his head buried in his job for years." He looked over his shoulder toward Lydia as they strolled across the shop-lined bridge. Mr. Cassidy had taken Cora's arm and the lead.

Lydia and Robert followed a few paces behind, allowing an easy discourse between the two couples . . . not that either of the two groups were a couple.

"It is called devotion, Mr. Cassidy. The law requires such devotion." Lydia squeezed Robert's arm as a sign of solidarity.

"Yes." Mr. Cassidy glanced at Robert yet again, grinned, and then faced forward.

Once past the last storefront of Pulteney Bridge, they turned to the left and headed down the hill toward the Bath Abbey church. The golden-colored Gothic tower rose above the green foliage of the park that ran alongside the river.

As they approached, it was soon apparent that Harrison's Walk was, indeed, well peopled. A place to be seen or not, the cloudless sky and warm spring breeze were likely what had brought out the numbers more than those wanting to impress and be impressed. Still, there was no lacking in finery, and Lydia was glad to have worn her new cerulean spencer and matching gloves.

With top hats bobbing and parasols waving, Mr. Cassidy led their small party down to the water's edge. Casual greetings from across the path, a shared guffaw or two, and Lydia found that she was quite in charity with Bath. She had always thought it to be a charming city, but she now had reason to feel comfortable with its populace. She might not have been accepted as readily, if at all, had the rumors of her *curious adventure* been bandied about.

But that danger had passed, and she had no need to be concerned about her reception.

As she glanced about, Lydia became aware that she was under some scrutiny. Lifting her eyes to Robert's, she raised her brows questioningly. "Is something amiss, Mr. Newton?" They were too close to others for her to be comfortable using his given name.

"Not at all, Miss Whitfield. I was just observing how flattering that color is on—"

"What-ho," Mr. Cassidy interrupted, waving to a trio gathered next to a weeping willow. "Look, Newton. I told you as much. Come meet my new friends." And then before Robert could even nod, the young man rushed across the grass.

Cora gasped.

Lydia dropped Robert's arm and rushed to her friend's side. "Cora. Cora dear, are you all right?"

"No, I'm feeling quite faint. I believe I want to go back to . . . back to Great Pulteney Street." She was staring at the willow tree.

Puzzled by Cora's heightened color, Lydia turned toward the group that Mr. Cassidy had joined. She knew them not. "I don't understand?"

"Please, Miss Shipley." Robert had joined her by Cora's side. "Trust me on this. Don't go."

Blinking back tears, Cora turned to stare at Robert. "You knew?"

"Yes. Forgive my subterfuge. My purpose will come to light soon enough."

"I can't do this."

"You don't have to do anything, Miss Shipley, nothing at all. There. Look, they are coming to us; you do not even have to move."

Lydia glanced over her shoulder to see that the group of two ladies and one gentleman were, indeed, approaching. And as they drew near, Lydia realized that she did know them after all. Suddenly she was filled with as much rage as Cora was filled with despair. "How could you?" she spat the question at Robert, shocked to the core by his betrayal.

There was no time for an explanation, and, frankly, Lydia did not know what Robert could have said to ease the situation. She had never been as hurt or as angry in her entire life.

*R*obert shifted so he was standing behind Miss Shipley, offering support by his presence, though not with his touch. He was afraid the poor girl might faint before the job was done. He could see by the expression on Lydia's face that he might have played his cards a little too close to the chest. He should probably have shared his plan with her.

Miss Shipley would never have agreed to this meeting had she been aware of it, but . . . well, yes, he could plainly see that he should have discussed it with Lydia. Too close to the chest and, perhaps, a little high-handed.

Cassidy walked across the grass, his new friends trailing slightly until, having gained their circle, Cassidy stepped out of the way to allow both parties a full and proper look at one another.

Instantly, tension filled the air, swirling around them in great clouds.

"Newton, I would like to introduce you to Lorne Granger," Cassidy began, pretending to be ignorant of the shared distress. "And his sister, Miss Gloria Granger. The lovely lady next to him is his fiancée, Miss Tatum Brownlow. Granger, I'd like you to meet my friend Robert Newton, Miss Lydia Whitfield, and *Miss* Cora Shipley."

The silence was heavy and uncomfortable as some complexions became ashen while others were inflamed. It might have lasted only a moment or two, but it felt interminable.

"We are acquainted," Lydia finally spoke, her voice surprisingly calm. "Old schoolmates." She lifted her cheeks.

Miss Granger lifted her cheeks as well, opening her mouth to show her teeth. Not appealing in the least. "Yes—"

"*Miss* Shipley? Excuse me, is that correct?"

All eyes turned toward Mr. Granger. Not a tall man, he was still a half head above that of Miss Shipley. He was only a few years older than Robert, clean-shaven but for the sharply chiseled side-whiskers, and he carried himself with authority. Granger's mode of dress labeled him a conservative, but his mouth looked ready to smile. Had Robert been pressed, he would have guessed that the man was usually a lighthearted fellow.

"Of course, Mr. Granger." Cora's voice shook ever so slightly. "We know each other well enough to not be mistaken in our identity."

"Yes, too true. But forgive me . . . I"—he glanced at his sister—"I understood you to have married. I was told—perhaps I misunderstood. You are to be congratulated on your engagement?"

"No." Cora lifted her chin, her eyes flickering to Miss Granger briefly. "I'm afraid that you were misinformed. I am neither married nor engaged to be married." She breathed deeply through her nose. "But *you* are . . . engaged."

"Yes."

Robert had never heard a single word laden with more distress.

*L*ydia clenched her fists behind the folds of her dress. Her jaw was equally taut, and yet she had to pretend that nothing was amiss, pretend that she was *not* trapped in a spiderweb of black widows, bold and deadly. At school, Gloria and Tatum had been the ringleaders of all things nasty and cruel—shaming and coercion their specialty. Yes, web spinning at its finest.

This was not where Lydia wanted to be, not where Cora should be.

Robert had a lot of explaining to do.

"I am not surprised that you were confused, Mr. Granger," Lydia said, tiptoeing around the explosive undercurrents. "You likely heard that Miss Shipley no longer resides in the family home at Fardover."

Mr. Granger pulled his eyes from Cora and blinked at Lydia

in a dazed, confused manner that spoke of a mind befuddled with thoughts—none pleasant, if his morose expression could be used as a guide.

"Miss Shipley has joined us at Roseberry Hall—become a member of *our* household."

"As a governess." Tatum snickered, then glanced at her fiancé and dropped her grin in a flash. She squinted her lovely blue, cruel eyes at her old schoolmate—casting the blame of her own *faux pas* on Lydia.

"You knew?" Mr. Granger asked, quietly, half turning in Tatum's direction.

"Well, yes. I believe I heard the rumor somewhere. It was such a surprise; we all thought Cora would marry well and yet . . . fate was not kind." The smarmy smile was back, but Mr. Granger did not witness it. He had returned his gaze to Cora.

"I am quite proud to be a governess," Cora stated with a lot more strength in her voice than moments ago. "Ivy and Tessa are lovely, kind girls, who think of others. Not a vile bone in their bodies. I have not had to suffer bugs in my bed or soaked shoes. No mockery and, certainly, no pretenses of friendship where there are none."

They were no longer talking about Ivy and Tessa.

Well aware of the sudden turn, Gloria sniffed in distaste. "I believe we should be on our way, Lorne. Tatum wishes to stop at the coffeehouse you so enjoyed the last time we took a promenade. Our own little Bath tradition."

"Oh, that is such a shame," Mr. Cassidy said, somehow

oblivious to the tension. "I hope we are still going to meet at the Pump Room later to take in the waters." He spoke to everyone, but his eyes were locked on Tatum Brownlow.

The flattered young lady blushed, glanced at the ground, and then looked up at him through her lashes. Lydia's belly rolled in protest.

"Oh, indeed, Mr. Cassidy. That would be most enjoyable," Gloria answered for the three of them. "And perhaps Mr. Newton would care to join us?"

It was extremely rude to make such a request while excluding Lydia and Cora. But the only appearances Gloria and Tatum ever worried about were those that looked back at them in the mirror.

"Thank you for your kind invitation. However, I must get back to work," Robert replied.

Lydia smiled genuinely. She greatly appreciated the smooth, mellow sound of his refusal—even if she was furious with him.

"Work?" Both Gloria and Tatum reacted with horror.

"Indeed." Mr. Cassidy nodded. "Newton here is a law apprentice."

"You are in law? I thought . . ." Gloria glanced at Mr. Cassidy and then back to Robert. "I thought that you were the Earl of Wissett's son."

"Third son," Robert explained.

"Oh." Gloria sniffed again. She took a step back and flicked her fingers at Cassidy. "Are you a first son?"

Mr. Cassidy laughed as if the question were part of a jest, not an inquiry meant to assess his worthiness of their company. "Of course. I will be Lord Tremont one day. But not too soon, I hope. I quite enjoy flitting about, meeting interesting people." Again, he smiled exclusively at Tatum.

Lydia's appreciation of Mr. Cassidy was sinking by the minute. Gentlemen can be so easily swayed by a pair of fine eyes.

"I do not mind if you wish to accompany the Grangers now," Robert encouraged. "I can see Miss Whitfield and Miss Shipley home."

"Oh, excellent . . . I mean, are you certain?" Mr. Cassidy was stepping forward even as he asked.

"Yes, indeed."

Lydia watched Mr. Cassidy; he hesitated before Tatum, as if he wished to offer her his arm. Then he looked at Gloria and lifted his elbow. And yet, as they strolled away, Mr. Cassidy continued to look over his shoulder and engage Tatum in conversation.

Lydia was unimpressed with Mr. Cassidy's boorish behavior, which included deserting their company with barely a wave. While Robert's earlier comment made it plain that he had instigated the encounter—likely to jolt a reaction from Mr. Granger—the whole mess was ill-considered. Distressing both Cora and Mr. Granger had been pointless and downright cruel. Mr. Granger could not, now that he knew Cora to be unfettered, back away from his engagement. Not only would his honor be ruined beyond repair, but he could also be sued for Breach of Promise.

No, Robert had put them all through this awkward ordeal with no gain possible. It was imprudent, foolhardy, and irresponsible. Try as she might, Lydia could not tamp down her burning anger. If he had spoken to her first, this whole scene might have been avoided.

It was almost a relief to focus her attention on Cora and getting her friend back to their town house. Had Lydia not been so distracted, she might have made any manner of waspish comments, might have given Robert a full dressing-down, and asked him to restrict any upcoming visits to number nineteen Great Pulteney Street for the time being. That, actually, would have been of benefit to their friendship. Time would allow her pique to blow itself out and give her some emotional distance.

While she knew that her sense of betrayal had been an overreaction, she was not above describing his actions as high-handed. They needed to have a talk, establish a few rules, such as: *Thou shalt not bring about the distress of my best friend . . . without express permission.*

"It is worse and worse again," Cora lamented as soon as the door closed, leaving Robert out on the street to make his way back to work. Lydia led Cora to the small parlor, holding her arm as she did. The poor girl was shaking like a leaf.

"It was one thing to think that he did not care. That he had found someone else—that he was happy, even if I was miserable. But to learn . . . to know that he was tricked." Cora stopped in the center of the room and placed her hand on Lydia's arm. "Did you see his face?"

Lydia nodded. She didn't want to comment; her friend's control was on the edge, and anything might push her over.

Such as a silent nod.

Cora burst into loud, ragged sobs. Allowing her knees to collapse, she slumped onto the settee. Lydia dropped down beside her.

"I'm so sorry, Cora." Lydia *tut-tut*ted and rubbed her friend's back. Had she believed in fairy tales, she would have told Cora that all would be well. True love would win out. But it seemed unlikely. Only Tatum Brownlow could break the engagement without any consequences. The nasty creature must have known that Mr. Granger had feelings for Cora, or the marriage lie would never have been invented. Tatum would not set the man free because of something as trivial as being in love with someone else. No, Tatum Brownlow was the type of young woman who would see to her own needs first and foremost. She always had.

*T*wo days later, while sitting across from her mama in the white-and-beige drawing room overlooking the tiny back garden, Lydia had cause to regret the hasty note she had penned to Robert the evening of the fiasco. She was greatly disappointed. She had asked him to give Cora and her a little time to regain their equilibrium, and he was doing just that. What was wrong with him?

Lydia had said nothing of her own displeasure, though her choice of words might not have hidden her pique. Two larger-than-necessary bouquets of flowers *had* arrived the next day. They now graced the entrance hall, allowing the seductive floral scent to waft up through the stairwell into every room in the town house . . . and served as a reminder—that it had been two days since she had seen Robert.

Lydia sighed.

She was still mad at him.

She sighed again and picked up a letter to read. It had been sitting atop the overfull silver tray that Hugh had brought in moments earlier. Replies to their invitations were arriving almost daily; most were acceptances.

"How many is that now?" Mama asked, without looking up from her magazine.

"Oh." Lydia glanced at the paper in her hand as if only just seeing it. She looked to her side and found a growing pile of notes and letters. Lifting them, she counted. "Twelve or so, that means . . . now, let me calculate. About thirty attendees to add to the list . . . and I have not finished reading the others yet."

"Oh, most excellent. It will be a veritable crush."

As this was said with the intonation of glee, Lydia refrained from complaining about the inconveniences of a crush. She sighed again.

"Are you quite all right, Lydia? You have a most serious countenance." Lifting her eyes, Mama stared intently. "How is Mr. Newton? We have not had the pleasure of his company for several days."

"Two, Mama."

"Is it only two?" she said in an exaggerated casual tone. "*I* was not counting."

"Please, Mama, don't. We are just friends."

"Yes, I have seen how you look at each other, very friendly."

Lydia laughed; it surprised them both. "I know what you are thinking, Mama. Any bachelor within twenty miles makes your eyes light up, and you start scheming. Except for Lord Aldershot, of course."

"If I thought you would be happy with Manfred Barley, my dear, I would support your father's arrangement completely."

"Would you?"

Dropping her magazine onto her lap, Mama straightened and smiled. "Yes, Lydia, I would. But, and I know you don't want to hear this, I believe your father to have been wrongheaded. He always said, '*What's good for Roseberry Hall is good for the Whitfields.*' I believe, what's good for the Whitfields is good for Roseberry Hall. He put the estate first—I would put the family first."

Lydia stared at her mother and blinked stupidly. "Mama? I . . ."

"Shocking, isn't it? I can be right once every so often."

"Of course—"

"With that in mind, I have some advice."

"In regard to?"

"Unexpected suitors."

"Oh." Lydia wasn't sure she liked where this conversation was going.

"If you were to find yourself attracted to a young gentleman working to attain a career, such as in the law, and said gentleman was a true gentleman, he would feel the weight of your disproportionate fortunes. He would not want to be perceived as a fortune hunter to you or to society."

"What are you saying?"

"This gentleman, no matter how strongly he felt about the matter, would *never* make an offer."

Lydia's heart sunk. "Never?"

"Most unlikely."

Suddenly the mildly gray day was looking stormy, and Lydia considered joining Cora for a good hearty cry.

"There is a solution, of course."

Lydia swallowed and met her mother's sympathetic gaze.

"You could propose to him."

"Mama!" Lydia was shocked. "That just isn't done." Granted, she had come dangerously close to doing so with Barley, but that was different; her father's approval had already been secured—years earlier—and she knew Barley would be making an offer eventually. But with a young man of such short acquaintance, it bordered on vulgar.

Mama shrugged and picked up her magazine again. "Marry Lord Aldershot, then. Life will not be nearly as complicated. Love is both heady and messy."

"I have not said that I am in love with . . . anyone—*anyone*, Mama. I don't know what that would feel like."

"That is true."

"And, more important, I do not know that . . . *anyone* loves me. He has not said so."

Flipping to the next page of the magazine, Mama smiled; it

was a slow-growing expression that blossomed into a grin. Perhaps it was the article in the *Lady's Magazine* that she found amusing.

Lydia huffed in frustration. She could hardly make an offer to a gentleman when the object of that quandary refused to pay a call simply because she had asked him not to.

Really, the male gender made no sense.

Chapter 18

*In which a sudden realization changes
Miss Whitfield's entire world*

For the better part of a day, Lydia chuntered over her mother's suggestion. First, it was outrageous. Second, ladies did *not* make offers to men. Third, how could Lydia be so bold without knowing if Robert held her in high regard or in great affection? Fourth, it just wasn't done. And fifth . . . well, it was outrageous.

She would think on it no longer!

It wasn't hard to divert her attention, as there was no short-age of enterprises to keep her busy. Shelley paid a visit to discuss the two orchestras that were available to play at her birthday ball, and a great deal had to be said about decorations and dresses. Cora joined them for that discussion while Mama took herself off else-where so they could gossip and commiserate in private.

Shelley was devastated to learn that poor Mr. Granger had

been taken in. Though, upon hearing about Robert's role in Gloria and Tatum's exposure, Shelley suggested that his greatest sin was in having tried too hard. Neither of the girls felt, as Lydia did, that he had overstepped. Even Cora, who had recovered from the shock, though not the melancholy, had decided that the truth was best, after all. And that it was comforting to know that she had not been mistaken in Mr. Granger's attachment.

Lydia found the turnaround and Cora's easy forgiveness of the person who had revealed the travesty rather baffling. She ignored the significant looks that passed between her friends every time Lydia mentioned Robert. It was only after they fell silent for a few moments that Lydia heard the echo of her conversation and realized that Robert's name had come up a fair number of times. She changed the subject.

Fortunately, just as Lydia was about to send another note to Robert—this time asking why he had *not* called—Sunday happened upon them. The Bath Abbey church was within easy walking distance and required no carriage, which was just as well as the coach and landau had been sent back to Roseberry to accommodate the Kembles' journey.

It was the first time that Lydia had been in the church, which had begun its days as a monastery, and she found that she was much impressed. She spent a fair amount of time staring at the fan vaulting in the nave and then switching her gaze to the vivid display of stained glass above the altar. Her mother elbowed Lydia whenever her inattention to the service was overlong, but the drone of the parson's voice was not engaging. Lydia's eyes continued to wander around the church unabated.

Eventually, her gaze lowered to the congregation. She paused to observe the straight and stiff father at one end of a pew, the round-shouldered mother at the other, and five children between them. There was a group of ladies with a marvelous display of bonnets, each more splendid than her neighbor's. And then there was . . . a young gentleman seated across the aisle, two rows ahead. Only a slight portion of his profile was visible, but Lydia was almost certain . . . yes. Her heart's steady rhythm began to quicken, and her breath caught in her chest.

It was Robert.

Swallowing, Lydia tried to control her breathing. She felt Cora shift in her seat and then heard her chuckle softly. Prying her eyes away, Lydia fixed her gaze on the parson, who was standing in the ornately carved pulpit. She had no idea of the subject of his sermon or how long said sermon continued. Lydia could think only about Robert sitting so near. Was he aware of her? Did he miss her as much as she missed him? It had been four days! Would he stop to speak to them after the service? What would she say?

All too soon, and not soon enough, the congregation rose for the final hymn. As they did, Lydia glanced over—casually—to find that Robert had turned slightly for a quick look in her direction. Their eyes locked, and Lydia could see that he was very aware of her presence; his glorious smile and nod said so.

With blinding realization, Lydia knew—beyond a shadow

of a doubt—that she *was* in love with Mr. Robert Newton, Apprentice in Law. Not a light fancy, not an inclination—but a deep, forever type of love. There was no going back from this; her world had just changed.

Forced by convention to face forward once again, Robert turned away . . . but Lydia continued to stare at the back of Robert's head—falling deeper and deeper into this thrilling pool of emotions, elation and contentment rising to the fore.

All her hesitance, all her indecision about Barley disappeared. She could *not* marry him. Ever. To live a calm, staid life with none of this excitement would be a prison sentence. Being Lady Aldershot was *not* worth the price, and if that would disappoint her father—he would have to deal with it as best he could on the other side of the veil. This was *her* life.

Lydia would send Barley a letter this very afternoon. She would ask him to visit her sometime before the ball; it would be most unkind to deliver such news any other way. It had to be done in person. She would want to impress upon him that they could remain good friends and agreeable neighbors. They could still rely on each other's goodwill, and there would be no need for awkwardness whomever he chose to marry . . . especially when a generous bridal gift could be applied against his debts.

She would not mention Robert. Barley need not know that Lydia had fallen completely and surprisingly in love with someone else. No need to admit that she had been wrong, that she was, indeed, capable of a deep, abiding *romantic* love.

Lifting her chin, Lydia joined the congregation in full voice as she sang "Ode to Joy."

$\mathcal{R}$obert crossed Pulteney Bridge with a light step. He grinned at the boy raking odiferous horse manure to the curb and tipped him well for his service. He nodded—with a grin—to the puzzled driver of a hack heading into the city. And he bowed—with a grin—as he stepped aside to allow the weary-looking woman with two toddlers to pass.

None to see him would realize that Robert had fallen under the hooves of a racing carriage and risen from the other side unscathed—metaphorically speaking, of course. He looked whole and hearty now, but until Lydia signaled a desire to reestablish their friendship, he had been in great danger of being deep in the doldrums.

He had made a mistake—a terrible mistake. Something on the order of a calamitous mistake! Robert would readily admit it. The problem was that the mistake had been so significant that Robert feared he might never get the opportunity to apologize properly. Bouquets of flowers were hardly a substitute.

All that had changed the day before.

While his conversation with Lydia outside the church had been brief, it had filled him with hope. Her smiles, her gestures, her stance, all were signs of a return to their previous footing. Yes, he could apologize, and she would forgive him.

Had he not accompanied Cassidy to the service with the Grangers and Miss Brownlow in tow, Robert would have been able to express his regrets right there and then. However, he *had* been so encumbered and found that he was pulled toward the Pump Room after the briefest of brief conversations with Lydia. They discussed something about the weather and the well-being of the family. Robert could hardly remember; so focused on the brightness of her smile and the jubilance shining in her eyes, Robert could barely articulate a word . . . or listen to himself . . . oh bother; he could barely do so now, his thoughts were bouncing around his brain with little rhyme and no reason.

Still, of one thing he was certain. Lydia had every right to be thoroughly put out with his high-handed behavior in the Brownlow affair. He used the word *affair* with all its implications. How else could the matter be described? Cassidy was doing his best to gain Miss Brownlow's interest, implying that he was disappointed to find that the young lady was no longer *on the market*. As a firstborn son, with title and lands in the wait, Cassidy would be a superior catch for someone who prized position over affection.

It was a charade, of course, bent on encouraging Miss Brownlow to become *dis*engaged. It was also a tightrope from which Cassidy could fall should his attentions become too overt. A challenge or, worse yet, a marriage trap waited for Cassidy should he step in the wrong direction. . . . Though Cassidy saw it as a lark.

The surprise meeting in the park had been part of the

charade—meant to awaken Mr. Granger to the manipulation of his sister and fiancée. It had done the job but hurt Miss Shipley and infuriated Lydia in the process. Not one of his finer moments. Right after he apologized profusely, Robert would explain the whole to her. They both had Miss Shipley's best interests at heart. He would be forgiven, and then his world would be righted again.

It was a marvelous day—or, at least, it was about to become one.

As Robert approached the tawny-colored row of town houses on Great Pulteney Street, he saw that a travel coach was stopped out front of number seventeen. It did not worry him overly until, as he stepped around the coach, he found that various trunks, bandboxes, and satchels were being unloaded into the lower floor of number nineteen.

The Kembles had arrived.

Robert's grin faded, and he pursed his lips in great disappointment. This was not a good time to pay a social call. He looked up at the entrance, hoping Shodster would somehow be aware of his presence and throw the door open, welcoming him in at this most inconvenient time. He willed it for some moments to no avail. The door remained closed, and Robert stood on the step staring at it stupidly.

Well, the good butler could hardly be blamed. The man would have only just arrived as well and was not likely yet up to snuff. His uncanny awareness and ability to see through doors might take a few more days to perfect.

Before pivoting and trudging back up the street he had just

strolled down, Robert glanced at the window off to the right, where he knew the small parlor to be. There, too, was no reward. A face came and went. No identification could be made; it passed in a blur.

With a grunt of dissatisfaction, Robert pivoted, heading toward the bridge and hill beyond. It would not take long to walk back to the office, where he would be able to continue—

"Mr. Newton!"

Robert turned and saw that it was still a marvelous day.

Lydia stood on the step in a lovely dress of some light pastel color. She had thrown an ornate shawl across her shoulders and was leaning forward waving.

"Ah, Miss Whitfield, what a surprise," he said in a teasing tone as he returned to the sidewalk in front of number nineteen. He doffed his hat.

"Really? I thought you to be on your way to visit us?" Lydia frowned prettily, not truly puzzled.

"If that were true, I would be headed in the wrong direction, would I not?"

"That is a certainty." She made a show of looking up and down the road. "Where then, if I might ask, were you headed?"

"Bristol." Robert nodded to emphasize his assurance.

"Oh, indeed." Lydia laughed. "Then I believe you to be lost, for you have traveled east instead of west."

"Really? Oh dear, that is a problem." Robert looked at the ground, mournfully shaking his head. Then he jerked his head up as if being suddenly put in possession of a new idea. "Perhaps

I should call upon my good friend Lydia Whitfield, instead. She lives nearby."

"That is a splendid idea. I believe she is looking forward to your visit."

"Is she?"

"Absolutely." There was a great deal of warmth in that one word.

Robert smiled and leaned on his cane, adopting a studied casual air. "Most excellent. However, I believe that her relatives have just arrived and she might be overly taxed with counting windows and burning menus, scaring unruly children . . . you know, domestic sort of chores."

"Well, it is most fortunate that Miss Whitfield is in possession of an organized character. All windows have been counted and menus duly burnt hours ago. Scaring children is slotted for this evening . . . though only if Miss Shipley is in need of assistance. So you see, Miss Whitfield is in desperate need of an occupation. A stroll and breath of fresh air would do handily."

"Something I can accommodate. What a happy chance."

"Most happy, indeed. Come inside. I will see that she is suitably bonneted and gloved in a trice, if you would be so good as to wait in the parlor."

Robert gestured Lydia ahead of him across the threshold of number nineteen. Once inside, the atmosphere was entirely different from his previous visits. Silent calm had been replaced by chatter, laughter, and scolding that bounced into the three-story entrance from various regions of the house. There was a smell of newly lit fires, and the accompanying puffs of smoke, as well as the enticing aroma of cooking wafting up from the kitchens. It was a bustling, busy household.

Shodster stepped into the hall and rushed toward Robert, hands outstretched ready to take Robert's hat and cane.

"Thank you, no. Miss Whitfield and I are going for a walk." Robert took a half step back. "We will be leaving shortly."

Looking to Lydia for confirmation, Shodster nodded. "I do beg your pardon, Miss Whitfield. I was not here for the door. It will not happen again."

"Worry not, Shodster." Lydia shrugged. "I learned how to open a door some time ago. The trick is to turn the handle."

The butler blinked at Lydia's lightheartedness. "Yes. That would, indeed, be the trick."

*L*ydia climbed the stairs to the second floor with great dignity. However, once there, she glanced around, decided that the hallways were empty, and sprinted to her room. She grabbed her brown spencer, her high-crowned bonnet with the matching ribbon, and a pair of gloves that set her gown to its best advantage. She was back down the stairs in the trice she had promised—just in time to see Shodster closing the door.

"Shodster?" Lydia said . . . gasplike. Then she saw the letter in her butler's hand. A quick glance confirmed that Robert was still in the parlor, tapping the brim of his hat against his cane. With a smile—she took the proffered paper and joined Robert.

"Ready to go?" she asked as if he had been the one preparing for the jaunt.

"Almost," he replied, though his tone was serious. His smile faded, and his expression carried a hint of trepidation. "Before we go anywhere, I would like to apologize for my high-handedness the other day. I should have informed you of what I was about and solicited your opinion."

Lydia laughed, clearly surprising him. "I accept, and counter your apology with one of my own." She lifted her hand as he opened his mouth to speak. "I overreacted. And I will be honest about this, my friend, I have thought long and hard as to why that would be. I am not known for being excessive in my emotions. . . . But I believe I now know the cause."

Robert stared at her, his eyes switching between her eyes and mouth, with such . . . um . . . concentration that Lydia could no longer remember what it was that she was going to say.

"And that would be?" he prompted.

"What would be?"

"The cause of your pique."

"Oh, yes. I beg your pardon." Lydia shook her head. "I am used to being, well . . . dare I say it . . . I am used to being in control—the one planning and deciding. It is required of me at Roseberry, and it has become a habit."

"I still should have—"

"Yes, yes. We could talk circles around this issue all day. Let us put it behind us." Then, taking a deep breath, Lydia touched on the subject that had been the biggest source of her disquiet since meeting Robert Newton, third son of the Earl of Wissett. "Robert?"

"Yes."

"I should like to tell you something."

"Oh."

The sound from the street faded into the background, and Lydia let the words spill out.

"I have decided not to marry Lord Aldershot. We do not suit. I would ride roughshod over him without intending to. I don't care about joining our estates. Nor about being Lady Aldershot. I . . . I . . ." She had run through all her reasons, except, of course, the most important one. "I . . . I . . . wrote him yesterday to request an interview."

Robert swallowed and took in a deep breath. "Is that his reply?"

"Reply?"

"Yes, the letter in your hand."

Lydia frowned and lifted her arm. "Oh. No. Well, I don't think so. The writing is vaguely familiar but not his, I don't believe." She broke the wax seal.

With a gasp, Lydia froze—immobilized by fear and fury. Instantly, Robert was at her side, and though it wasn't necessary, Lydia leaned against him for support—just for a moment.

The sound of footsteps in the upper hall brought Lydia out of her trancelike state, and she straightened, away from the safety and security of Robert. She dropped onto the nearest seat and felt, rather than saw, Robert move to behind her chair. When she lifted the letter to reread it; she knew he could see it, too.

Fool,

You ignored my warning. It was little enough to ask, a mere four hundred pounds. And yet you spurned me.

I had no choice. My lips moved, and your secret is told. Little voices behind your back.

Such a sordid tale. A night with your lover, your lawyer. A night of passion.

Now, he will pay, too. Watch as his world crumbles; his career is forfeit. All because you love money best.

But I can find it in my heart to still these little voices. Calm the flood of rumors. Save his career. All is not lost—yet. But there is a cost.

One thousand pounds.

Put the money in a box—addressed to Tommy Goode. Leave it under the fifth pew from the front on the right side of the Abbey church. No tricks.

I will be watching. You have three days.

"No," Robert said, stepping in front of Lydia, leaning down to look straight into her face. "Don't even think of it."

"Robert . . . your career. I can't have you lose something you cherish because of lies."

"Lydia, a thousand pounds! It is a fortune."

"I can ask Mr. Selleck about the barns—which repairs can be held off. Ivy's pony will have to wait. Yes, and if the birthday gowns are muslin, not silk—it can be done. Of course, I will have to get approval from Mr. Lynch and Uncle Arthur. What can we tell them? What can *I* tell them?"

"No. No, Lydia, it is the principle. People like this . . . this monster cannot win out. And you know the threats and demands will never end if you give in."

"I have to consider it."

"No, you don't."

"Mr. Newton, what an exquisite pleasure," squealed a voice from the parlor doorway. "Your timing is impeccable, as always— we have just arrived. Are you well, Cousin? You do not look your best. If you need to rest, I can entertain Mr. Newton." Elaine swayed from side to side, arms clasped behind her back, thrusting certain parts of her person forward. "You must apprise me of Bath's entertainments, Mr. Newton—the theater, assemblies . . . Oh, yes, we have *much* to talk about."

Robert straightened. "Thank you, Miss Kemble. Lovely to see you, too. Miss Whitfield has accepted my invitation for a little exercise—a stroll along Harrison's Walk."

"No." Lydia shook her head and chewed at her lip. "I think I need to rest, as Elaine suggested. I have a sudden headache; please forgive me for canceling. But . . . perhaps we can continue our discussion tomorrow? I will have had time to consider your point of view and will let you know what I have decided."

"Very good." Robert bowed to both ladies and headed to the entrance hall. He turned back at the threshold, catching Lydia's look. He held it for some minutes but remained mute. Then he nodded, turned, and bid Shodster farewell.

"That was badly done, Lydia. I could have taken Mr. Newton up on his offer of a walk to the park, if you had not sent him away so quickly." And then, as if only just realizing that the conversation she had overheard was slightly irregular, she frowned and stepped closer. "Are you still working on your marriage contract? Really, Lydia, you should not be so particular. Poor Lord Aldershot, he will not know whether he's coming or going."

"Too true, Cousin. Now, if you will excuse me, I will lie down for a bit."

Lydia fled to the sanctity of her room and stayed there the rest of the day. She rose the next morning determined. She would speak to Mr. Lynch and Uncle Arthur. She would pay the blackmail this time. She would not see Robert's career ruined! When the threat was uttered again—and she was certain it would be renewed—she would be ready. She would have already contacted Mr. Warner—and would simply not let the Runner leave until this fiend was caught.

But until then, she had to make Robert understand.

On edge, Lydia waited in the drawing room with the family—most of the family. Uncle Arthur had already found an excuse to visit the nearest club—something about old friends and acquaintances. Lydia had not paid much attention at breakfast; she had been lost to her thoughts.

Even now, as the others chatted around her, Lydia sat in the corner, book in hand, watching the clock as the afternoon rolled around to the hour for callers. It seemed as if the clock had forgotten how to tell time as the hands barely moved.

At last, there was a knock at the door. However, Shodster did not usher Robert into their midst but Mavis and Mrs. Caudle. Lydia stood and dipped, but she was not best pleased.

Mrs. Caudle settled herself with the matrons, while Mavis joined Lydia by the window.

"Welcome to Bath," Lydia said quietly to Mavis, lifting her cheeks and making an effort not to sigh.

"Oh, thank you," Mrs. Caudle called from across the room. "We are so pleased with these turn of events, aren't we, dearest Mavis?"

Mavis nodded kindly to her mother. "Oh, yes, what could be better than a few days in the city, shopping." Her expression brightened. "We are so looking forward to the ball that we made a special trip to buy a turban for Mama and shoe roses for me." And as she spoke, Mavis pulled a paper from her reticule. "So kind of you to include us." She passed the note to Lydia.

Again, Mrs. Caudle joined in their conversation from across the room. "Yes, quick, Mavis. We must be one of the first to accept your invitation."

Lydia glanced at her mother and allowed her to correct the

rector's wife. "Not the first, Mrs. Caudle, but one of the most welcome." It was a lovely fiction—well executed. It had the ring of truth if not the weight.

"That is wonderful to learn. I did so hope that the rumors would not deter your guests. I, for one, must say I do not believe a single word of it." Mrs. Caudle nodded.

Mama looked puzzled.

Lydia's belly turned sour, and she swallowed. "Rumors?" She glanced to Mavis.

"Something about a night in Bath without a chaperone."

"Really? Who?"

"Why, you and . . . well, Mr. Newton," Mavis said, staring at Lydia with undisguised interest. "Worry not. We paid it no never mind. But I must say, there are some who will not be as indulgent. But we will stand by you, dear Miss Whitfield." She leaned forward and patted Lydia's hand in sympathy. "Even if we are the only ones in attendance at your ball, it will be an exemplary evening."

"Don't forget Lord Aldershot, Mavis. He will be there, too, of course."

The expression of their youngest guest stilled; her eyes turned glassy. "Of course, Mama." Then she reapplied her smile. "Tell me what color you are going to wear, Miss Whitfield. Cream? Ivory? Off-white? So hard to decide, is it not? Though all are excellent choices."

Lydia was slow to answer; her mind was a riot of concerns, her thoughts in chaos. Was it too late? Was Robert's career already ruined?

"So, Mrs. Caudle, did you come by stage or did you hire a coach?" Mama asked the rector's wife. It was a pedestrian but safe subject. She had dropped her volume, but in the silence, Lydia could hear the discussion without strain.

"We came with Lord Aldershot, in his carriage. He is to stay in Bath for a few days, as well, and asked if we would care to join him. Wasn't that kind?"

"Most kind."

Lydia noted the sarcasm in her mother's tone, but Mrs. Caudle did not. "Lord Aldershot is always so accommodating—often at our house. He and the Reverend get along like boyhood friends despite the difference in their ages. So refreshing to meet someone of the peerage who is not all caught up by their position in society. Although we do have an ancient lineage, as you probably know . . ." And so the lady continued outtalking Mama and skipping from topic to topic with the best of them.

Lydia was thoroughly confused. If Barley was in Bath, why had he not come to see her as she had requested? Had he been affected by the rumors already? Avoiding her company? The day seemed to be getting worse.

"We must be going."

Mavis stood up, startling Lydia from her reverie.

"Oh, yes, of course," she said stupidly, standing for the good-byes. Their guests had stayed the requisite quarter hour.

As soon as they were gone, Mama left her perfectly comfortable settee and approached Lydia with a serious expression; it bordered on annoyed. "Lydia, I think we need to talk."

Rubbing at her forehead, Lydia dropped her eyes to the table . . . and the acceptance letter from Mavis. She blinked. And blinked again.

The florid style of the writing was unmistakable. Had she placed the threatening note beside it, they would be a match. This was the same hand . . . the hand of her blackmailer.

Mavis? It couldn't be! Mavis?

Grabbing the letter, Lydia raced for the door.

"Lydia! Where are you going?" her mother called after her.

Lydia was going to stop Mavis. She was going to confront her. She was going to accuse the rector's daughter of avarice of biblical proportions. She was going to end the blackmail once and for all.

Running to the balcony overlooking the entrance, Lydia shouted, "No. Shodster, don't let them leave."

But it was too late; he had been in the act of closing the door, not opening it.

Chapter 19

*In which control and puppetry draw Miss Whitfield
and Mr. Newton onto the field of honor*

Robert marched up Great Pulteney Street with purpose.
He adroitly dodged his fellow pedestrians and the vehi-
cles clogging up the thoroughfare. He had much on his mind; he
had reached a conclusion.

He was on his way to number nineteen to assure Lydia that
while they might talk, discuss, debate, or engage in any other
manner of communication, he would not let her beggar herself
for him, not his career, not his person . . . not . . . just *not*. He
cared too deeply to let her make *any* sacrifices on his behalf.

This conclusion was not dissimilar from that of the day before.
He was nothing if not consistent.

Wending his way between horses and wagons, Robert crossed
the street. He glanced up to assess his distance to the town house
when he watched someone—someone Lydia-shaped—hastening

from the building, arm in the air, waving a paper. She seemed to be rushing toward a carriage-and-two, but it pulled away from the curb, unaware of her urgency.

Seeing Lydia lift her skirt above her ankles to give chase spurred Robert to quicken his pace. He could cut off the carriage and allow Lydia to catch up; her purpose must be significant to flout convention by running—running down a crowded sidewalk. It was fortune that this end of Great Pulteney Street narrowed toward the bridge and slowed traffic. He did not have to step in front of a cantering team.

As the open carriage approached, Robert recognized Lord Aldershot, though not the two ladies at his side. Robert stepped off the curb just as the team slowed for the upcoming turn. He reached out to grab the reins of the lead horse, and though he was pulled backward a step or two, Robert retained his balance and brought the phaeton to a standstill.

"What is the meaning of this?" shouted Lord Aldershot. A stream of very ungentlemanly words followed his question, for which the man received a glower or two from those within hearing.

"Beg your pardon," Robert said, moving to the back of the team, so that their conversation would not require raised voices. As he did, he glanced and met not the stare of Lord Aldershot but that of a stubby-nosed man behind him, standing on the back of the carriage: Lord Aldershot's groom.

Robert was thunderstruck. The groom was none other than the third villain from the barn.

The implications were staggering.

This was a man who would not be wandering about the countryside without the express permission of his employer—who would be housed with said employer and at his beck and call—who . . . who had last been seen in the company of Les and Morley. There was only one conclusion that could be derived, and Robert derived it!

Aldershot was involved in Lydia's kidnapping.

"You!" he shouted, just as another voice shouted likewise. Robert jerked and turned his head.

Lydia had attained the carriage and had stepped up onto the running board. Holding a paper in one hand, securing her balance with the other, she stared with great hostility, not at Aldershot, but at the younger of the two ladies beside the baron.

"I know who you are! Visiting with the pretext of friendship while spreading your lies. Your arrogance, stupidity, and greed will see you *no* richer." Lydia's color was excessively high and her voice excessively loud. "I will *not*, do you hear me—"

Everyone in the vicinity could hear her.

"—give you a single shilling. Not a single solitary shilling for your betrayal." Shaking in anger, she turned her head. "The writing is the same, Robert. The same. Mavis Caudle is behind the threat."

The name did nothing to clarify who this young woman was, why she would do such a terrible thing, or how she was connected to Aldershot, but Robert felt Lydia should know the worst.

"Lydia, look—" He pointed to the face behind Aldershot.

But the groom was gone.

In an instant, Robert dropped the reins and rushed to the back of the phaeton. The groom was *not* gone; he had crouched behind the hood so that he was no longer visible from the front— away from Robert's discerning stare. It had been a wasted effort.

Robert grabbed the groom's coat and hauled him off the carriage; he dragged the accomplice to where he was visible to all concerned.

Lydia, still clinging on the side of the carriage, took one look at the groom and swung her head around to confront Aldershot.

"How could you do this, Barley?"

Lord Aldershot opened his mouth and then snapped it shut without saying anything. He turned to the young woman beside him and gaped wordless once again.

Mavis Caudle shook her head and then lifted her chin. Staring back at Lydia, she raised her voice. "I have never been so insulted in my life. You have insulted my honor." Half turning, she flicked her eyes toward Aldershot. "Defend my honor, Barley. Challenge Mr. Newton."

"What?" he and Lydia said at the same time—his inquiry was a squeak, hers a shout.

"But it was Lydia, not Mr. Newton, who insulted you, Mavis-dear. I have no quarrel with—"

"My honor has been insulted before this throng of people." Mavis-dear swept her arm across the front of the silent woman beside her and gestured toward the few pedestrians trying to make their way around the stopped carriage. "Challenge Mr. Newton."

To Robert's great surprise, Manfred Barley, Lord Aldershot, did just that.

"You cannot insult the honor of Miss Caudle, Mr. Newton, without answering to me." Aldershot nodded, pursed his lips, and then looked at Mavis-dear for what appeared to be approval.

Without looking his way, Mavis-dear reached across and gave Aldershot's arm a squeeze. It was so casually done that their intimacy was instantly revealed.

Robert started and exchanged a questioning glance with Lydia just as Mavis-dear spoke again.

"Tomorrow at dawn."

"Tomorrow?" Aldershot's voice was high and thin.

"Yes, now go. Barley, walk on!"

"But Lydia is still holding—"

Before Lydia could step down and away from the carriage, Mavis-dear grabbed the reins and flicked them. The horses stepped-to, and Lydia was knocked off balance. Throwing the groom aside, Robert lunged forward and caught Lydia before she could hit the stone sidewalk.

They tumbled into a heap, both safe but severely rumpled. Standing as quickly as a tangle of skirts and limbs would allow, they watched in silence as the released groom chased and then caught the phaeton, jumping up as it turned the corner and disappeared.

"So." Robert sighed. "Aldershot and . . ."

"Mavis Caudle, Reverend Caudle's daughter."

"Oh dear."

"Yes. Exactly." And then she sighed, too, very deeply. "I would never have conceived of it. Barley. The very man I was planning to marry. How could I have been so blind? Papa would be so very disappointed."

Robert thought the gentleman would more likely be livid, but he refrained from saying so.

"And Miss Caudle. I don't know her, but I would think a parsonage upbringing would have included the rule that one must not snatch people off the street without a by-your-leave."

"Yes, I would hope so."

"And then threaten to blackmail said person for a situation not of her making. I mean really, can they be any more despicable!"

"I think not."

Lydia heaved yet another heavy sigh and pulled her gaze from the end of the Pulteney Bridge. "They cannot—will not—get away with it!"

"Absolutely not."

And then Lydia lifted her eyes to Robert's face. She frowned and tipped her head as if trying to understand his expression.

Robert was smiling.

"What are you thinking?" she asked, her frown unfurling, her eyes losing their stormy glare.

Robert stepped to Lydia's side, offering her his elbow. "If we play our cards right, justice will be served." Stepping forward in a slow but steady pace, they headed back toward the rented town house.

"But Barley is a baron. We cannot have him arrested—even if we have proof." She looked down at the letter still in her hand. "Which we have against Mavis—for blackmail, at least. But as to the kidnapping and Barley's involvement, we have nothing."

"Nothing in hand as yet. If we get hold of his groom, we might have a case—a good case. And any gentleman of the peerage can call Lord Aldershot to task or anyone acting on behalf of a peer, such as a Bow—"

"A Bow Street Runner! Robert, that is brilliant. There is no need for the duel after all; we can set Mr. Warner on him. He can find the evidence."

"If we don't seem to comply, they will disappear."

"They don't have to disappear. Barley can simply go back to Spelding—minus his groom, of course. Mavis, though, is in the suds. . . . But no, you are right, he wouldn't go home without her. Mavis has Barley wrapped around her finger. Whatever they do, it will be together. In fact, what is to stop them from disappearing right now?"

"Pardon?"

"If I were them—caught, as it were—I would have immediately turned the carriage toward London . . . no, Bristol, and boarded the next ship to the Americas."

"I don't think they have the funds to do that."

"They could earn their way across the ocean, working."

Robert gave Lydia a significant look.

"You're right," she said, though he had not said anything. "They would never consider doing anything so demeaning.

Still . . ." She frowned. "What then would be the purpose of this duel? They can't very well sell tickets. Where is their profit?"

"There is only one way to find out."

"What kind of person challenges an apprentice lawyer to a duel?" It was a rhetorical question, for all and sundry knew the answer: a very foolish person.

"Robert, you are not going to participate, are you? You can't; it's against the law."

"Indeed. It is."

"Robert," Lydia's voice was plaintive. "You can't. . . . You could be killed."

"Worry not. I'll think of something." Robert squeezed her arm and led her past the door being held open by an unseen hand.

It was not in Lydia's nature to sit around—or stand around or pace around—unoccupied whilst waiting for Robert to devise a clever plan. No, she would not let Providence, or Barley, end the life of the man she loved. Just partaking in a duel could cost Robert his career. So let him be clever, let him arrange, and solicit, and whatever else he had in mind. She was going to the source of the problem, the person who would be holding the other pistol. She was going to talk to Manfred Barley.

And avoid her mother.

It took Hugh the rest of the afternoon to find the hotel at which Barley had hidden his sorry self and report back to Lydia. That the villain had spurned York House was not unexpected, as it was one of Bath's most expensive hotels, but he had also rejected the Christopher and the Pelican, picking the less genteel White Hare. His economic situation could not have been more obvious.

Lydia walked to Stall Street—actually, it was more of a march, as poor Jane could hardly keep up. The maid was forced to sprint sporadically just to stay at her side. Cora would have been the more logical choice of companion on this errand, but Lydia was quite certain that Cora would have tried to calm her down.

Lydia did not want to be calm. She wanted to be angry and articulate. She wanted to decimate Barley and disembowel his challenge. Not one to condone violence, Lydia found her palms itching to slap his face, each side!

The stout, dirty-aproned innkeeper of the White Hare opened his private parlor with a smarmy grin, gestured her in, and offered Lydia a drink while she waited. She would have none of it, and she paced the length of the room as soon as he left to summon Lord Aldershot. Jane stayed in the hallway next to the open door, out of the way.

Surprisingly, it didn't take long. The reason was soon apparent.

"Mavis," he said with great excitement, until he was through the threshold and saw who was standing in the center of the room. "Oh, Lydia. I was not expecting you." He turned as if he were going to leave.

In a flash, Lydia stood in the way of his exit. "We need to talk."

Shifting first to one side and then the other, Barley tried to step around, but Lydia would not allow it. "We need to talk," she repeated.

With a huff, one part sigh and one part anger, Barley drew himself up to his full height. "No, we do not. I will *not* marry you, and that is all there is to it."

"Apparently this is going to come as a bit of a shock, Lord Aldershot, but I haven't wanted to marry you, either, for quite some time." It wasn't all that long. . . . It just seemed like forever.

"Really?" His expression relaxed. "Oh, that is excellent. We thought your note was going to be another demand to set a date. You are so overbearing, Miss Whitfield, ordering me about—oh, may I call you Miss Whitfield again? Wonderful. Mavis will be so pleased. She was wrong. . . ." His brow furrowed. "Dear, dear, she does not like to be wrong. I think I'll just say that I was mistaken; she doesn't mind if *I* am not correct." His smile returned. "Yes, that will do."

"If control was the difficulty between us, Lord Aldershot, I believe you have gone from the frying pan into the fire."

"No," he said too quickly. "Mavis simply knows her own mind, but she does not order me about." He shook his head as if to clear it. "If you had been clearer on the purpose of your summons, we would not have sent that last threat. . . . Lawks, that would not have done, either. I am sorely lacking in funds—"

"Not enough blunt to keep your light-skirt happy? She wants *your* title but *my* money."

"Miss Whitfield! Really! You cannot use such a term—and certainly not in reference to Miss Caudle."

"The truth is the truth."

"What a terrible thing to say about a gentleman's daughter. Our feelings for each other, our deep, abiding love, cannot be so labeled. You make it sound sordid. Fie and for shame, Miss Whitfield, fie and for shame. You are besmirching a timeless love. We are meant to be together for all eternity in poverty or luxury."

Lydia stared at Manfred Barley in disbelief; these were not his words. She could hear Mavis Caudle behind every syllable. "If that were so, then why did you not simply tell me that you had reconsidered? Whence came the suggestion of kidnapping and blackmail?"

"Mavis, of course. She pointed out that the wealth of Roseberry Hall has been carried on the back of Wilder Hill Park for generations. She is the more clever of us two, but I quite agree. Your wealth should be *my* legacy."

"Really. Here I thought the Whitfield fortune was derived from sugar, excellent management, and restraint."

"Exactly. It isn't right that someone of such plebeian heritage should have so much more than those of us with ancient ties to the aristocracy."

"You are being manipulated."

"I am not."

"That is wonderful. For as much as I enjoy listening to blathering nonsense, I am not here to discuss the folly of uniting our estates but the challenge that you issued a few hours ago. If, as you say, you are not buckling under the machinations of your hussy, then you will have no problem canceling the duel."

"Well, I can't do that."

"Oh, and why not?"

"You are supposed to offer me some generous amount so that I will not go ahead with the challenge."

"Ah, so that was the purpose. . . . It keeps coming back to money. Miss Caudle is nothing if not consistent."

"Well . . . Mavis thought that we should double the request."

"Two thousand pounds. Fine. Done. Call off the duel."

"She'll want the money first."

"Barley, you know that I cannot collect two thousand pounds in"—Lydia glanced around for a clock, of which there was none, then speculated—"fourteen hours. Banks are no longer open, and arrangements would have to be made with Mr. Lynch and Uncle Arthur. I do not have access to such a sizable amount of money."

He winced. "Yes, I thought it might prove difficult. Mayhap a letter would do. Yes, I might be able to persuade Mavis with a promissory note."

"Persuade her? Barley, do you not realize that Mavis is pulling your strings? You are her puppet. She has dragged you from the straight path and pushed you down the slippery slope of vice. Have you not fathomed yet that you can be arrested for what you have done!"

"No one will speak of the duel. It's an unwritten rule."

"Not for the duel, Barley. For arranging my kidnapping and trying to extort money from me. Call it blackmail, call it fraud, it is all illegal."

"But I am a baron."

"It is still illegal, Barley."

"What is going on?" A new voice echoed throughout the room.

Lydia whirled around to find herself nose to nose with Mavis Caudle. "Ah, speak of the devil, and here you are." She lifted her cheeks in a semblance of a smile.

The pretty, young rector's daughter flushed angrily and glared with animosity. Her jaw clamped, her mouth pursed.

"I am here to answer your demands, dearest Miss Caudle. Crass, vulgar, and plebeian though it might be, I am here to buy you off—just as you predicted I would."

Mavis Caudle smiled. It was a far uglier expression than her pursed lips. "Excellent. We have a deal. Well done, Manfred."

"She'll have to give us a promissory note, Mavis-dear. The banks are . . ."

"Not good enough."

"You were the one to set the impossible timeline."

"Be that as it may, banknotes are the only currency I . . . we will accept."

"I cannot get them in time."

"Try."

"But—"

"Good-bye, Miss Whitfield. We will see Mr. Newton on Daisy Hill at dawn. If you have furnished him with the necessary funds, Manfred might not aim at his heart. It is up to you whether they stand at twenty paces or share a handshake and walk away."

Bile rose in Lydia's throat, and she opened her mouth to protest, but Mavis Caudle shook her head. She smirked and grabbed Lord Aldershot's arm; she walked past Lydia with perfect posture and a chin so high in the air it was doubtful that she could see ahead.

The effect was spoiled when, after having gained the hallway, Lydia could hear Mavis snap, "A promissory note can be traced, you fool."

*F*ourteen hours can be experienced in many ways—to Lydia they were an eternity and a moment. Calling upon the goodwill of her nearby friends and family, with no questions asked—at least none directed toward her—Lydia was able to collect five hundred and ninety-three pounds. It was far short of the two thousand demanded, but she hoped, prayed, that it would be enough to sway the harlot to walk away from Daisy Hill with no blood on the field. Lydia was not worried about her good neighbor's opinion, gullible, malleable sap that he was. He would go along with whatever Mavis-dear directed.

Somewhere in the middle of the night, Lydia penned a note to Robert, letting him know what she had arranged. A note returned with a cryptic and unhelpful message.

Excellent scheme, though I have thought of an alternate to try first. As I was the one challenged, the choice of weapons is mine. Will let you know if the funds are needed.

His words were not reassuring.

The predawn rising was not as difficult as Lydia had thought it would be. Excessive trepidation foils a restful night. Even Cora, who insisted on accompanying Lydia to Daisy Hill, looked wide awake when they met to tiptoe down the stairs.

Shodster watched them descend with sorrowful eyes, hesitating before unlocking the door. "Jeremy and Hugh will go with you, Miss Whitfield," he whispered.

"But—"

"Mr. Hodge will need to stay with the carriage, Miss Whitfield. I will not have you traipsing through the dark without proper protection. I don't know what Mr. Newton is thinking."

"He isn't expecting me to be there."

"More fool him," Cora said, maneuvering Lydia through the door.

"Thank you, Shodster." Lydia nodded in a way that she hoped conveyed her appreciation of both her butler's efforts and his concern. "I will return as quickly as I can." The door shut behind them, and she heard the bolt shoot home. She shuddered at the sound and then joined Cora in the coach.

Daisy Hill was not far from the city, and yet there was a sense of complete isolation. An owl screeched, and the leaves rattled in the wind, but of humanity there was no sound. The air was crisp, far cooler than one would expect for the beginning of May. But then, Lydia had never been up at dawn before. Perhaps this was the norm.

The sky was marginally brighter when Mr. Hodge pulled alongside another carriage. The other driver was huddled in a blanket, leaning on the side rail in an indolent manner. His unemotional stare did not invite queries. So Lydia was left to wonder if it was Robert or the terrible two who had arrived ahead of her.

Wordless, they alit and stared across the mole-hole-dotted field to the hill beyond. It seemed logical that this was their destination, so they lifted their skirts several inches and climbed; Lydia's over-stuffed reticule bumped against her thigh as she walked. She was glad to have worn her brown pelisse, as it not only blocked the wind but also kept her person hidden in the dark. Cora, too, was shadowed, swathed in gray. Hugh and Jeremy followed behind—somewhat more visible in their green livery and cream breeches.

The hill was not overly high; the climb did not take long.

Movement up ahead directed their path, and Lydia did not know if she was relieved or disappointed to see that the group of four resolved into Miss Caudle, Lord Aldershot, his groom, and a stranger carrying a black satchel.

Taking a deep breath, Lydia approached.

Before she had closed the gap, Robert burst through the bushes, evidently having gained the hill from the other side. It was a far more convoluted route if Lydia's inquiries had been correct—a more arduous climb.

"Excellent, we are all here." His voice cut through the silence, sounding loud and invasive. He glanced toward Lydia with a slight frown of surprise, but just slight. He shrugged, smiled, and then turned to face the terrible two. There was no sense of nervousness about him.

His bonhomie manner intensified Lydia's disquiet by leaps and bounds. Was he not taking the whole process seriously? She increased her pace until she stopped twenty or so feet from the confrontation.

"Lower your voice, Newton. We do not want to attract attention," Aldershot snapped.

"Don't see why not." Robert's reply was louder if anything. He half turned to the person beside him. "There we go, Cassidy, mark off the twenty paces. Looks like the sun is coming up."

"Mr. Newton, voices carry in this kind of stillness—"

"Don't you know it!"

"And we do not want anyone to know what we are about." Miss Caudle's tone was caustic.

"Why? Are *you* doing something you ought not to be doing?" Robert spread his raised arms, gesturing dramatically, very un-Robert-like.

Lydia began to fear for his reason as well as his person.

Robert watched Mr. Cassidy mark off an area—counting as he did so. "How is that?" he asked Robert, ignoring the other party entirely.

"Excellent, excellent. Yes, that should do. Plenty of room for everyone. What say you, Aldershot?" Robert pivoted, looking in every direction. "Time to discuss the terms of *your* challenge."

"Finally, you are seeing reason."

"Yes, indeed. You accused me of insulting Miss Caudle." He flicked his hand in her general direction without glancing toward the young lady. "Though it was not true, you issued a challenge nonetheless."

"This is all water under the bridge, Newton. We have come to terms—monetary terms. Let's get on with it."

"I was not present for any discussion of monetary terms, and as this challenge was offered to me, I see my lack of involvement in said discussion as a great oversight on your part. Therefore, the agreement is invalid."

"What! That cannot be. It was the very purpose of this exercise. If you do not agree to the payment, then I will have to shoot you."

"Sounds more like murder than a duel."

"Call it what you will. Pay me or you shall suffer deadly consequences."

"I don't believe that even you can kill with my choice of weapons."

"Do you think to best me at swords, Newton? Really, while you were grubbing about in books, I was learning from a fencing master. No, the only way for you to survive unscathed is to provide the funds that were discussed with Miss Whitfield." Aldershot snorted a laugh of great derision.

It curdled Lydia's stomach.

"Still, as the one challenged, it is *my* choice of weapons."

"Fine, Newton. I see that your brain is a featherweight. You don't seem to know the meaning of deadly consequences. Choose away."

"Thank you."

Lydia gasped. "No, Robert." Thrusting her shaking hand into her reticule, she stepped forward. Before she had a chance to pull the banknotes free, the shrubs around them shook, and several figures stepped out of the trees.

Chapter 20

In which life hangs in the balance of five hundred and ninety-three pounds

The shapes solidified into three young gentlemen of various girths, heights, and facial hair. They, in turn, were followed by two more, and then more again. In all, nearly a dozen young gentlemen sauntered out of the woods and over to the staring combatants. The newly risen sun added a pink glow to the tops of their felt hats and caped shoulders. Their walking canes left pockmarks in the soft ground.

"Welcome." Robert smiled to the newcomers; he offered a general bow.

There were murmurs of greeting and a fair amount of smiling—accompanied by a guffaw or two. The atmosphere was carnivalesque, as if the whole affair were some sort of lark. They collected along Mr. Cassidy's paced-off arena on either side of Lydia, and when it became somewhat crowded, several skipped across to the other side. Jockeying for position, they all wanted to see.

Macabre. Lydia was repelled by this morbid fascination. She straightened, lifted her chin, and drew a deep breath, preparing to give them all a proper set-down and send them on their way. . . . But she hesitated.

What was Robert about? For it seemed evident that he had brought this horde, this large group of *witnesses*, with him. It was dangerous—a very dangerous tactic. Should any of them mention this gathering, Robert would find himself incarcerated, without a career. He was not a cavalier young man. . . . There must be a purpose.

"What are you about, Newton? This is not the way of it." Aldershot sounded indignant, but there was a tremor to his words. He glanced around nervously, and sweat formed at his temples.

"You and Miss Caudle took it upon yourselves to besmirch Miss Whitfield's good name. When called on it, you feigned insult. I have never considered truth to be an insult; it is simply the truth."

Lydia recognized the sentiment, of course. Robert had stated the same to her uncle a week or so past. Still, she cared not a whit about truth at this juncture; she cared about Robert. Opening her mouth to add her objection to that of Aldershot, Lydia felt a touch on her arm.

"It will be all right; worry not," Mr. Cassidy whispered over her shoulder.

Only Cora and Lydia heard the request. They shared a look, and while Lydia didn't try to mask her confusion and fear, Cora tried a facade of false composure.

Lydia's frown deepened; she turned back—lips pursed. She took a deep breath and then another. She swallowed against the bile that clawed at her throat and then clenched her jaw.

"And now before all these witnesses, I accept your challenge. My weapon of choice"—Robert paused dramatically—"is wit: a duel of words."

"Words!" both Lydia and Aldershot exclaimed at the same time.

However, while Lydia smiled and felt knee-buckling relief, the same could not be said for her greedy neighbor. Aldershot scowled and shook his head in short jerks.

"Words are not a weapon," Mavis Caudle entered the fray with a sneer. "This is trickery, nothing else."

"Indeed? Words have great power, Miss Caudle. Of all people in this company, you more than any would know that they can be used in deeply harmful ways—the damage can be catastrophic." Robert turned back to Aldershot. "Wits will have to be your pistol, old man, though I fear you to be unarmed. Bearing in mind that this is a somewhat unusual tactic, I will give you leave to choose what manner of words we will use: riddles, poetry, or insults. Our friends here"—he swept his hand, gesturing toward the strangers—"they will be our judges. Three each—an extra if needed to break a tie."

"What asininity is this? Are you demented?"

"Aha, insults it is." Robert grinned and looked quite gleeful.

The crowd laughed and clapped—though it was more in amusement than appreciation for such a weak volley. Aldershot would have to do better than that if he was going to lock horns . . . or wits with Robert.

"As insults go, that was nothing more than milquetoast. We shall have to call it practice or the game is already won. Hardly fair to make you concede so soon—unlike some present, I believe in honesty and fair play."

"Was that your first insult?"

"No, no, not at all—we shall call that slur practice as well—or truth. Either will work."

"Mr. Newton, you are not playing by your own rules," Mavis said. "Every word out of your mouth is an insult."

"I do beg your pardon, there is just something about your lover's weak chin and lackluster discourse that brings it out of me. I shall endeavor to behave." He nodded with finality, though his grin showed exactly how heartfelt was his apology.

Walking past Lydia to the far end of the designated area, Robert planted his feet and bent his arms as if readying for a fight. "All right, Lord Aldershot. I thought you to be bird-witted and cow-handed. Now, I have discovered you to be the opposite." He stretched his arms out, paused, and then delivered the last line. "You are bird-handed and cow-witted."

He looked toward the crowd, and while acknowledging the mild applause, Robert nodded at a thin figure half hidden in the shadows. Lydia squinted; she could see the newly risen light glinting across a row of brass buttons. She smiled to herself—if she had a propensity toward gambling, she would have bet that the figure wore a blue overcoat and the top hat of a Bow Street Officer.

"Was that it?" Mavis Caudle asked. "You are not as clever as you thought."

"No, no, Miss Caudle. My game of words is with Lord Aldershot. You might have a lifetime of manipulation on which to stand, but derision is not an insult, and you were not invited to speak." Shifting his eyes to Aldershot, Robert addressed his opponent. "Do you wish to concede? I will not be insulted by you both."

"No, no. Mavis-dear, best let me handle this."

"What does this accomplish? Nothing!"

"As much as any duel." Robert sounded bored, though Lydia was fairly certain it was a feigned tone.

"There is no point to this, Manfred. The outcome is immaterial; we were playing the game for a different reason, if you remember? For *profit*." Lydia watched Miss Caudle's stance become taut. "We have already lost."

Glancing at what amounted to an audience, Aldershot swallowed roughly. "I cannot walk away, Mavis-dear. How would it look?"

"Like you were manipulated into a pointless duel of *words*."

"Perhaps Lord Aldershot prefers that to being shamed before a group of his peers." Lydia stared at Miss Caudle.

Miss Caudle sent Lydia a withering look—well, she attempted

to do so; Lydia stood steady and firm, not wilted in the least. Then Mavis stepped back behind Aldershot. The conniving young woman continued to put distance between herself and Aldershot until she was some three or four feet from the baron.

Was Mavis Caudle deserting her lover? Lydia smiled. The allure of his position in society was only of interest if it came with a big purse. Returning her attention to the battle, Lydia continued to watch Mavis Caudle from the corner of her eye as the woman slipped slowly and deliberately around several boisterous spectators.

"Ah, yes, well, hmm . . . yes." Aldershot scratched at his ear, oblivious to his abandonment. "Hmm, yes. Have you had your head examined? I fear the physicians will find it quite empty."

The onlookers were less than impressed. A voice shouted out, "You can do better than that," while a fair number of gentlemen shook their heads and clicked their tongues. All eyes returned to Robert.

"Your insults barely register, Aldershot. How did you learn to be a dullard in so many different ways?"

Lydia smiled. Momentarily distracted, she glanced around for Mavis Caudle. Frowning, she leaned closer to Cora. "Did you see where Mavis went?"

Cora shook her head, still watching the duelers.

Slipping behind the group, Lydia craned her neck to look down the hill. The upper portion of the meadow was visible now, the sun was slowly climbing the sky. . . . And yet there was no fleeing figure.

"You have your own category in entomology you are so beetle-brained."

This time, the crowd laughed at Aldershot's words.

Shifting so that she could see down to where the carriages waited, Lydia was startled by a sharp tug on her reticule. It jerked her sideways, away from the group, and snapped one of the two drawstrings attaching the bag to her wrist.

"It is senseless to mock you; it will take you the rest of the day to take my meaning." Robert's insult drifted through the crowd.

Lydia's gasp of surprise was lost in the echo of the laughs and jibes that followed. She tried to draw her arm back, but the solid hold on her reticule pulled her forward instead. Once again, she was nose to nose with Mavis Caudle.

"Miss Caudle! What do you think you are doing? This is out-and-out thievery. I would not think that even *you* would stoop this low."

"This money is mine. You brought it to give to us, and I want it."

"This money was to free Mr. Newton from a grave threat. The threat is gone—so you do not get *any* of these funds!"

"Give it to me now, or I will force you to."

"Miss Caudle, you are stepping deeper and deeper into illicit water. Do you not realize that you can be arrested for all your attempts to extort money from me?"

"Manfred is a peer. You cannot accuse him of anything."

"Lord Aldershot is a baron . . . not a prince. A fellow peer can easily be found to assist in the course of justice. I am not without my resources, you know. That being said, you, Miss Caudle, would not be treated likewise. You would not be given any leeway no matter how intimate your relationship with Lord Aldershot."

"Unless I were his wife," Mavis Caudle smiled in a manner that made Lydia want to step away . . . far way. "We were married by special license two months ago."

"If that were true, then why would you not be open about it? Celebrate your joyous union with the neighborhood. No—"

"You, *you* are the reason we have had to wait. *You* are the reason for all our woes."

"I don't see how—"

"Everyone believes that *you* will marry Manfred. As soon as his creditors know the truth, they will be on us like locusts. We will have to retrench. You owe us this money."

Lydia spurted a laugh. "Really? That is your excuse. Your husband ran up his debts, and I am to blame? That is the most illogical justification that I have ever heard." She tried to yank the reticule free but stopped upon seeing the glint of steel. "What? Mavis . . . um, Lady Aldershot, what are you doing?"

In a flash, the knife came down, severing the last string on Lydia's bag. Mavis shoved Lydia with such vigor that she fell backward, landing with a jarring thump on the cold ground. Mavis Barley, Lady Aldershot, picked up her skirts and ran toward the waiting carriage—stepping carefully around the mounds of mole dirt as she raced away.

"Lydia!" Cora cried out, and in doing so silenced the crowd behind them.

Suddenly lifted to her feet, Lydia turned to find Hugh at her side. Jeremy stood next to him, holding firmly on to Barley's stubby-nosed groom.

"Beggin' yer pardon, miss. We was distracted. Thought you might be interested in talkin' to this here fella." Hugh looked crestfallen. "Never expected herself to be given ya trouble. You want we should go after her?" He nodded toward the fleeing figure.

Before she could answer, Robert pushed through the crowd. "Lydia, are you all right?" He nudged the footman aside and grabbed her about the waist as if she were about to fall again . . . which she wasn't—but she leaned ever so slightly nonetheless. "What happened?"

"What is going on?" Aldershot joined them, glaring at Lydia and then turning his gaze to the far side of the field.

"Your wife stole my reticule, Lord Aldershot." Ignoring his look of astonishment, Lydia continued. "I do not know what nonsense she has been feeding you, but neither a baron nor his lady can act with impunity."

"That is the truth of it, Lord Aldershot." Mr. Warner stepped out from the shadows. "Kidnapping, assault, blackmail, and now thievery—all very serious crimes. Perhaps we should explain the realities of life to Lady Aldershot."

They all glanced toward the figure that had now reached the carriage at the bottom of the hill. The driver, throwing back his blanket, jumped down from his perch, revealing the uniform of a constable.

Rolling back on his heels in a studied casual manner, Mr. Warner continued to address Lord Aldershot without looking his way. "I thought you might try to make a getaway, my lord, once you saw that the jig was up. But I see that I underestimated your lady. Fortunately, my constable is quite capable of assessing the situation."

In silence, they stared for some minutes as the scene at the bottom of the hill dissolved into a drama of shouting, kicking, and some very surprising language.

"Yes, well, I think we should probably offer assistance to poor Constable Johnson." Mr. Warner turned and nodded a bow to Lydia. "I will return your funds forthwith," he said, and then turned to Hugh and Jeremy. "Bring the groom along, my good fellows. He can languish in jail with his inept cousin Morley Goode and his cohort in thievery, Les Niven. Come, Lord Aldershot, let me be your escort." Though his words were light and frivolous, his tone was anything but. Silently, Lord Aldershot started down the hill.

Lydia turned to Robert, though disappointed that in doing so, he was forced to release his hold on her person. It had been a great comfort. "Poor Barley, what a mess he has made of his life."

"Indeed. But I believe he had help. His wife?"

"You noticed that, did you?"

"It was hard not to." Robert gently touched the side of her

chin and then turned to watch the men as they reached the bottom of the hill.

The anxiety, the fear, and the tension that Barley and Mavis had brought into her life faded away. And yet there was no sense of exhilaration or even simple satisfaction—just a great sadness for lives gone miserably astray.

*B*ath, as promised, was rife with distractions in the spring—chief among them was Miss Lydia Whitfield. Robert found that on every day leading up to her birthday ball an excuse . . . er, reason . . . could be found to spend time in her company. Occasionally, he could label the encounter a meeting, but in most cases it was an outing. And a pleasurable one at that—despite including various family members, there was always a moment when they could stare at each other without censure. They partook of such opportunities as often as possible.

Rising early, Robert found that he could complete the bulk of his duties at the firm by midafternoon. A leisurely stroll in Sydney Gardens, on fair days, and a gossipy taking in of the waters, on rainy days, followed. The evenings included a card assembly, concert, or night at the theater. Robert had never known the city to be so lively, exciting, and fascinating.

One meeting, which truly was a meeting, occurred just days after the dawn adventure. Lydia had decided that a formal arrangement should be set up for the security of her aunt and cousins upon her marriage or reaching the age of majority. Knowing that this monetary compensation would also aid her uncle gave Lydia little pleasure, but she knew that she could not destine her family to his frantic schemes. The Kembles' manor had to be repaired and the estate brought back to snuff if they were ever going to be self-sufficient again.

The meeting went well. Mr. Kemble put questions to Mr. Lynch, but he was not caustic or belligerent in the asking of them. His bloodshot eyes demonstrated how much he continued to appreciate a nightly overdose of port, but there were no hitches to his speech, and he was clear-thinking. After all the papers were signed, he stood and bowed formally to his perplexed niece.

"I believe it customary for a show of appreciation under these circumstances, and as such I will express some gratitude. However, before I do so, I would like to state that had I not been required to vacate my own estate to assist in the running of Roseberry, there would have been no need of your generosity. Still, my excellent management and husbandry of your property has provided the means to rebuild my estate, and with that in mind, I thank you."

It was a convoluted acknowledgment at best, but more than Robert had expected.

Lydia nodded with as much solemnity as her uncle and sighed deeply, very deeply.

The night before the birthday ball was purposefully unexceptional. Resting up for the celebration was the purpose of a subdued evening, though Robert found that he was still included in the company. He was more than pleased, as he had news to impart—but not to all.

After the meal, the family adjourned to the drawing room—a long room with two seating arrangements, one clustered by the fireplace and the other by the windows at the far end. Most of the family chose to collect near the fireplace, so Robert gestured invitingly toward the windows. Lydia immediately veered to where he indicated, though she looked mildly disappointed when he included Miss Cora in his solicitation.

Miss Elaine started across the floor to join them when Mrs. Whitfield touched her arm and suggested that she might be more comfortable on the settee beside her mother. Miss Elaine's expression could be characterized as sour. She sighed loudly and dramatically and then slumped into her seat, crossing her arms and staring daggers at Lydia.

Those across the room paid scant attention.

"I have news," Robert said, sweeping his tails behind him and perching on the chair closest to Lydia.

The young ladies, seated together on a floral-patterned chaise, stared up at him expectantly.

"Indeed?" Lydia prodded.

"Yes, I have heard that there will soon be a notice in *Boddely's Bath Journal*. Couched in discreet language, of course, it will announce the amicable dissolution of the engagement between Miss Tatum Brownlow and Mr. Lorne Granger. It would seem that the lady has changed her mind. I don't believe that there will be any mention of greener pastures."

"Dis . . . dissolved? In tr . . . truth?" Miss Cora, not one to stutter under normal circumstances, was having a hard time conveying her thoughts to her mouth.

"How do you know?" Lydia came to her rescue.

"Cassidy dropped by my office this afternoon. I will probably regret setting him to this task; you should have seen him strut. So pleased with himself."

"But is he safe? Did he become entangled—caught—in Tatum's web?"

"I don't believe so. Cassidy is quite sure that he is still unshackled, and did not balk at my suggestion to visit his cousin for the London Season. He will head east right after your birthday ball."

"Oh, Mr. Newton, I don't know how to thank you for your intervention. You are a saint."

"Apprentice, actually . . . though I can see how you might confuse the two."

The three shared a loud and boisterous laugh, garnering interested looks from across the room—and a scowl from Miss Elaine.

The day of Lydia's birthday ball did not begin with promise—gray skies and light, almost misty rain. By afternoon, the clouds opened up and poured, but only for a few hours. And then, miracle of miracles, the sun chased away the clouds and pulled in the warm airs from the hills, blanketing the city with comfortable, sweet-smelling breezes.

As dictated by the Beau Nash rules of proper conduct, the ball was scheduled to begin precisely at the hour of six. This required Robert to leave the firm at midday to prepare. It was just as well, for he found it difficult to concentrate. His thoughts were entirely taken up by memories of the wit, figure, and laughter of one Miss Lydia Whitfield.

This was both a beginning and an end, and as a consequence, he was both elated and heavyhearted. Tonight, he would dance with Lydia. In fact, he had been given the great honor of opening the ball with her. The first set would be the minuet. Halfway through the night, Robert would lead her to the floor for their second dance. She had chosen a quadrille. But that would be all. Any more than two dances would start tongues wagging.

Once he returned her to her mother's side, he would have to vie for Lydia's attention through the hordes. Robert had no doubt that Lydia would take. There was no reason to assume otherwise. Lydia Whitfield was a cultured, beautiful, wealthy young woman of marriageable age. Bachelors would arrive at her doorstep in droves from this day forward, until she made her choice.

Robert didn't want to think about who that might be; at least it wasn't Lord Aldershot. Lydia needed a husband of excellent morals—she would respect nothing else—and someone who could make her laugh but also stand up to her with knowledge and true understanding of the ways of the world. Someone who could benefit from a well-ordered life. His conversation would need to be more than hounds and horses. No, Robert did want to think about it.

To the end of his days, Robert would never forget the

glorious sight of Miss Lydia Whitfield waiting just past the portico in the principal entrance of the Lower Rooms. He had just stepped out of his sedan chair, pulled straight his coat, and fixed the seam of his gloves when he looked through the door and beheld her.

He knew her gown to be of white with a pink sheen, covered with some sort of lace and beads; she had described it to him some days before. He knew her to be wearing pearls in her hair—real pearls, ten of them. He knew that her shoe roses sparkled with silver ribbon, but he saw nary a one. He was too busy watching Lydia's face, drinking in the joyous expression, the happiness in her eyes. And she was staring at him.

Tired and yet exhilarated, Lydia looked around the beautifully appointed Assembly Room. With high ceilings and brightly glowing chandeliers, there was no sense of overcrowding—a crush though it might be, it was a comfortable one. The music was lively, the dancers smiling, and the night appeared to be a great success.

Lydia had done her best to attend to her guests in equal measure. She had danced with a physician, two barons and an earl, a magistrate, and, unfortunately, a ne'er-do-well—though he was polite and an adequate dancer. She had made a round of the matrons and chaperones hovering near the fireplace at the far end of the ballroom, chatting for a few moments with each. And she had seen to the partnering of Elaine and Cora to suitable gentlemen throughout the evening. Though, with Cora there was little to direct. Her friend had already danced three sets with Mr. Granger and looked to be agreeing to another. They had eyes only for each other—and if some considered their behavior unseemly, none in the family would fault her.

There were only two sets of dances left before the fateful hour of eleven, when all would call for their carriages or sedan chairs, and the night would be over. Overheated, more inclined to stand near the open doors to the terrace than twirl and skip through another set of steps, Lydia looked around for her next partner and met, instead, the eyes of Robert Newton, dancer extraordinaire.

He was leaning on the paneled wall next to one of those tall fresh-air-wafting doors, and Lydia watched him straighten, look slightly puzzled, and then shrug.

Choosing to take this as an invitation, Lydia whispered to her mother and then skirted around the room, doing her best to avoid the dancers. Elaine skipped past her, laughing uproariously to the comment of her partner, and then she, too, disappeared into the multitude.

As Lydia neared Robert's position, she could feel the waft of a cool breeze, and yet her skin began to burn, and she found it increasingly difficult to breathe. And still she continued, locked onto his gaze. After having traversed the entire length of the room to speak, they stared at each other in silence. Eventually, Lydia smiled, Robert winked, and they found their voices.

"No partner?" Robert asked, raising his tone above the din.

"Mr. Wilson has not come to claim me." In fact, Lydia knew Mr. Wilson to be engaged in an energetic conversation with a

Mr. Dorchester near the library entrance. Lydia had not sent her uncle after him, nor would she do so with Robert. She was quite content to stay exactly where she was.

"I would call this a triumph, Miss Whitfield. Are you enjoying the night?"

"Absolutely, Mr. Newton. Though, if I had one regret, it would be that we, you and I, cannot dance together again." She sighed overdramatically, though her words were true.

"Not seemly."

"But really, who would know?" she asked.

Robert laughed. "Well, all those who are watching us at this moment. Can you not feel their eyes? You don't want to appear particular; it might limit those who come to call over the next few weeks and months."

"As long as *you* come to call, Mr. Newton, I don't see the problem."

A frown flicked across Robert's face; though it was hurriedly replaced with a smile that did not reach his eyes. "Now that you are out, Miss Whitfield, I will not be able to visit as I have been doing. It was a little untoward, though kindly tolerated by your family because of my position as your solicitor's apprentice. It doesn't mean that our friendship has to end, just that we will be able to see each other only on occasion."

"No," Lydia said with far more force than she intended. Robert's countenance was that of a dispirited man, wounded to the heart, and it made her want to cry. There was no need of this.

They could spend as much time as they liked together if he would but offer her his hand.

But he wouldn't. Her mother was right.

Touching his arm gently, Lydia drew Robert across the threshold onto the terrace. The cooler air helped clear her head, helped shore up her nerves.

"Lydia, we cannot be out here. You have to be careful of your reputation—very careful, you—"

"We are in full view of the entire room, should anyone choose to look."

"And they are, Lydia. I know this affords us some privacy, but it is that very privacy that will cause—"

"Hush."

"I beg your pardon?"

"I wish to speak to you about something very significant and you keep distracting me. I find it difficult to . . . I . . . Robert—" Lydia drew in a great lungful of air, coughed slightly, and then blew it out slowly. "Robert?"

"Yes."

"Can you think of any reason why two persons who care deeply for each other . . . who *love* each other . . . should not make a match of it?"

His silence was deafening.

Lydia waited, her heart pounding. Robert knew her too well not to understand the gist of her question. She watched him swallow before opening his mouth.

"There are times when emotions, even if they are shared"—he smiled briefly and then returned to his sober expression—"are best ignored when the union would only be for the benefit of one party, namely the one less prosperous."

A boisterous laugh burst out of Lydia, surprising them both. She turned it into a giggle and then smiled—broadly. "Excellent. Just as I thought. We are not talking about the lack of affection. We are talking about the ridiculous notion that a couple should allow a difference in finances to stand in their way."

"Of course."

"No 'of course' about it. Why is it acceptable for a penniless baron to marry money with no expectation of returned affection and yet the same financial disparity would cause great consternation and gnashing of teeth merely because it is a love match?"

"It wouldn't. No gnashing."

"The sky would fall?"

"Of course not."

"Then what is the problem?"

"I will not be called a fortune hunter or, worse yet, a kept man."

"What would these names be against a lifetime of happiness?"

Frowning, Robert shook his head despite agreeing. "Yes, what indeed. However . . ." Taking a gulp of air, he continued. "What of my career?"

"Your career?"

"Yes. I am not a gentleman of leisure. I have obligations and schedules." He smiled at that word . . . though why, Lydia could not fathom. "Especially now that my apprenticeship has begun. Until just recently, you believed that you were going to marry a peer, and now . . . well . . . to be the wife of a solicitor? Your social position would plummet. . . . I would have to give up the law. Yes, there is no way around it."

Lydia tipped her head, as if in doing so it might make the conversation clearer. "Being a solicitor is part of who you want to be. I would never ask you to give it up."

To Lydia's surprise, Robert's frown deepened. "Truly. You would not find it demeaning?"

"Demeaning? To be married to an up-and-coming solicitor who earns his fortune with honesty and hard work?"

"Hardly a fortune, Lydia. I will never be your equal."

"Aha, so it is our financial disparity, after all. We have just come full circle."

Robert snorted a laugh. "I am utterly confused."

With a quick glance into the room, noting the inquiring faces, Lydia reached out for Robert's waistcoat and slowly pulled him into the shadows. "There is one matter that counts above all else. Do you love me?"

This time, there was no hesitation. "With all my heart, until the day I die, and beyond, if there is an afterlife."

A flood of relief washed over Lydia, leaving her speechless . . . for all of a moment. "Then, I will marry you, if you will ask."

Before he had a chance to say anything, Lydia leaned forward.

She wrapped her arms around his neck and lifted her mouth to his. She could feel his heart pounding out a quick-time rhythm as he slipped his arms around her waist and pulled her closer.

When their lips met, she thought her insides would melt into a puddle of ecstasy. Filled with a delicious, undefined longing, Lydia leaned in closer, wishing that she could stay locked in his arms forever. But all too soon, Robert lifted his head, taking a ragged breath.

"Lydia, my dove?"

"Yes, Robert?"

"I have just thoroughly compromised you."

"Thoroughly . . . what ever shall we do?"

"We will have to announce our intentions this very evening— before there is any hint of scandal."

"Excellent idea. What are our intentions?"

Robert chuckled and leaned over to kiss her forehead, but Lydia lifted herself up on her toes, initiating another session of excellent compromising.

"Lydia, my dove?" Robert said again, eventually.

"Yes, Robert."

"Will you grant me the great privilege of your hand in marriage?"

Lydia closed her eyes and savored his proposal—the offer of a union for life. Exquisite joy, overwhelming and eternal, filled her to the brim; the sensation was so marvelous that she forgot to breathe for a time.

The air around them stilled, as did Robert. He was waiting.

How could he not know her answer? She had encouraged the pro-posal. And still he waited.

Lydia opened her eyes and grinned. "I would be honored."

The relief on his face nearly brought tears to her eyes. She lifted her hand and cupped his chin. "I would be *honored*," she repeated. "I love you so very much."

As her future husband lowered his head once again, Lydia sighed dreamily. "We should go in," she whispered, tightening her hold, preventing him from going anywhere.

"Absolutely," he said, nibbling at her lower lip.

All thoughts of ballrooms and inquisitive glances were instantly drowned by the flow of marvelous sensations coursing through her body and a sudden desire to drag Robert deeper into the shadows.

They would go back into the ballroom soon . . . but not yet.

GLOSSARY

Chimneypiece: a British term for the construction around a fireplace, also called a mantelpiece

Chunter: to mutter, grumble, or grouse—a British term

Gig: a light, two-wheeled, one-horse carriage

Land agent: a British term for the steward of an estate who supervised the farm, laborers, and tenants as well as collected rents and other money

Landau: a four-wheeled carriage pulled by two or four horses with facing seats and two folded hoods that could be raised to enclose the passengers

Marionette: a puppet controlled by wires or strings

Nonplussed: to be bewildered and confused about how to react

Retrench: to drastically reduce expenditures; for the gentry it often entailed moving to an urban center, employing fewer servants, getting rid of carriages and horses, etc.

ACKNOWLEDGMENTS

Duels & Deception was written before, during, and after the publication of *Love, Lies and Spies*. There is absolutely no doubt that without the encouragement and calming influence of the Swoon Reads team, *Duels & Deception* would not have come together in a timely or cohesive manner. Many thanks to the entire group, but particularly Emily and Lauren for their enthusiasm and brilliant suggestions, Christine and Holly for their faith and excitement, and Anna for the beautiful cover design.

Also part of Swoon Reads, I must thank the amazingly talented authors who are unfailing in their support and eagerness, especially Kelly, Danika, and Kim. It is a very good thing that we do not live in the same place or mischief would occur!

I would also like to thank all the readers who have contacted me through Facebook, Twitter, Goodreads, and the Swoon Reads website. There is nothing more uplifting than knowing that I have added a touch of humor, contentment, romance, and a few sleepless nights to your lives.

Last, but *never* least, I would like to thank my family. Thank you, Mike, for being the best sounding board ever and your remarkable knowledge of . . . well, of everything. Deb, I would not be the writer I am if you had not challenged me to be better, argued about how to ride tandem on a horse, and corrected my grammar over and over. Christine, you are a photographer extraordinaire, my go-to media girl, and the perfect alpha reader when I am uncertain. Dan, your energy and laughter are contagious; you energize my creativity and humor. Mom, there is no fan like you—if I were half the writer you thought me to be, I would be content!

FEELING BOOKISH?

Turn the page for some

Swoonworthy EXTRAS

THE RULES FOR DUELS

There were three main reasons for offering a challenge: taking liberties with a female relative; dishonorable behavior (cheating, defamation, etc.); or attacking physically.

Once the challenge was accepted, seconds would be chosen to act on behalf of the principals. They were close, trusted friends—the protocols were in their hands.

The second's first duty was to try to resolve the dispute without having to resort to "pistols at dawn." There was no dishonor in offering an apology or admitting an error.

Most duels were held in early morning, just outside of town.

It was the duty of the second to check the pistol, load it, and mark out the distance—generally, between ten and fourteen paces.

The principals saluted each other before stepping to their mark and turning sideways—pistol arm outstretched—waiting for the handkerchief to be dropped.

Principals could fire at each other or into the air.

After, if they were able, both parties would salute, express regret, and leave the field. The last fatal duel in England was in 1852; the winner was tried for murder.

MARRIAGE LAWS
AND CUSTOMS

- Marriages were valid only if they had been advertised by banns (read out in church on three consecutive Sundays) or were sanctioned by a special license; they also had to be recorded in a church register.
- Parental consent was required for anyone under twenty-one: even if betrothed at an earlier age, most married in their early twenties.
- A "smock" wedding required a bride to be naked (although she usually wore a shift for propriety). It was believed that a bride without clothes or property did not bring debts to the union, either—however, this was a custom, not a law.
- The wedding ring was placed on the fourth finger on the left hand because of an old belief that a small artery ran from the finger to the heart.
- Weddings took place in the morning by canon law. It decreed that they could be solemnized only between eight AM and noon.
- The meal after the ceremony was a wedding breakfast. Elaborate weddings could continue throughout the day, with music, dancing, and games.
- A honeymoon did not exist in the Regency period, but the well-off took an extended tour (sometimes called a bridal tour), and they did not go alone, bringing friends and/or family and, naturally, servants.

A Tea Date

with author Cindy Anstey and her editor, Emily Settle

"Getting to Know You (A Little More)"

Emily Settle (ES): What book is on your nightstand now?

Cindy Anstey (CA): I often read more than one book at a time, but *Ancillary Sword*, by Ann Leckie, is the one keeping me from turning out the light . . . right now. A space opera might seem a strange choice, but my taste in books is quite eclectic.

ES: A space opera is never out of place, in my humble opinion. What's your favorite word?

CA: I love words too much to have a favorite—but today (notice how I'm qualifying) I would choose *addlepated*, *swoony*, *bombastic*, *whiffler*, and *amalgamate*. I do overuse *excellent*, but it's more of a habit than a favorite.

ES: If you could travel in time, where would you go and what would you do? I mean, based on your writing, I'm actually pretty convinced that you are, in fact, a time traveler, so . . .

CA: (Laughs) Thank you. I wish I were a time traveler. First-person research would be amazing! I would love to spend a summer getting to know, truly know, Jane Austen. I would sit at her feet and listen as she explained her society and culture, her writing methods, and her life philosophy. (I specify the summer because I would freeze without central heat in the winter, and all those unwashed bodies in closed, smoky rooms would be rather (gag) stinky to the twenty-first-century nose.)

ES: What was the most fascinating or funniest thing you discovered while doing research for *Duels & Deception*?

CA: I discovered a little-known fact that doesn't really play in the book but I have to use sometime. When a gentleman married, there was no assumption that his bachelor friends would be accepted into his new life. Only if the friend(s) were invited to meet the bride (at the wedding or a dinner or invited to "call") would the relationship continue as it was. Otherwise, the boys would only meet at the club, or races, etc.; but if they crossed paths while out, they would pretend to not know one another, so as not to cause the bride discomfort.

ES: I would read that book!

"The Swoon Reads Experience (Continues!)"

ES: What's your favorite thing about being a Swoon Reads author so far?

CA: I thrive on positivity, and so I would have to say that my favorite aspect of being a Swoon Reads author is the enthusiasm that permeates everything from the team to the other authors to the readers.

ES: How has the Swoon Reads community affected your experiences as an author?

CA: I think every author suffers from self-doubt to some degree, but the Swoon Reads community offers such great support that it crowds out the doubts and energizes my creativity. It spurs me on!

ES: Did the publication of *Love, Lies and Spies* change your life?

CA: Absolutely! You couldn't get better affirmation for all those hours spent at the computer. I walk much taller now—metaphorically speaking.

Better still, my husband has taken over the cooking so that I can keep writing—which is fantastic because he always was the better cook.

ES: Aw, that's so sweet. And we appreciate his efforts so you can keep writing, too! Do you have any advice for aspiring authors on the site?
CA: There is no fast track to learning how to write well, but every word, sentence, and chapter that you type is a step closer to that ultimate goal. So, keep at it. Write and read . . . repeat.

"The Writing Life"

ES: Where did you get the inspiration for *Duels & Deception*?
CA: At any given time, I have five or six plots running around in my head. It is soooo hard to remember the seed of inspiration. It usually springs from research; and if pressed, I would likely attribute learning the rules of honor in regard to duels as being the beginning. It was hard to fathom the foolishness of placing your life on the line for something as minor as an insult.

ES: What's your process? Are you an outliner or do you just start at the beginning and make it up as you go?
CA: I am absolutely an outliner. However, even as I write out the plot, I know that the characters will alter the plan. I adjust as often as I need; it's always a better story if I give the characters free rein. I tried to wing it one time and wrote myself into a corner.

ES: What do you want readers to remember about your books?
CA: Do I get a list? . . . I would hope that my books have made the time period come alive, that it makes the readers want to explore the Regency era. But more important, I would hope that the readers have found my books uplifting and funny—a happy escape from life's stress, even if only for a short time.

Duels & Deception

DISCUSSION QUESTIONS

1. How would you characterize the relationship between Lydia and her female relatives? How do you think they have affected her character?

2. To what extent do you feel Lydia's challenges in gaining control of her family farm are due to her youth and which aspects are due to her gender?

3. What drives Robert? What are his motivations to become a lawyer, and how does that change throughout the book?

4. How important are Lydia's friends, Cora and Shelley, to the story? How significant is the role of female friendship to Lydia?

5. Robert and Cassidy seem to have very different natures, but they also have a tight bond. How important was this to your understanding of Robert?

6. Lydia's kidnapping was designed to ruin her reputation. It is implied that Lydia's good name is her worth. Do you feel that society still has the same expectation of young women?

7. The characters are skeptical about the utility of Scotland Yard. Do you think that Burt Warner has redeemed this institution?

8. Who did you first suspect was the culprit behind the plot against Lydia? When the villain's identity was revealed, how did it change your perception of the book?

9. Were you surprised that after Lydia and Robert discussed the challenges to their communication, they both still operated as individuals trying to save the other at the duel? How do you think this reflects real relationships?

10. Do you like Lydia's proposal to Robert? Do you feel, considering their characters and situations, that this was realistic?

In which plans for a Season without romance
are unapologetically foiled.

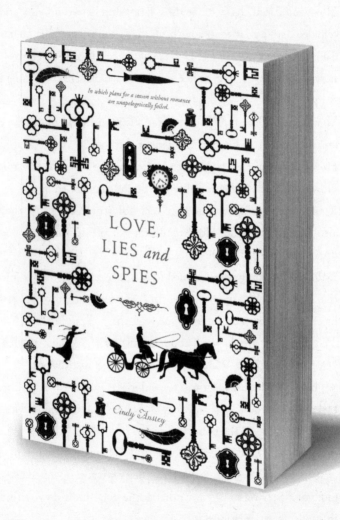

In which plans for a season without romance
are unapologetically foiled.

LOVE,
LIES *and*
SPIES

Cindy Anstey

In this hilarious homage to Jane Austen, a lady with a penchant for trouble
finds a handsome spy much more than merely tolerable.

CHAPTER
1

*In which a young lady clinging to a cliff
will eventually accept anyone's help*

"OH MY, this is embarrassing," Miss Juliana Telford said
aloud. There was no reason to keep her thoughts to herself, as she was alone, completely alone. In fact, that was half of
the problem. The other half was, of course, that she was hanging off the side of a cliff with the inability to climb either up
or down and in dire need of rescue.

"Another scrape. This will definitely give Aunt apoplexy."

Juliana hugged the cliff ever closer and tipped her head
slightly so that she could glance over her shoulder. Her high-
waisted ivory dress was deeply soiled across her right hip, where
she had slid across the earth as she dropped over the edge.

Juliana shifted slowly and glanced over her other shoulder.
Fortunately, the left side showed no signs of distress, and her

lilac sarcenet spencer could be brushed off easily. She would do it now were it not for the fact that her hands were engaged, holding tightly to the tangle of roots that kept her from falling off the tiny ledge.

Juliana continued to scrutinize the damage to her wardrobe with regret, not for herself so much as for her aunt, who seemed to deem such matters of great importance. Unfortunately, her eyes wandered down to her shoes. Just beyond them yawned an abyss. It was all too apparent how far above the crashing waves of the English Channel she was—and how very small the ledge.

Despite squishing her toes into the rock face as tightly as possible, Juliana's heels were only just barely accommodated by the jutting amalgamate. The occasional skitter and plop of eroding rocks diving into the depths of the brackish water did nothing to calm her racing heart.

Juliana swallowed convulsively. "Most embarrassing." She shivered despite a warm April breeze. "I shall be considered completely beyond the pale if I am dashed upon the rocks. Aunt will be so uncomfortable. Most inconsiderate of me."

A small shower of sandy pebbles rained down on Juliana's flowery bonnet. She shook the dust from her eyes and listened. She thought she had heard a voice.

Please, she prayed, let it be a farmer or a tradesman, someone not of the gentry. No one who would feel obligated to report back to Grays Hill Park. No gentlemen, please.

"Hello?" she called out. Juliana craned her neck upward,

trying to see beyond the roots and accumulated thatch at the cliff's edge.

A head appeared. A rather handsome head. He had dark, almost black, hair and clear blue eyes and, if one were to notice such things at a time like this, a friendly, lopsided smile.

"Need some assistance?" the head asked with a hint of sarcasm and the tone of a . . .

"Are you a gentleman?" Juliana inquired politely.

The head looked startled, frowned slightly, and then raised an eyebrow before answering. "Yes, indeed, I am—"

"Please, I do not wish to be rescued by a gentleman. Could you find a farmer or a shopkeep—anyone not of the gentry—and then do me the great favor of forgetting you saw me?"

"I beg your pardon?"

"I do not want to be rude, but this is a most embarrassing predicament—"

"I would probably use the word *dangerous* instead."

"Yes, well, you would, being a man. But I, on the other hand, being a young woman doing her best not to call attention to herself and bring shame upon her family, would call it otherwise."

"Embarrassing?"

"Oh, most definitely. First, I should not have gone out in the carriage alone. Carrie was supposed to come with me, but we quarreled, you see, and I got into a snit, and—" Juliana stopped herself. She was beginning to prattle; it must be the effects of the sun. "Second, if I had not been watching the swallows instead of the road, I would have seen the hole before my wheel decided to explore its depths—very scatterbrained of me. And third, if I return home, soiled and in the company of a gentleman with no acquaintance to the family, I will be returned to Hartwell forthwith in shame. All possibility of a Season and trip to London will be gone completely."

"Well, that is quite an embarrassing list. I do see the problem."

"Is there someone down there?" another voice asked.

The head with the blue eyes disappeared, but Juliana could hear a muffled conversation.

"Yes, but she does not want to be rescued by us. She says she needs a farmer."

"What?"

Juliana leaned back slightly to see if she could catch a glimpse of the other gentleman, but that dislodged a cloud of dirt.

"Achoo."

"Bless you," one of the voices called from above before continuing the conversation. "Yes, it seems that we are not the sort—"

Juliana's nose began to itch again. She scrunched it up and then wiggled it, trying to stop another burst. To no avail. *"Achoo."* This time her left hand jerked with the force of the exhaled air and broke several of the roots to which she was clinging. Slowly, they began to unravel, lengthening and shifting Juliana away from the cliff's side, out into the air.

"Oh no." She let go of that handful and reached back toward the rocks for another, hopefully stronger, group of roots. But she was not so lucky. Twice more she grabbed, praying that the tangle in her right hand would not get the same idea.

Just as she had decided the situation was now possibly more dangerous than embarrassing, a hand grabbed her flailing wrist. Relief flooded through her, and her racing heart slowed just a touch.

"Give me your other arm."

"I beg your pardon? You cannot expect me to let go."

"Well, if I am to pull you up, you are going to have to."

"Oh dear, oh dear. I really do not want to."

"I understand completely. But I am afraid we have no length of rope, no farmer is in sight, and your predicament seems to be proceeding into the realm of peril. Not to worry, though. I have this arm firmly in my grasp, my feet are being held—sat upon, to be exact, so I will not topple over—and all that is left for you to do is to let go. I will grab your other arm, you will close your eyes, and up you will come. Back onto terra firma."

"This is terra firma." Juliana pointed with her nose to the rugged cliff wall.

"Yes, but I doubt very much that you want to stay there."

"I like the idea of dangling in the air so much less."

The head nodded sympathetically. "Life is full of these trials, I am afraid."

"They seem to follow me around. I am a magnet for trouble."

"That is sad news. However, perhaps it would be best to

discuss your penchant for interesting situations when we are on the same ground level—say, up here. It would make the discussion much easier to conduct."

"In other words, I should stop dillydallying."

"Exactly so."

"I really do not want to do this."

"I understand."

Juliana took a deep breath. "I am only eighteen, you know."

"I did not."

"That is much too young to die, do you not think?"

"I quite agree, which is why we are going to do everything we can to help you make it to nineteen."

"All right, I will do it."

"Brave girl."

Juliana felt anything but brave. Her knees were starting to wobble and her hands had decided to shake. She took several deep breaths, counted to three in her head, and then let go.

Check out more books chosen for publication by readers like you.

Cindy Anstey spends her days painting with words, flowers, threads, and watercolors. Whenever not sitting at the computer, she can be found—or rather, not found—traveling near and far. After many years living as an expat in Singapore, Memphis, and Belgium, Cindy now resides with her husband and their energetic chocolate Labrador, Chester, in Nova Scotia, Canada.